DARK EMBERS

Book 3 of The Path of Ashes

a post-apocalyptic series by
Brian Parker

This is a work of fiction. Names, characters, places and incidents are the product of the author's imagination and are used fictitiously. Any resemblance to actual events, locales, or persons, living or dead, is purely coincidental.

Notice: The views expressed herein are NOT endorsed by the United States Government, Department of Defense or Department of the Army.

Dark Embers
Book 3 of The Path of Ashes

Works Available from Brian Parker

Five Roads to Texas
Five Roads to Texas: A Phalanx Press Collaboration
After the Roads
The Road to Hell

Easytown Novels
The Immorality Clause
Tears of a Clone
West End Droids & East End Dames
High Tech/Low Life: An Easytown Anthology

The Path of Ashes
A Path of Ashes
Fireside
Dark Embers

Washington, Dead City
GNASH
REND
SEVER

Stand Alone Works
Grudge
Enduring Armageddon
Origins of the Outbreak
The Collective Protocol
Battle Damage Assessment
Zombie in the Basement
Self-Publishing the Hard Way

Plus, many more anthology contributions and short stories

PROLOGUE

His feet were bloody and torn. When they'd taken him, he'd been in his thin sleeping clothes with nothing on his feet. The miles of rough, uneven terrain that he'd been forced to run across had quickly ripped them open, causing the group to stop and place ill-fitting shoes over the bloody mess. They didn't want to leave a trail for his family to follow.

At first, the slavers kept Varan and his older brother Caleb separated as they fled, herded along with several other children from the family compound. Eventually they shoved all of them roughly together and forced the children to run as a group into the night. He'd thought about stopping, refusing to go any further, until the knives that his kidnappers brandished encouraged the youth to continue.

Varan remained hopeful that his family would come charging across the foothills to annihilate his abductors. It was an illusion that he clung to, desperately wanting to believe in his family's infallibility. They would come. Traxx don't abandon their own. It was a lesson drilled into them their entire lives: the family stuck together, no matter what. Their father and uncles would come to save them. The boys just had to survive until they did.

They ran for days and when they made camp, there was no fire to give away their position to potential hunters. The nights were the worst. Slavers often took screaming children to the boundaries of their camp to have their way with them. By the time the animals were finished, the screams died down to whimpers.

The children huddled together against the cold nights as their sweat-soaked clothing cooled. They weren't offered any of the kidnappers' blankets nor provided any answers to why they'd been abducted. The only information that Varan could ascertain was that they had to be somewhere by a certain time. Where, he had no idea.

After three days of almost constant movement and little food, they met up with another group of ragged men at a crossroads. This group was heavily armed with a mixture of old world weaponry and the type of swords that the children had learned to use at the Traxx compound.

The newcomers had a giant cage mounted on wheels, drawn by horses. The cage was already crowded with a wretched collection of people. The boys soon learned of their fate as their abductors bartered with the slavers. Eventually, the men agreed on a price and their new owners grabbed the children by the shoulders, tossing them shoving them roughly into the cage with the rest of the prisoners.

The caravan rode toward the setting sun for more than three weeks, stopping only to add new prisoners and discard the dead from the cage. They rode high into the mountains, passing snow-covered peaks and then descended into lush, green valleys, always traveling westward. After successfully navigating the highlands, they passed into a massive desert, the heat and press of bodies conspiring to end their miserable existence. The boys began to measure their life in hours, not months and years. It was only a matter of time before they died of starvation or from exposure to the elements.

Somehow, Varan and Caleb survived the journey and arrived at the remains of a city. It was like one of the massive places that their grandfather had described to them in his many stories around the cooking fire. Varan had begun to despair that his family wasn't coming after all. Why had the Traxx abandoned them? Were the lessons of commitment, honor and justice simply stories that had been told to children to keep them under control?

Miraculously, the same buyer purchased Varan and his brother at an auction, while the other children from his family's compound went to other owners. Lucas Miller, the man who'd bought them, owned a stadium where men fought all manner of people and beasts to entertain the crowds. The boys were too young to be gladiators, so they had to clean the warriors' cells while they were away training and bring them food and water once they were safely secured for the night.

As he settled in to his life as a slave, hauling away the buckets of shit from the gladiators whom he would one day train beside, Varan's heart hardened against the Traxx family. They had betrayed him. They were secure in their tidy little compound with enough food for everyone, laughing and drinking in the courtyard as their grandfather regaled them with fabricated stories of the family's past.

Over time, he grew into a man. Both Varan and Caleb became gladiators, fighting for the glory of the House of Miller in local and regional contests. As their fame grew the memories of home lessened, but the sting of betrayal remained.

Varan became the Primus, the most skilled warrior in the stable of slaves owned by Lucas, and he hated the Traxx family for abandoning him to this life.

ONE

Garrett Traxx struggled along the jagged pathway leading to the top of the mountains dominating the terrain around him. Homelake lay almost sixty miles from the mountain, far out into the foothills where the weather was milder and more predictable. The people had insisted that he consult with the Seers before they made his coronation official, so he'd set out on the journey with a few men and his twelve year old nephew, Brandt.

The years since they left Texas had been a strange and often confusing journey for the Traxx family. When slavers abducted Caleb and Varan, along with nine other children from families in their compound, people had understandably been devastated. The security that they'd thought their pitiful walls would provide had proven false. The guards were easily overwhelmed and the fence scaled.

The compound's leadership realized that they hadn't isolated themselves far enough from other communities, so they decided to move once again. After the harvest, the Traxx family gathered their belongings and left. Another forty people from various families in the compound joined them. There was too much heartache and too many memories to remain in Texas any longer.

They went further north, away from the old homestead, crossing into what had once been Colorado. An abandoned hotel along an overgrown highway within sight of the mountains provided the shelter that they needed. The old town was far enough onto the empty plains to be able to grow their crops and near enough to the mountains for safety. Even in the old world, the hotel had been in the middle of nowhere, more of a rest stop for road-weary travelers than a destination of any consequence.

The Homelake Hotel and nearby lake provided their small group with shelter and an ample supply of water once they purified it. Over time, they converted the hotel into a legitimate stronghold with real walls built of earth and wooden timbers. Others began to flock to the area to make use of the abandoned homes and arable cropland nearby, building a small community around the Traxx family's home.

The winters in Colorado, like everywhere else, were cold and miserable with deep snow that blanketed the land and kept people cooped up inside their homes. The season lasted much longer than anyone could remember, even his aging father, Aiden who was born just a few years after the old world ended. In the summer, though, the fields surrounding the hotel were fertile. Their farmers surmised that the surrounding mountains had caused most of the acid rain that plagued the country after the war to fall to the west of their location. The growing season was short, but productive, yielding more than enough food to make it through the long winter.

The Traxx family had lived in the hotel, known as The Keep after they'd built the fortifications, for almost ten years. Then, last month, the surrounding community had shocked Garrett by voting for him to be its king. His friend Nicholas read of the kings who ruled their lands hundreds of years before the end the old world and convinced the villagers to crown Garrett. It was only an honorary title, but the sentiment remained. The residents respected him enough to make him their official leader instead of simply being one of the men who lived in The Keep.

Like everything in life, there was a catch to him being crowned king. The merchants insisted that he speak to the Seers of the Valley Lodge, a reclusive group of women who secluded themselves in the mountains and were renowned for their ability to perceive events that might happen. The people wished to know whether the election of one man to lead them was the right move.

Garrett was wary. His father had told him often enough that his aunt Mary had the Gift as a child and that she'd even been instrumental in helping to save the old city of San Angelo from certain doom. The visions often twisted a person's perception of what may come to pass, he'd cautioned Garrett before the journey. The Seers could likely see one possibility for the future; it wasn't set in stone and events could be altered.

Garrett had met with them a few years prior. They'd had a particularly dry spring on the heels of a near disastrous winter and he'd gone to ask them about the harvest. The Seers had predicted rainstorms in the late summer that ended up saving the crops. The following winter was hard, but they'd survived and had bumper crops ever since.

The Seers even told him that a Traxx would become lord of The Keep. At the time Garrett laughed at their obvious attempt at trickery; he was already the head of the family, living in the hotel with his brother Blake and a few other families who'd traveled with them from Texas.

He glanced sideways at Nicholas with a slight frown. His friend had been present when the Seers proclaimed that Garrett would be elevated to royalty and had been the one who led the people in the vote. He often wondered if they'd foreseen Nicholas' involvement in the bid to have Garrett elected as king or if Nicholas got the idea from the Seers, effectively fulfilling their prophecy. He'd never know.

"Are we here?" Brandt asked, stirring him from the memories that had crept up on him.

Garrett's face flushed from embarrassment as he realized that he'd allowed himself to stop walking. For once, he was thankful of the cold that permeated his limbs, hiding the color in his cheeks. "Almost," he replied. "At the crest of this rise, we'll take the path down into a small valley. The Seers live in an old lodge in the center of a clearing."

"A lodge?" the boy asked excitedly. "What's a lodge?"

He grinned at his nephew, of course he wouldn't know what a lodge was; he'd only learned of it himself when he visited the first time. "It's a big house. You'll see soon enough, Brandt."

The boy frowned, "So it's like The Keep?"

"No, not anywhere as big as that; it's a big house where hunters used to stay when they would go hunting. It's designed to look like a wood cabin, but it's not real wood, it's—"

"What's 'not real wood,' Uncle?"

"It's… Well, it's something from the old world. You'll see when we get there."

Nicholas chuckled at Garrett's frustration. The family hadn't taken children beyond the walls in years. After the coronation, Brandt would be second in line for the throne behind the king's daughter, Tanya, so he'd reluctantly agreed to allow the boy to come.

"Brandt," Nicholas coughed, diverting the boy's attention away from Garrett. "Look up ahead. How far do you reckon we are from the top of this path?"

Brandt looked up at the crest of the hill they were traversing and Garrett could tell that he was attempting to estimate the distance. After a moment he said, "Maybe three hundred feet."

"Okay, so in three hundred feet, you'll get your questions answered. Stop pestering the king."

"I—Yes, sir," the boy replied. He bent his head down so he could focus on the path's treacherous footing and pulled ahead of the group.

When he was out of earshot, Garrett said, "Thank you, but I'm not the king yet. It's been a long time since I've had to be responsible for a nine year old. His father and mother were always around so they dealt with the constant questions of his."

"Well, m'Lord, the—"

"Don't start that shit again," Garrett cut him off.

Nicholas bent slightly at the waist as they walked, "As you command." He darted quickly out of reach as Garrett threw a playful punch in his direction.

"Seriously, though," his friend continued. "The questions are how they learn about the world around them. It's a good thing that he's curious."

He acknowledged the fact with a grunt. "I know. I'm just not used to being the sole recipient of his questions. Tanya turns eighteen after the next harvest, so it's been a while, and even then Peyton handled most of them while we worked in the field."

Snowflakes drifted across their vision, causing them to look skyward. The clouds were a light grey, not the angry dark grey and green that indicated a poison snow, so they were fine to continue along in the open. Nicholas gestured upward, saying, "I hope these aren't the first flakes in a blizzard. I don't want to be stuck up here with the Seers... They're creepy."

Garrett continued to examine the sky as they walked. "It shouldn't be; too early in the season. The harvest was only last week. We haven't even finished storing everything yet."

Ahead, Brandt had stopped at the crest, staring down into the valley, hidden from view of the rest of the party. He pointed excitedly toward where Garrett knew the Seers' home was located in the valley below.

"Looks like we're here," Nicholas stated.

Garrett waved his arm over his head to get the boy's attention. "Remember, stay on the trail," he called, mindful of the defenses hidden in the fields surrounding the lodge.

Brandt paused long enough for his uncle to catch up before picking his way down the trail toward the structure in the center of the valley.

The Valley Lodge was exactly as Garrett remembered. Situated between several rows of mountain peaks, the dell before them was well hidden from outsiders. Waist-high grass, turned brown with the changing of the seasons, circled the vale's floor. Garrett knew that the tall grass held a nasty surprise for unwelcome visitors and raiders. It bent in the wind that swept constantly from the north, hiding the old world magic that would kill any who stepped away from the path with an explosion that sprayed jagged shards of metal in all directions.

Closer to the lodge, an old chain-link fence kept a small herd of cattle and flock of chickens confined to the area immediately surrounding it. The animals kept the grasses trimmed short, allowing for excellent fields of view for five hundred feet all around the building. The explosives in the grass, coupled with the long standoff distances—as well as the ability to see danger in the future—gave the Seers an easily defensible home against any medium-sized raiding party.

The Seer's home sat directly in the center of the little valley. It was a moderate-sized hunting lodge, once used by sport hunters when they'd vacation in the wilderness of southern Colorado. He chuckled to himself. *The hunters of old must not have liked to leave the comforts of home behind when they went out to pursue their quarry.*

The lodge wasn't nearly as large as The Keep, but it was large enough to house all of the Seers and the small guard force they kept on staff. When he'd been here before, there were five of them. Three performed the ritual that gave the idea to Nicholas to nominate him for king, while the other two sat in the shadows of the room they used for their ceremony.

The women had surprised him. He'd been expecting old cronies covered in warts and moles; the women who'd been present had all been wart-free. While none of them stood out in his mind as particularly attractive, each of them would have made good wives for some of his people if they hadn't been cursed with the Gift.

"*HALT!*" a disembodied male voice echoed across the valley.

Garrett had been expecting this as well. The Seers had a system of pipes buried in the ground that all lead from a central point inside the building to the edges of the valley. Someone could shout in one end of the pipe and be heard on the other end. He'd liked the idea so much that he had one installed on either side of The Keep's walls so they could talk to people while the gates were closed. Theirs didn't work nearly as well as the Seers' pipes though.

His group halted, except for the youth, who continued to work his way down the path, heedless of the orders from the lodge. "Brandt, stop!" Garrett shouted.

The boy paused to look back toward his uncle. At that moment, an arrow embedded into the ground five feet in front of Brandt. His nephew's head whipped around to focus on the quivering shaft and he slowly raised both of his arms.

"*What do you want?*" the voice demanded, echoing once again from everywhere around them.

Garrett looked around for the end of the pipe and saw it near where the arrow rested. The mottled green and brown tube blended perfectly into the landscape surrounding it. The arrow indicated a stronger level of security than the Seers had the last time that he was here, so he followed Brandt's lead, raising his hands. Then he walked slowly toward the copper pipe and bent down to talk into it.

His breath clouded as he pulled the scarf away from his mouth. "My name is Garrett Traxx. I came to—"

"*We know you, Traxx,*" a new, female voice stated. "*We've been expecting you; however we didn't know you to come with a war party.*"

He looked back at the ten men who'd journeyed with him and his nephew. It was a small war party to say the least. "These men are here to protect me, not to raid you."

"*Protect you from whom? Yourself? Foolish Traxx.*"

"Now, wait a minute."

"*You have nothing to fear from us, King Traxx.*"

"How did you— Never mind." He glanced back at his traveling companions. They could hear everything that was said through the tube as clearly as if they were standing in front of it and not him. He looked back toward the lodge and continued, "I've come to speak to you about the coronation."

"*Coronation? You have greater things to worry about than a celebration.*"

Garrett bit hard on the inside of his cheek. He knew before he came that speaking in riddles was the way of the Seers. It was a trick they developed to help with their prophecies, allowing enough room for multiple interpretations of a statement, thus, when an event came to pass, they could claim credit for it. It was a delicate game they played and his people took much stock in what the women had to say.

"Life amongst the wastes is tough. What do we have to fear that we don't already experience on a regular basis?"

"*Pride. So much pride, like your famous ancestor. It was his undoing.*"

"Famous ancestor… Do you mean Aeric Traxx?"

"*Yes, of course. You may enter our valley, along with three others, plus the little Traxxling.*"

There was a pause and the original male voice returned, "*Just the five of you. Everyone else will stay where they are or they'll be killed, no questions asked.*"

He grunted his approval into the pipe and turned to survey the party. Nicholas would be one of the three to go with him of course; he picked two others, both the sons of prominent merchants around Homelake. Brandt would round out the party.

"You men stay here," Garrett told the seven who would remain. "Make sure to stay on the path, don't wander off. The rumor is that the fields surrounding the Seers' lodge are seeded with explosives that will take a man's legs completely from his body."

Several of the men edged warily back from the grasses and one of them spit out the plant stalk that he'd been idly chewing. Garrett thanked the stars that his companions hadn't wandered too far into the grasses while he set the order of business with the speaker in the tube. He certainly didn't need a death or maiming overshadowing the coronation.

"Alright, let's go," Garrett sighed. "Don't do anything stupid, you can bet that whoever shot that arrow at Brandt's feet is watching us."

He trudged ahead of the small group down the cleared path toward the lodge. Three men sat on the front porch, watching their advance until they came to the chain link fence, then one of them stepped off onto the grass and made his way slowly toward the gate. The same man had been here the first time he visited the Seers.

"You could have met us at the gate when we got here," Garrett stated, annoyed that they'd waited in the cold for several minutes while the man ambled over from the lodge.

"Not the protocol that Darci has established," the guard replied gruffly.

"I didn't meet Darci last time I was here. Who is she?"

He snickered and pointed back up the path, "She's the one that shot that arrow." The man, Garrett thought he remembered his name to be Garth, pulled a set of keys from his pocket and inserted one into the padlock linked through the chain holding the gate closed. "She was hired after the incident."

Garrett was slightly confused. "What incident?"

Garth shrugged, "A few years ago, there was a guy who didn't like the prophecy that Erika gave him. He slit her throat before I was able to react." He gestured toward the bleached bones resting in a cage near the center of the front pasture, "That's him. Bastard begged for death by the time I was done with him. Unfortunately, the fire underneath him burned out one night and the cold finally took him.

"After Erika's death I was finally able to convince the rest of them to employ more security. We've got the four of us, plus several men who range through the forests surrounding the valley, and Darci. Finding her was truly a blessing."

Garrett scanned the rooftop of the lodge while Garth fed the chain through the fence. To be able to shoot as far across the valley as she had, he figured she had to be up high on the roof. He didn't see her at first, but then, resting against one of the chimneys, he saw her. The cloak she wore was the same dull brown as the rock chimney, allowing her to blend in easily with her background at that distance. If he narrowed his eyes, he could make out the stock and limbs of a large crossbow.

Garrett whistled softly and pointed toward the archer with his chin, "That's her up on the roof?"

The guard stepped out of the way to open the gate. "Yeah, that's where she normally stays while we have visitors coming down from the mountains."

The king looked from the lodge to the crest of the valley where his men waited, measuring the distance. "Geez, that's got to be, what, three thousand feet? How'd she shoot that far?"

"Roughly." Garth shrugged, "Maybe a little longer. She can hit everywhere in the valley—accurately."

"That's impossible," Nicholas chimed in.

Garth sputtered and then laughed aloud. "Maybe for you. Darci has this old book about world records that she showed me once. In the old world, people could shoot for double that length with a specially made bow and arrow. She's something special, though. She can hit anything she can see. That's why the Seers hired her."

They spread out inside the fence as Garth closed the gate and put the chain back through it. "I've seen her kill four men before they made it past the first marker stones."

Garrett glanced back up the pathway. Sure enough, large boulders broke up the tall grass at regular intervals. The stones looked to have been there for all time, causing him to wonder if they'd been placed before the fall of the old world. The hunters may have used the markers to increase the accuracy of their weapons at different distances.

"Damn, she's really good to have around then," he muttered, falling into line with Garth as the guard led the way back toward the lodge.

"The Seers are in high demand," the man replied. "Everyone wants to know what the future holds. Sometimes people don't want to pay the price for their services or want to take what they think the Seers have stockpiled, so we need security. The truth is that we're scraping by here, just like everywhere else."

"Except you don't have to farm the land yourself to get the resources," Nicholas countered. "All of that is given to you by people trying to get answers about their future."

"That's true, I guess," Garth admitted. "We do get paid in food and supplies—like clothing and firewood, sometimes other random things— but we have to supplement with our own meat and there's a large garden the Seers tend to when not talking with travelers."

Garrett didn't begrudge them earning a little bit of food or clothing like Nicholas did. The Seers provided a service for people and they charged for their services so they could continue to survive. Part of their survival was the employment of guards to help keep away the raiders and slavers so they had to charge enough of a fee to cover the guards' cost as well. It was the same economy as in Homelake; they simply offered a different product than the merchants at home.

They continued in silence until they reached the porch. The rough-looking men posted there asked them politely to leave their weapons. Nicholas started to protest that they hadn't relinquished their weapons when they were here years ago, until Garrett unbuckled his weapons belt. The gesture was enough to end his friend's objection. If he was willing to give up the sword of Aeric Traxx, then Nicholas could leave his own sword.

Nicholas held up his empty hand, the other was busy digging into his boot to pull out the knife he had stashed there as well. "The Seer who was murdered couldn't see what the guy was going to do?" he asked.

Garth sucked at his teeth and seemed to arrange his thoughts before answering. "From my experience with them, I've learned that they can't predict their own deaths. Crimes of passion, often spur of the moment with no forethought, are hidden from them as well."

"They can tell others all about what will happen to them, but they can't take care of themselves?" Nicholas scoffed.

"That's why we're here," a woman's voice surprised them from behind.

Garrett turned to see the dark-haired woman in the brown cloak who'd been on the roof earlier. She wore rough leather leggings and a homespun shirt, offset by high-cut boots that looked to be from one of the old world militaries and a metal composite crossbow topped with a metal tube. "Hello, Darci."

She inclined her head slightly. "King."

Simple and to the point, Garrett liked that. "I was telling Garth here that I was impressed by your skill with the bow."

Darci hefted the crossbow and patted the tube centered above the trigger. "This is the best scope I've ever seen. Traded four demonbroc paws and eight jackrabbit carcasses for it; probably fed that merchant for two months if he preserved the meat properly."

"A scope?" Garrett asked.

"It's like a pair of binoculars. You've seen those, right?"

"Yes, of course."

She rolled her eyes. "This is exactly like a binocular except there's only one tube. I can see thousands of feet with the scope, like it was right in front of me. They used to put them on the top of *guns*, but most of them have been lost or broken over the years. This one is special."

"Because it's yours?" Garrett guessed.

She smirked, "Exactly, Traxx. Are you prepared to meet with the Seers?"

He patted his coat and replied, "Yes. We've surrendered all of our weapons."

"Good. Garth will escort you inside."

"You're not going in?"

Her smirk turned dark. "I'm a much better long-range fighter. Garth and Ryan will be inside the sanctum with you."

"Well, I'm glad that you'll be out here watching our backs while we're inside."

"You'll be safe," Darci stated and turned to return to the roof.

*****

The *sanctum*, as Darci had called it, was a large space set off the common room. Garrett sat uncomfortably on a cushion waiting for the ceremony to begin. As he did so, he looked idly around the room and tried to focus his mind, which was already becoming a fuzzy from the smoke swirling foglike along the floor. He couldn't decide what the room was originally designed for. Outside, the remains of an old sign hung above the door and the letters "**SA**" were the only readable section left of the title, lending to his belief that it was a sanctum in the old world as well.

The room was square with some type of wood, perhaps cedar, lining the walls and ceiling, while the floor was simple concrete. In the middle of the floor, a drain was set in the sloping foundation to allow liquids to escape. Garrett wondered if the hunters used the sanctum as a slaughter room for their game, and the drain was to catch the blood. Two rows of wooden shelves or seats of some kind lined each wall, adding to the room's oddities. Did the hunters gather in the room and watch the victor carve up the animal? Was there some type of connection between the kill and honoring the beast?

He'd never know the true nature of the room, of course. The Seers tried to soften the room's appearance by placing pillows and rugs everywhere, using the wooden structures as a combination of storage and seating. When he was here before, Mistress Erika and two other women had formed the points of a triangle around him while two more fed twigs of an aromatic bush into an ancient brazier set in the corner. Garth had stood outside, peering through the little glass square set in the door—which was how the merchant had been able to kill Erika before he could get inside.

The current set-up was much like the first time, except Garth and Ryan, one of the guards who'd been on the porch when they arrived, were inside the sanctum with the Seers. Nicholas and Brandt were allowed to enter the sanctum with Garrett while his remaining companions sat in the common room drinking wine with a young girl.

Nicholas and Brandt sat along the wall next to Ryan. Garth stood in the doorway, blocking the window with his height. As before, two women sat near the brazier peeling leaves from small sticks and setting them aside before throwing the wood and roots into the fire. Garrett sat on a pillow, roughly in the center of the floor near the drain that he'd noticed before. Once he sat, one of the Seers had drawn a triangle on the concrete in chalk, placed a cushion at each point and then returned to sit on the bench.

The three Seers who would perform the ritual sat across from him on the wooden benches. They wore heavy robes of wool with strands of silver and gold intertwined around their wrists and upon their brows. Idly, his mind thought that their adornments must have cost a fortune. The women focused on a point behind him, seemingly ignoring the fact that he was even present.

The woman directly in front of him was stunning. Her dark hair framed olive skin that could only have come through breeding and not years of toiling in the sun. She appeared slim and of average height, but he could tell that she was well endowed as well. His mind began to wander even farther as the thick smoke curled around him and he found himself thinking about the woman more. What else did those robes hide?

He sat for an uncomfortably long time, waiting for them to begin the prophecy. Sweat dripped down the crevasse between his shoulders, continuing to trail along his spine and mingle with the wetness between his cheeks. It was incredibly hot in the sanctum and the acolytes continued to feed twigs into the fire.

Garrett began to get an ache in his lower back from sitting cross-legged, so he straightened his legs and arched his back to stretch it out. Still the women stared at him.

He wondered if he should open the conversation, but that felt wrong. *Are they already in a trance, learning of Homelake's future?* He was dimly aware of the pungent odor of pine and something sweet permeating the air. When he looked toward the brazier, he was surprised to see thick layers of smoke pouring forth from it; they'd begun to pile the leaves of the plant directly on the coals.

"Garrett Traxx, I am the Mistress of the Valley Lodge."

The violation of the silence in the chamber surprised Garrett, making him jump and whip his head back toward the Seers in front of him. The woman in the center had spoken. Her voice was scratched and battered, sounding as if she had something stuck in her throat and the words had trouble passing it.

His reaction must have played across his face, for the woman smiled. "Do I surprise you, little king?"

"No, I just wasn't expecting the rites to begin yet," he lied.

She laughed, the noise grating down his spine like a child rubbing a rock across a washing board. "You must learn to lie better once you are truly a king in the land of Homelake, Traxx."

His face flushed in embarrassment. *How can such a beautiful woman be cursed with that voice?* "I'm sorry... ahh, Mistress?"

"You may call me Diane or Mistress; both are acceptable in our home."

He nodded dumbly, feeling compelled to tell her the truth. "The sound of your voice startled me, Mistress. You are a beautiful woman, I wasn't expecting—"

"Traxx, you flatter me," she replied in guttural tones that made him wonder if she was even human.

The mistress pulled her robes away from where they'd gathered around her neck. She leaned her head back to expose ugly scars along both sides of her throat. "My father attempted to cut out my voice when I was a child. He thought that if he could remove my voice, the Gift would go away and I could be married off to a man who preferred a silent woman."

Her head snapped back down to stare icily at Garrett. "It didn't work. The visions intensified and I fled to the Valley Lodge, a place of legend where I was told the Seers were accepted by all." She held up both hands in front of her companions as she said the last word. The two women stood and grasped her delicate fingers, lifting her gently from the seat.

As one, they moved forward. Diane stopped near a pillow directly in front of him and the other two continued to their own cushions behind him on either side to form the human points of the triangle around him.

"I know why you are here. Tell me why you think you came to us today, Traxx."

Her word choice disturbed him. Why he *thought* he was there?

Garrett cleared his throat before beginning, "Mistress, I am to be crowned king of the people of Homelake at the full moon—"

"That is only two weeks from now," Diane interrupted him.

"Yes, Mistress. The people demanded that I speak to the Seers before my coronation. They wanted to ensure that crowning one, singular person as the leader is not a mistake."

"And the inevitable passage of the title on to your descendants," she surmised.

He nodded. The idea of succession had been a heated point of contention among the Council, dividing them on the issue. Generally, the farmers had liked the idea of the stability a royal family could bring; while the merchants wanted the title to be voted upon after Garrett's death. He preferred the hereditary nature of royalty as well, but had chosen to keep his opinion to himself so as not to sway the Council one way or another.

"Yes, that's one of the concerns," he admitted. "The other is whether or not crowning a king is the right thing for our people. Both the Council and myself share this concern."

Diane smirked at him through the haze of smoke. "Does it *really* matter what your title is? Are you not already the leader of the people of Homelake and the head of the governing council there?"

"Yes, but—"

"You waste our time, *King* Traxx," she growled while she gestured for the two women feeding leaves into the flames to increase their pace. Garrett waited patiently while the smoke built, allowing Diane to get into the element that she desired.

She inhaled deeply from the thick cloud around them. "What are your other concerns? You surprise me, Traxx, for you've not scratched the surface of the real problem. I have dreamt of other…issues for Homelake—and for everyone in the region."

"Issues? What issues?" Garrett demanded.

"All in good time," she replied as she inhaled deeply once again. "For now, talk to me about your concerns."

Behind him, he could hear the other two Seers breathing deeply as well, taking in as much of the smoke into their lungs as possible. He'd seen it before, with each breath, the women would begin to lose themselves in their trance. "I want to know about the crops," Garrett began. "We have a little wheat and some oats set aside, but everything else is ground-to-mouth; most of our food doesn't last much longer than a month once it's harvested. When will the ground produce enough to allow us to begin saving for the leaner seasons?"

"This is the lean season!" the Seer to his right shouted, causing him to jump.

"Forgive Arielle," Diane spoke softly, drawing his attention back to her. "She is usually the first to succumb to the effects of the Calamus."

Garrett watched, mesmerized as the Mistress' chest swelled and deflated with each breath. The fuzziness in his mind was beginning to deepen as the drug's effects intensified. "Calamus?" he asked, the word slurring off his tongue.

"Maybe you know it as Sweet Flag?" the Mistress said. "We use the root to help bring our visions while guests are present. Otherwise, we wouldn't be able to tell you of your future until you'd already gone—not a good business practice."

"Sweet Flag?" he was having difficulty thinking straight. The smoke was much more intense than it had been the first time he visited the lodge.

"Yes, but it smells awful," Diane's ruined voice cut through the fog. "That's why we also use pine needles to cover up the scent. When I became the Mistress of the Lodge, I also added the leaves and seeds of the Prickly Poppy to help ease the terror of the visions, which allows us to understand them and interpret them a little easier. As it turns out, they smell nice too."

He nodded his head dumbly in the smoke. The Seers wouldn't be able to see his movements; it just felt like the right thing to do. He had to acknowledge her somehow and he didn't trust his voice anymore. In fact, Garrett wasn't sure he trusted any part of his body at that moment.

"Garrett Traxx," Diane spoke, pulling his attention back from the edge of the abyss. "Do not panic. It is natural to feel isolated and that your body will betray you. When we—"

"Betrayal!" the woman named Arielle, gasped. "Your friends will betray you!"

"Yes, sister, tell us what you see!" the youngest of the three women in the triangle called from his other side.

"The past is not dead!" Arielle stated. "It will come for you. The sins of the past will be your undoing."

The fogginess in Garrett's mind cleared away, remaining in his limbs. He felt that he couldn't move, but could hear everything perfectly. The Seer's words painted a picture in his mind, "A jungle… Traxx in the jungle with the lizard-men… They fly! So beautiful, graceful…"

"The Earth Mother demands a sacrifice to end her pain!" the young Seer screamed.

The two of them played off each other, yelling things back and forth about flying men and the repair of damages. His head began to swim with all of the things that they said until one voice, the voice of a devil cut through the smoke.

"Your ancient enemies have returned." It took him a moment to focus on the voice. It was vaguely female, but not quite. There was something wrong with the way the words were put together, forced through ruined vocal chords. Then, he remembered the Mistress. Her face emerged from the smoke as she leaned forward.

"The wild men have returned from the grave. Their army, always ravenous, has conquered the homeland of your fathers. They rule all of the brown land to the south, demanding more and more from their people."

She grunted as if she'd been struck, then, "They know of the Traxx prosperity in the foothills of the giant mountains. They've been told of the never-ending food supply, the abundance of women who are not marked by disease, even the cooler weather draws them.

"Plotting. Planning. Scheming. The Vultures have returned. Beware little Traxxling. When you are older, they will come for you and everything before them will burn anew.

"But, all is not lost. Prepare yourselves! Make your places strong. Defeat them or you will never know peace."

The sudden silence in the room was more maddening to Garrett than when all three women had spoken at once. His mind raced with questions and clouded with the images that her vision created. Had the Vultures really returned with another army? Were the flying lizard men that Arielle saw the same as his family's ancient enemy? He remembered his father's tale of how the young Seer, his Aunt Mary, had been off a little with identifying the gang.

Diane said that they'd return when he was older, but had failed to say whether that was one day older or forty years. Then there was the part about the Earth Mother and healing… Did that have something to do with mending the soil so they could grow healthy crops instead of the stunted, shriveled fruits that they were able to produce now?

So many questions without answers. He knew better than to ask the Seers, they often had no idea what they spoke about when the words flowed through them during a ritual. One thing he knew was that The Keep had to be fortified with stronger walls—first around the Traxx home and then around all of Homelake. When he was a boy, the walls of San Angelo were destroyed through sabotage and giant metal beasts that smashed through stone like a rock through glass. That wouldn't happen this time; machines of that kind no longer worked and only haunted his nightmares.

The smoke began to clear from the room as he sat silently waiting for the women to indicate that the ritual was complete. The two Seers behind him rose wordlessly and went to Diane, once again helping her to her feet before filing out of the room.

As Garrett watched them go, his eyes drifted to Nicholas and Brandt, still positioned near the door. Seeing his nephew triggered something in his mind that Arielle had said before she began ranting about flying men. *My friends will betray me… Who?*

TWO

Balroth's massive bare foot swept a wall of sand into Vengeance's face, temporarily blinding him. He didn't wait for what he knew was coming and dove to his right. He'd watched the giant's other fights from the cages before. The man—more beast than human—was known for his dirty moves among the other gladiators.

Vengeance felt the monster's adze pass mere inches over his spine while he was still airborne in his dive to the side. If he hadn't reacted instantly, the head of the tool would be buried eight inches into his side. No one could survive that kind of damage—and no one had.

Balroth was the champion, the man who brought the crowds to the stadium by the thousands, the one who devoured all who dared to stand before him... And Vengeance had called him out for his shot at the title.

The youth had little to lose. His only possession in this world was his life. He'd been a gladiator for seven long years, fighting in every little backwater hellhole that Lucas could find and had paid dearly for it. By all accounts, he should have been dead long ago, so it didn't matter to him that Balroth collected men's heads like some men collected women.

The only real problem, as far as Vengeance saw it, was that he'd gotten Chaos, his older brother, involved in the fight.

Vengeance hit the ground hard. He'd thought that he'd be able to roll back to his feet, but the sand in this stadium was thicker than he'd anticipated, causing him to sink into it. "*Oof!*"

The crowd roared in response to his acrobatic move to elude the giant's weapon and he smiled into the dirt. He heard Chaos yelling to distract Balroth and knew the giant was on the attack once again. The whistling of the blade made him roll away from his adversary. Sand flew in all directions when the axe buried into the ground where he'd been a moment before.

Balroth grunted, pulling his weapon from the earth before blocking and sidestepping Chaos' thrust with a farmer's pitchfork. He clamped his upper arm down hard onto the shaft of the farm implement and then rotated his torso, sending the smaller of the brothers tumbling away to land in a heap beside the bodies of the three inexperienced slaves who'd made up their team of "gardeners" doomed to fight against the champion, the "woodsman."

The giant turned once more to face Vengeance. He gripped his garden hoe with both hands across his body, cursing his owner, Lucas, for agreeing to the theme of settlers versus a marauding invader. Their farm implements were woefully inadequate against Balroth's adze, a wickedly sharp tool used to split and shape wood. Two of his companions lay face down in the sand, their heads crushed by one massive sweep of the champion's axe. The other stretched gruesomely towards the safety of the gladiator cages, murdered as he tried to run. Balroth had buried the adze all the way up to the handle in the kid's back.

His adversary lumbered toward him, grinning with the confidence born from surviving countless fights in the wasteland matches. "You will die like the others, boy," he grumbled.

Vengeance smiled back. He'd endured twenty-four matches—he knew how to win as well. "Today is your day to go to the halls of the fallen, Balroth. I—"

He didn't have a chance to finish the witty comment that he'd prepared for the benefit of the crowd before the giant closed the distance and swung the adze. Vengeance blocked the axe with the shaft of the hoe, shattering the wooden handle and jarring his shoulders with the impact.

He stepped lightly backward, holding both pieces of his ruined weapon. The champion glanced quickly over his shoulder to find Chaos, but Vengeance's brother was nowhere to be seen. The youth didn't have time to wonder where Chaos had gone; Balroth charged toward him, causing him to backpedal.

Vengeance ducked under the champion's clumsy swing as he barreled past. *Balroth should have known better than to try an attack while running*, he thought, swinging the lower part of the hoe at the backside of his foe.

The crowd roared in approval. They assumed he was playing with the champion by slapping him on the ass with the stick. Vengeance raised his arms to the side, encouraging them to cheer. He loved the crowds; they were what made this life bearable.

Balroth almost surprised him while he soaked up the mob's adoration. He caught the man's movement out of the corner of his eye and threw himself backward. The head of the adze whistled past, a mere foot in front of his face. If he hadn't moved, it would have crushed his skull.

Vengeance took advantage of the giant's momentum and smashed the stick against the back of his head as he wheeled past. To his disappointment, it did little to the champion. He was simply too large to get any real advantage against him, especially with a half a length of garden hoe.

He turned and sprinted back to where the other slaves had died. One of them had a pitchfork that his brother had tried to use against Balroth. He reasoned that the tines on the fork could do some damage to the champion, regardless of his size.

Vengeance's feet burrowed into the blood-damp sand as he stopped to search for the weapon. It wasn't there.

Balroth's pounding feet caused him to turn. The big man was bearing down on him once again. Vengeance planted his feet and hurled the part of the hoe without the blade. It whirled through the air and smashed into the champion's face. Blood exploded from his nose, covering his face in the dark substance.

The giant stopped and wiped the gore from his mouth, smearing it across his cheek. His teeth were bloody as he smirked at Vengeance, "You've blooded me, worm. Thank you. It's been a long time since anyone lasted more than a few seconds against me. You've earned your place in *Fólkvangr* today."

Vengeance inclined his head, accepting Balroth's compliment. The momentary truce ended and the bigger man raced toward him, swinging the axe theatrically above his head for the benefit of the crowd. He had a moment to think that the champion really didn't have any technique and must have relied on his size and strength to win his battles... Then he was ducking the blade.

He swung the half-hoe hard, gashing a wound into Balroth's thigh. The champion yelled out in pain, bending down to grasp his leg. "Goddamn it, you fucker! I'm going to tear you apart and fuck your corpse."

"This is your day—" A darting shadow behind Balroth caused Vengeance to pause. He recovered quickly, so as to not ruin the opportunity. "This is your day to die, Balroth."

The champion's rumbling laughter echoed across the sands of the arena. "You think you're gonna— *Arg!*"

Balroth swung his elbow blindly behind him, hitting Chaos across the chest to send him flying backward once more. He clutched at his low back, pawing uselessly at the dagger buried to the hilt in his kidney.

"I'm gonna kill you!" the mammoth shouted. The sand scattered wildly when Balroth turned toward Chaos with a growl. He lumbered toward Vengeance's brother, raising the adze above his head to take a swing at the small gladiator who'd stabbed him. Chaos scrambled on his backside away from the hulking beast.

"Hey! Hey, you big bastard!" Vengeance yelled to get his attention. Chaos was a capable fighter, but the simple truth was that he'd have been dead twenty times over if he'd fought on his own instead of as part of a group or doubled-up with Vengeance.

It was no use, though. The knife Chaos jabbed into the big man's back had injured him and he wanted revenge. The axe went up and fell amazingly fast toward his brother, stirring a cloud of dust up from the ground as it hit.

"*No!*" Vengeance screamed. "Caleb!"

He sprinted toward the two of them. Balroth swung his axe back and forth wildly into the dust cloud. Vengeance launched himself, hitting the giant low in the back. His shoulder smashed up against the hilt of Chaos' knife, plunging it almost all the way inside Balroth's body.

The giant's back straightened and he switched the axe from one hand to the other. Vengeance tucked up close behind Balroth to avoid the sweep of the axe behind his back. The blade passed closer behind him than it had before when he was on the ground as the seat of his trousers whipped sideways.

He squeezed with all of his might around the giant's midsection, attempting to drive the knife further into the man's stomach. Somehow, impossibly, Caleb—*Chaos*—appeared through the dust and rammed a pitchfork into Balroth's shoulder and the adze tumbled to the ground.

Vengeance released him and snatched up the axe. He pivoted away on one foot and swung it sideways as hard as he could. The curved blade of the adze impacted just below the giant's kneecap. The weight of the weapon's head carried it through the meaty tendons around the knee, passing through the smaller, rubbery ligaments and continuing nearly unimpeded between the bones. The adze hacked through the same tissues on the inside of Balroth's leg, emerging and then imbedding itself into his other leg.

The massive gladiator stood silently in shock on one leg for a moment before toppling over. He began screaming and cursing Vengeance before he'd even hit the ground. "You mother fucker! Godsdamned, goat-raping, son of a whore."

The roar of the crowd was almost deafening. Vengeance allowed himself a moment to glance up from the bloody, spurting stump of Balroth's leg. The bowl of the stadium stretched around him, impossibly large. Seats extended skyward, so high that he couldn't even make out the faces of the fans in the top rows. *All of these people are here for me*, Vengeance thought.

"Varan!" Chaos shouted as he ran up to him. They hugged each other fiercely as Balroth continued to bellow obscenities toward them. "Great fight, Brother!"

Vengeance accepted the praise and then held Chaos at arm's length. "Are you okay? I thought you were done for."

"I threw up a cloud of sand and got out of the way. Then, when he was swinging madly, without looking, I circled around and took Steven's pitchfork. He didn't need it anymore." Chaos laughed at their friend's demise like only a man who'd accepted death as his mistress could.

"I'm glad that you did. I didn't know what I was going to do after I got him wrapped up," Vengeance admitted.

"You'd have fucking died, worm!" Balroth shouted. The man had dragged himself nearer to them, the adze trailing alongside of him.

"You're beaten, Balroth. Admit it and you may live."

Individual shouts emerged from the crowd, "*Finish him!*" "*Cut his head off!*" "*Kill him!*"

Vengeance looked up at the crowd as Chaos leapt onto the giant's back, kicking the axe away before wrapping his arm around the man's throat in a chokehold. Then he began squeezing.

The onlookers wanted a death. They'd paid for a championship match—that *always* meant a battle to the death. It didn't matter how many men had died today, it was one group of warriors against Balroth. Only one of those would be allowed to leave the sands of the arena floor. Vengeance knew the rules and Cooper would beat him if he tried to violate them. But he was the champion now; would Lucas dare to injure such a precious commodity?

Balroth had always been nice enough to him when they were caged near each other; his personality didn't change until he went into the arena. Should he let the man live? They could fashion a fake leg for him and he could retire to train the next generation of gladiators.

That thought stuck in his gut. Did he *want* there to be a next generation of gladiators? He'd lost so much in his lifetime because of the slavers who'd taken him. A rhythmic chanting from the crowd caused him to stop the nonsense going through his mind.

"*Kill him. Kill him. Kill him…*" On and on the chant continued.

"Stop, Chaos," Vengeance ordered.

His brother released his hold on the giant. The smaller man had almost knocked him out, but once Chaos let him go, he began taking deep gasps to replenish his air supply.

Vengeance walked confidently over to Balroth and crouched down. "You fought well today, Brother." He surveyed the bloody scene around them. Of the six men who'd entered the stadium to fight the giant, armed with daggers and a few farm tools in some sick joke that the organizers had designed, only Chaos and Vengeance remained alive. "Many men went to be with *Týr* today."

"Send me to Him, then," the giant replied, still gasping from the chokehold Chaos had placed on him.

"Are you ready to go to the God of the Sun? To walk the fertile fields of Fólkvangr and live amongst the other warriors forever?"

"I value death more than you will ever value life, *Champion*. Do it. Send me to Him."

Vengeance stepped away and retrieved the adze that had been Balroth's weapon of choice. The fresh blood of his three companions coated the head and shaft already stained by the remains of countless others. Balroth had been a mighty warrior; surely he had earned his place in heaven with the souls of those he'd sent there.

Chaos stood apart from them, throwing his arms up and down to incite the crowd into frenzy. They would get the death they commanded. Vengeance walked back beside the man who he emulated in secret and studied when he had the opportunity.

He placed the axe on his shoulder and opened his stance. "Boy," the giant said quickly before the strike came.

"Vengeance. My name is Vengeance," he corrected.

Balroth nodded his head. "Vengeance, don't let this life use you up like it did me."

The curved steel fell against Balroth's neck and his head tumbled free.

The masses in the seats roared their approval. This is what they'd come to see. Life in the wastes was hard; their sole source of entertainment was the traveling fights that made their rounds through the old stadiums.

As his brother embraced him, Vengeance drank deeply of the crowd's exaltation.

THREE

Tanya tugged at her dress. It felt so...*restrictive* after wearing pants for as long as she could remember. There was a time, when she was a young girl at the old home, when she wore dresses. Then, not long after her cousins were abducted, the family went on the road, so she traded in her skirts for breeches and she'd kept her legs covered ever since then.

Today was a special occasion though; for today, her father would officially be crowned the King of Homelake. His coronation was supposed to have been almost a year earlier, but he'd refused to do anything except prepare the city for war after he returned from his visit to discuss the future with the Seers of the Valley Lodge.

He drove the people of Homelake hard as they geared up and fortified the city against the family's ancient enemy. In between working in the fields, they harvested boulders and timber from the mountain slopes to build the walls. They'd completed massive structures only two weeks before today—which is why Garrett had finally agreed to allow the coronation ceremony to move forward.

While the walls were constructed, the blacksmiths had been busy melting scavenged metal from the useless self-propelled carriages that seemed to be everywhere in the old world. From the light metal panels on the sides of the vehicles, they'd made arrowheads by the thousands and developed a durable and tough design for helmets and ring mail. They reformed the vehicles' massive steel frames into short swords, fighting knives, pikes and spears. Financed from Garrett's own pocket, they'd forged a massive armory for the city's militia and the newly established Traxx Guard.

The Traxx Guard had a two-fold mission; their primary duty was to protect members of the Traxx family. Secondly, they were to act as the sergeants and captains of the militia during drills and if they were called upon to fight. The initial force numbered thirty-four men and six women, chosen from among the militia, who'd applied and passed the grueling two-week tryout; special emphasis was given to those who showed exceptional skill with individual weapons. Her father chose to focus on a recruit's ability to fight alone with their chosen weapon because the guards would be spread thin across The Keep and would need to be able to fight alone if the outer perimeter was ever breached. The militia, on the other hand, would fight in close-knit groups similar to how the old history books described the Greek phalanx, or as archers from the walls.

The city of Homelake had become an island of armor and warfare in little more than a year.

The regular militia was given a two-week reprieve from drilling so they could observe the tryouts for the Traxx Guard. Of course, Tanya watched the tryouts as well, when her duties afforded her the opportunity to slip away for a couple of hours. There was little in the way of excitement for a girl on the eve of her eighteenth birthday in Homelake...until she met *him*.

At the end of the first week of the trials, she was ladling out water to the candidates after a long day when a boy her own age accepted a cup from her. Frederick was glistening with sweat. It ran in thick lines down his face and dripped from the tips of his black hair, disappearing into the dampness of his filthy shirt. He'd made small talk with her for several minutes, never discovering that she was the king's daughter. Tanya smiled at herself in the mirror as she remembered meeting the handsome young candidate.

They became friends during breaks in the action and she'd made a point of watching his tryouts, viewing the sword matches through her fingers as he fought against other candidates. The final trial was against her father's friend, Nicholas, recently named Captain of the Traxx Guard.

Afterwards, the announcer called out the names of the men and women who were to be the inaugural members of the Guard. To her delight, Frederick was one of the names called.

He'd sought her out after the ceremony and excitedly asked her to a date along the lake to celebrate. She'd accepted, but almost immediately, someone called her "Princess Tanya" and Frederick became embarrassed to discover that the water girl he'd been talking to was actually the princess. He apologized profusely for his ignorance, so she'd told him the only way he could make it right was to take her on the date he'd promised her.

They'd begun dating exclusively and not long afterwards, they became lovers. She often thought they were ready for the next step in their relationship, a formal proposal of marriage from Frederick, but those thoughts stalled when they met with his staunch commitment to the Guard.

It wasn't forbidden for members of the Traxx Guard to be married, but Frederick professed to her that he refused marriage while he was an active member of the Guard. He feared that others would think he received special favors from the king as his son-in-law. Instead, he chose to live a simple life in the barracks on The Keep's first floor so he and Tanya could be close together.

She pulled at the area of the dress that seemed to cut into her midsection. Tanya remembered the seamstress telling her that a flattering look was one that clung tightly around her stomach, but she certainly didn't think that the woman would make it *so* tight.

Her pants sat across the back of the chair where she'd left them the night before and she looked longingly at them. She'd had that particular pair for years, receiving them as a gift for her sixteenth birthday, long after her teenage growth spurt. The last several weeks, though, she'd noticed them getting tight around her waist—like the cursed dress—and wondered if the seamstress could remove a few stitches or add little more fabric around the beltline.

Part of her mind told her to just have a new pair made, but she couldn't justify wasting the fabric that was still good, even after all this time. She wondered why she seemed to be getting thicker. Her diet was the same and she'd been conducting drills with the Guard for almost as long as they'd been an organization, so she should have remained the same size, not getting big—

"Wait a minute," she muttered to her reflection.

Tanya hurried away from the mirror to her desk and pulled out the little handwritten calendar that she had in the desk. She glanced at the top of the calendar where the words, "*111th Year Since The Reset*," were written darkly. She found today, her father's coronation day, marked with a flower that she'd drawn weeks ago. She began searching each entry for the last day of her menstrual cycle.

She hadn't thought anything was out of the ordinary. She certainly didn't feel any different; she'd just been busy with her weapons drills and helping to oversee the coronation. Her finger trailed along the neat little boxes that she'd drawn and was surprised when she had to flip past two pages. It had been more than two *months* since the end of her last cycle.

"Oh shit…"

FOUR

A metal cup banged against Varan's cell door. He raised his head off the straw mat to see who it was and felt the pressure of last night's woman on his shoulder.

"Get up, Vengeance. Lucas wants to see you."

He recognized the cell keeper's voice as the offender. "What does he want, Cooper?"

The cup banged harshly against the vertical bars. "He wants you to fucking get up, you worthless slave!"

Varan sat up as the nude woman beside him stared wide-eyed at the jailer. "I will kill you if the opportunity arises. You know that, don't you Coop?"

Cooper laughed. "I'm not worried." He grabbed his dirty crotch and thrust his chin toward the girl in Varan's cell. "When you go, I'm going to have a piece of that."

"Touch her and I don't care what Lucas says, you will die."

"You don't care what Lucas says?" Cooper asked loudly, raising his hands to shoulder level, encouraging an audience. "Do you all hear that? This slave doesn't care what his owner says."

He dropped his arms and leaned in close to the bars. "Just because you're the champion and get your pick of the house women doesn't mean that you're above the master's law, *Varan*."

The gladiator stood in anger. No one except his brother and Lucas were allowed to call him by his true name, not even the women who shared his cell with him. It was a reminder of his past that he'd just as soon stayed there.

"What did you call me, Coop?"

"It's your name, isn't it?" he asked, taking a step back, even though the impenetrable steel bars separated them.

"You know the rules. Lucas doesn't allow anyone to call me that. You know what happened to the last dickless asshole who tried…" he trailed off, letting Cooper's imagination finish the rest. Several years ago, another gladiator had dared to utter his given name as a curse while they cleaned themselves after a fight. He'd torn the man's testicle off with his bare hands.

He wore the crisscross scars from the jailer's whip on his back with pride and as a reminder to his fellow slaves that he wasn't to be taunted. It wasn't lost on either him or Caleb that the scars looked like the metal tracks that cut through countryside near some of the towns that they traveled through when they went to the various places that the Contest took them. Even though they'd abandoned him to his fate, the Traxx couldn't leave him in peace.

Cooper cleared his throat, "Well… Um, you know, *Vengeance*, the boss wants to see you."

Varan smiled, *Good, the jailer can be taught.* "Leave her alone, Cooper," he said as he indicated the woman. "She's done nothing. Don't try to take out your anger at me on her."

The man's eyes searched up and down her body, "Eh… She's too skinny anyways. My giant cock would stab straight through her bony back." He clapped his hands and then rubbed them together. "Put your clothes on, champ. You know the drill."

The jailer watched him intently as he dressed, making sure that he didn't stow a weapon in his pockets. Once he was finished, he stuck both hands through an open section in the bars and Cooper placed a rusty pair of old world handcuffs on him before opening the cell door.

Cooper stepped back rapidly, hand on his knife, as Varan walked out of the cage. He locked the woman inside the cell behind them and directed the gladiator to lead the way toward Lucas' office. He'd been there many times, so he knew the way without needing to be prodded along by the jailer. As the Primus, he enjoyed certain freedoms that the others did not, which included regular visits with his owner to verify that he was properly fed and cared for.

Varan trudged wearily across a corner of the practice field and through the gates of the gladiators' compound. He needed to piss and wanted to spend more time with the woman before beginning his day of training. *What is this early meeting about?* he wondered.

The House of Miller's gladiatorial compound sat in the old world town of Trinity, in the area known as California. The compound itself was a large, odd-shaped field, completely encircled by ten-foot high stone walls. Rusted barbed wire topped the wall, more likely to cause a deadly infection than inflict any damage upon someone attempting to scale them. Secured behind the walls was the open training ground, large enough for the gladiators to practice every skill except for horsemanship.

Also within the compound was the gladiators' home. A large building with several roll-up doors—more than half of which no longer worked— held the cells of the slaves. The men and women that Lucas owned were lucky since there were enough of the small rooms for everyone to have their own space with cinder block walls separating the cells. Varan had been stacked six men deep in rooms the same size with only bars separating them when they traveled to other Contest locations.

Immediately outside of the compound was a two-story building. At one time, it had been the jail, which is where the dormitory's bars came from. Lucas and his family lived on the old jail's second floor and Varan had seen the family's living quarters twice. Normally, it was reserved for the Miller family and their house slaves, but he'd visited Lucas there when the man was bedridden with sickness. The various couches, pillows and blankets seemed odd to Varan, who lived his life either fighting, fucking or sleeping. He couldn't fathom the uses for the different pieces of furniture since it was just Lucas, his wife and their two children.

The first floor, which Varan had visited several times over the years, held the offices of Lucas' various business ventures. Aside from owning the small local stadium and providing his own gladiators for the matches all over the region, he also owned several inns and taverns throughout the town of Trinity. He was easily the most influential man in the city.

"Is that animal secure, Cooper?" one of the guards asked as they passed through the compound's gate and waited for the external gate to be opened. Varan's nose wrinkled at the man's fetid breath. He'd been taught from an early age that a man's teeth were extremely important. They provided him with a way to chew food, aiding in the digestion and absorption of nutrients locked away inside, and the vacant holes left where rotten teeth were pulled or broken away were prone to deadly infections. Most importantly, though, a healthy set of teeth worked well as a last-ditch weapon, born of desperation. He'd seen a man rip out another's throat with his teeth before; a glorious example of humanity's resolve to survive at all costs.

"As much as someone like him can be," Cooper replied. "The boss trains these beasts to kill someone with every conceivable method, though, so I wouldn't get too close."

The guard took a step back and Varan snarled at him for effect, causing him to trip over his own feet. He fell away to the guffaws of the other guards at the gate.

"Goddammit, I'll kill you, you sonofabitch!" he yelled as he drew his sword.

Varan stared defiantly at the guard. *Is this how it ends? Some piss ant nothing runs me through and it's all over? So be it.* He stepped back with one foot, raising to the balls of his feet in a fighting stance, totally relaxed and ready to kill the guard if he charged him. He'd been unarmed against an opponent more times than he could remember. He was not afraid. If this was his day to return to Fólkvangr, then he was ready. But he would go out fighting. Týr would banish him to *Niflhel* to suffer the underworld's torments forever if he died as a coward.

"You put that away, Greg," another of the guards, a sergeant Varan realized, told him. "Lucas will torture you for days if you injure the Primus. That man right there—and the rest of the gladiators—are what pay your wages; you'd do best to let him pass. Old Cooper has him locked up tight, no need to worry."

Varan dropped his handcuffed hands and fell back onto his heels. Today would not be the day to send these men to their deaths. That day was approaching, but their sergeant had earned them a stay of execution. *For now.*

The outer gate opened and he went through first, Cooper followed, ever watchful that the man would try something to escape. They followed the crumbling sidewalk around to the Miller home, passing through a newer wooden fence, constructed of timbers from the trees in the area. They passed through this barrier unmolested and entered the building.

Two women, sitting at chipped wooden desks, looked up at them when they came through the door. Varan had seen them sitting in the exact spots each time that he'd been summoned to speak with Lucas. He didn't think the women were slaves—they certainly didn't report to the slave cells in the compound each night. They must have been workers, hired like the guards, who went home to their families each night.

He tried to determine what it was that they did. They had stacks and stacks of thin rectangular paper that they scribbled notes and tally marks on furiously. It looked like they copied one page to another, not really creating anything, just making work for themselves. The sheets they copied to the clean paper were crumpled or folded and looked as if they'd been out on the road. *Maybe they're Contest announcements*, he thought.

Varan remembered his letters from when he was a child, but he'd never been good at them, and hadn't tried practicing them since the night he was abducted and sold into slavery. He tried to get either of their attention as he marched past, but neither of them paid any attention after the initial reaction to see who'd come into their busy office.

Lucas Miller's office was beyond the desks, down a hallway protected by two more guards. Cooper talked them through and within seconds they were standing outside of the spacious office, easily the size of four or five cells put together.

"Come in, Vengeance, come in," his owner called, beckoning him through the doorway. He pushed his chair away from the desk, where he'd been studying those same strange papers that the women out front were preparing and came around to pat him affectionately on the shoulder.

"Are you well, my Primus?"

"Yes, sir," Varan replied, careful to keep his tone even and bland. Regardless of the fact that Lucas had never beat him, the men who worked for him had, so he was just as guilty as the others in Varan's eyes.

"Old Cooper here hasn't been busting your balls too much has he?"

"No, sir. We're well taken care of in the compound. Thank you for your generosity."

Lucas nodded his head and Varan became fixated on the rolls of skin around his neck. He unconsciously tensed his abdominal muscles; a man shouldn't have so much to eat that he becomes fat, as his owner had become.

"Alright. You're sure there are no concerns?"

Varan thought a moment and then answered, "If I may have the woman who stayed in my cell last night returned to me, I liked her very much."

"Done. Cooper, make sure that she is locked in Vengeance's cell each night until he tires of her." Lucas sat down at his desk and as an afterthought said, "Oh, and Cooper?"

"Yes, sir?"

"None of your people—or you—are allowed to touch the girl. She belongs to Vengeance until I say otherwise. Got it?"

Cooper nodded his head slowly. Varan could tell that the man's plans to rape the girl just outside of his cell while he watched had been dashed. "Yes, sir. I'll make sure no one lays a finger on her."

"Good. We need to keep our champion happy and virile."

He looked away from the jailer to Varan. "Have a seat, Vengeance. We have a matter of business to discuss."

"Yes, sir," the gladiator replied woodenly. *This can't be good.*

"I've received a letter, signed by the members of the Commerce Guild. It's also been signed by most of the House owners from the coastal remains."

Varan clucked his tongue in suspense. The Commerce Guild was the organization that oversaw the fair distribution of supplies to all the remaining towns. They were not opposed to individual wealth–as the opulence of the Miller home indicated–but they did believe in a sense of fairness and ensuring that no town went without having enough food for their residents. He didn't know how far their influence spread, but he had to assume that everywhere he'd fought had been under the Guild's purview.

"They have decided that Contest co-champions are not to be allowed," Lucas stated.

The floor seemed to drop out from under Varan's feet. "What does that mean?" he asked, quickly reeling his thoughts back in.

"It means that you're going to have to fight Chaos. To the death."

Emotions warred within him. There was no way he could fight his brother in a death match. They'd been through too much together in the past fifteen years to have their world turned upside down. If either of them died in battle protecting each other, then he could accept that fate. To kill one's own kin was surely a sin that would banish him to Niflhel for eternity.

"Sir, I can't fight my brother."

"You will, or I'll make you!" Lucas bellowed. "You are a slave, Vengeance. I *own* you…" Miller patted both hands softly on the desk to calm himself before speaking again quietly. "You will do as I tell you."

Varan didn't take his eyes off of his owner, but the scrape of boots in the hallway told him that the guards had shifted in the doorway in case there was trouble. "Everything is fine. Leave us," Lucas ordered.

"I understand your frustration, Vengeance, I do, but—"

"You understand nothing," Varan shouted back. "My brother is all I have left."

He saw movement out of the corner of his eye and tried to avoid Cooper's swing, but the chair he sat in was too plush and caught him. The wooden club hit him across the bridge of his nose, causing an explosion of white light in front of his eyes.

"Hold!" Lucas yelled at the jailer, who had the weapon drawn back for another strike.

Varan twisted in his seat to stare daggers into Cooper, imagining the man's murder in a million ways. Blood poured freely from his nostrils, quickly covering the arm of the chair with the thick fluid.

"Dammit, Cooper. You've ruined my unblemished old world armchair. That cost me two slave girls." Lucas pointed at a cabinet and ordered, "Get him a towel."

He watched the jailer with hatred in his eyes. The man retrieved an old hand towel from a side cabinet and wisely tossed it in his lap, keeping his distance. "Clean yourself up; you're ruining the nice furniture."

"I will kill you one day, Cooper. And believe me, you will know that it's coming and it won't be quick or painless."

"Enough!" Lucas slammed his hand down on the desk. "Vengeance, I know this is difficult for you. Your brother has been with you for your entire life. He's your blood. And so on. I've thought about this and it pains me to order you to do this, but I can't go against the Guild."

"It's more than that, Lucas," Varan countered. "You're asking me to kill the last remnant of my past."

"I know what I'm *telling* you to do, Vengeance. The truth of the matter is that if I hadn't arranged to have you two together in most of your fights, he would have been dead ten years ago. I saw the potential in you, so for those two years that he fought in the arena before you were old enough to join him I staged all of his fights against men who'd seen the end of their days—and even some of those were close calls.

"Chaos is not a strong fighter," Lucas continued. "Yes, he's a great teammate and you work well together, but one-on-one, most of the gladiators in the arena could beat him."

Lucas' expression softened once again. "Look, you've kept him alive this long, but I have no choice except to schedule the fight. Without the support of the Guild, the people of Trinity would starve to death within a year. We have fresh water and timber for trade, but our crops don't supply enough to sustain everyone in this town. Anarchy would rapidly descend on this these hills."

"I would accept that over murdering my brother."

"You'd rather have the blood of two thousand people on your hands?" Lucas asked.

Varan shrugged, "What do I care about them? They are nothing to me. I don't know them. They're faces in the crowd at best."

"I've trained you well… Too well, it would appear."

"I won't fight my brother."

"Then he'll kill you in the arena and die the next fight that he's in. You know this. If you agree to fight him, you could make it a clean kill. Painless. Let him get into the ring with the likes of one of those monsters from Redding—or worse, from Crescent City. Their current primus takes his time, slowly slicing pieces of his adversary away and he eats it as they watch in horror. Is that what you want for your brother? Hardly an honorable death."

Lucas let that sink in for a moment before continuing. "*You* could honor your brother; give him a proper warrior's death. Don't let him die like that, to be eaten alive, toyed with and embarrassed…tortured in front of a crowd. If that happens, they will never remember your brother's feats in the arena, he would only be remembered as the man who was killed by the demon from the coast."

Lucas' words resonated with him. He didn't want the memory of himself or his brother to disappear into anonymity, forgotten and lost to the sands of the stadium. Would the gods even allow Caleb into Fólkvangr if he was cut down and murdered, an embarrassment to the men they'd sent to *Freyja's* fields together? "I don't want to kill my brother," he muttered.

"I know you don't want to fight Chaos, Vengeance. I'm feeding you rancid meat and telling you to enjoy your meal. But, you are both warriors and you'll do as you're told."

Varan knew it was a losing battle to argue with Lucas any further. The man would put them in the ring, regardless of their personal desires and if they refused to fight, he'd just have the guards shoot them from the stands. Yet, he couldn't live with himself if he murdered his brother. He needed to talk to Caleb and tell him what their owner planned.

"Yes, sir," Varan replied to Lucas' demand. "Do you know when the Contest will be?"

"No, the Guild hasn't given me any details yet."

"May I go?" he asked.

Lucas stared at him for a moment and then replied, "Yes. Go pray to your warrior gods and speak with your brother." He looked over to Cooper, "Allow him to speak with Chaos this morning before they begin their daily drills."

"Yes, sir," the jailer replied.

"Think on it, Vengeance. You know that I'm right. Either you face him in battle and honor him or the Commerce Guild will remove one of you in the name of progress. Good day, son."

Lucas returned to studying the strange marks on the paper, ignoring Varan and Cooper as if they'd already gone.

*****

Cooper pushed him roughly into his cell, telling him to wait there while he collected his brother. The woman was still there. She'd put on her clothing since he last saw her. The scent of stale urine in the chamber pot made him wrinkle his nose slightly as he sat down roughly on the concrete bench protruding from the wall.

How was he supposed to tell his brother what Lucas had planned? He couldn't simply say to him that they'd had a nice run, see you in the afterlife. Why had this trial come to him? Was Týr punishing him for something? Was his god making him atone for his sins through the sacrifice of his brother? Had he not fought bravely enough or done something against the will of the gods?

"Is everything alright, Primus?"

The woman's voice startled him from his thoughts. "Huh? I'm sorry, I was thinking."

"I could see that. You look upset; did your visit to the master not go well?"

"No, the visit to the *master* did not go well…" he allowed his voice to trail off as he imagined his sword running through his brother's heart.

"I believe there is still an hour until the morning work bells," she stated. "Do you want to talk about your troubles? I'm a good listener."

He smiled and examined her face. She was pretty—easily the prettiest slave in the household. Tight spirals of dark red hair framed her lean, heart-shaped face and bright emerald green eyes stared at him intensely. Varan got the distinct impression that everything about the woman was intense; their lovemaking the night before certainly had been.

"What is your name?"

"Freya, Primus."

He reeled. Was this a sign from the gods? "Like the goddess Freyja?"

She cocked her head slightly and answered, "It sounds similar. You said 'FRY-ya' but my name is 'FRAY-ya.' I can see where it's confusing, Primus. You may call me whatever you'd like."

He resisted the urge to slap her. "Dammit woman, we are equals. Both of us are slaves, regardless of what title they've given me. Speak freely."

She didn't flinch at his words. Instead, she glared back at him. "You will not beat me for telling you exactly what I think?" she asked?

Her words defused the anger inside of him and he sighed, "No, Freya. I will not beat you for speaking to me as you wish."

"Every man I've ever known has hit me for telling them the truth. Men often say that they would like to know what is on your mind, but when you tell them, they can't handle it and become angry."

Varan held up his hands, still shackled in the restraints. "I swear to the gods that I will not harm you for speaking your mind. Ever. There, does that ease your fears of me? I'm not so insecure in myself that I would need to hurt a woman for disagreeing with me or saying something that I didn't like."

She seemed to consider his words, her lips pursed as she thought about what he'd said. After a moment, she answered, "Okay. I will take your word for it, Primus."

"You may call me Vengeance if you like."

"I heard the jailer earlier; why don't you go by your given name?"

Varan grimaced. *Do I really need to explain things to her when my brother has been handed a death sentence?* It wasn't a hard question to answer, but the reason why he avoided the use of his name had defined who he was as a warrior.

"I was abducted from my family compound in Texas along with—"

"Is Texas a city?" Freya asked.

He chuckled, "No. Texas is a place far away; over the mountains, across a vast desert of sand and beyond."

She stared at his hands as he gestured outside and then slowly looked back into his eyes. "How big is the outside?"

"Huh?"

"How big…" she grunted in frustration. "How far away is Texas?"

Varan shrugged. "I was only ten when I was taken. It's a long ways away though. Do you often travel with the household when we go to the Contest?"

"Sometimes. I went to a place called Yuba City one time. It took five days of travel to get there."

He shuddered at the memory of Yuba. The town had been close to one of the fires that burned away the old world and created the wastes. The place still bore the scars of the destruction wrought so long ago. The worst part was the strange growths that seemed to protrude from everyone who lived there. He'd been worried about contracting whatever disease they had, but Lucas had ensured they stayed only long enough to participate in the Contest and then left promptly.

"Yuba was a long ways off—the farthest I've traveled to fight—but Texas is ten times as far away. And, I've heard people say that Texas is only halfway across all the land; that more lay on the far side."

"Then why do we stay here?"

"This is where the House of Miller is located. We're owned by Lucas, so this is where we stay." He returned to her earlier question before they'd gotten sidetracked by how big the land was. "I don't go by my given name because I believed with all of my heart that my family—all of whom are great warriors," he clarified. "I believed that they'd come and rescue Chaos and me. We waited and waited, the days turned to weeks, months and eventually years. The Traxx never came after us. They abandoned us to our fates."

"Maybe they tried to find you, but couldn't."

It was a possibility that he'd fantasized about, but he knew it wasn't true. The Traxx were renowned for being able to find whoever they were looking for. That fool old man, Aiden, had even told them the story of the first Traxx the night they were abducted. Aeric had traveled for months, all the way from Texas to some other place—he'd long forgotten the name—and found his mother and girlfriend. The ability to seek out lost people was a skill that he'd passed on to all of his family. No, they hadn't tried to find him or Caleb; they'd simply abandoned them to the slavers.

"That isn't what happened. They left us, probably glad to be rid of the mouths to feed."

"I heard it, but didn't understand. What is your given name? May I call you by it?"

"No!" he replied angrily. "No one calls me by that name except for my brother."

Freya stared into her lap. "Forgive me, Primus. I didn't mean to make you angry."

"Oh, now, dammit. I'm sorry. I didn't mean to get angry. Don't close up on me, Freya. I don't have anyone else to talk to."

She looked from her lap off through the bars where the sounds of feet in the hallway drew her attention. "It sounds like your brother is being brought in. I will go."

He nodded and remained in place as the cell door was opened. Cooper shoved his brother, similarly handcuffed, through the door. "Wait!" Varan called. "Freya wishes to return to her cell."

"You've already had a lover's spat?" the jailer roared in laughter. "Too bad. Lucas ordered that she'd remain in your cell. You're stuck with her now, Primus. I've sent for her things from the house slave cells. Guess she's going to learn all of your dirty little secrets now."

Cooper continued to laugh as he walked toward the jailer's office where Varan could smell that his breakfast sat waiting for him. The bastard was following Lucas' orders exactly, making Freya stay in his cell, regardless of whether he wanted the privacy or not.

"Brother," Varan said in a way of greeting as he turned away from the office.

Caleb inclined his head and motioned toward the girl. The Primus shrugged and muttered, "Looks like you're stuck in here, Freya. I'm sorry."

A look of confusion crossed her face. "Why are *you* sorry? Cooper's a broc's asshole."

"It's kind of my fault. I asked Lucas to allow you to come back to me tonight and he told Cooper that you were to remain with me for as long as I wished."

Caleb's eyebrows shot up. Varan figured that he wanted to say something about him never asking for the same woman two nights in a row, but he wisely kept his mouth shut.

For her part, Freya smiled. He hadn't noticed how straight and clean her teeth appeared—both a rare occurrence in his experience with women. "Thank you for taking an interest in me, Primus."

It's more intrigue than interest, he thought. There was something in the fire-haired woman, who shared her name with his goddess, that he wanted to know more about.

"We can continue our talk later. For now, I need to speak with Chaos before Cooper has him returned to his cell."

"Of course, I'll just go… Over here?" she stated, indicating the head of his cushion, which would give the brothers a few feet of privacy.

Varan and Caleb both laughed at the girl's obvious awkwardness. Varan had wanted to talk to him alone, but it couldn't be helped. Freya was here to stay.

"Sit, Brother. I have news from Lucas."

Caleb sat cross-legged across the bench, leaning his back against the bars. "What has he come up with this time? Are we to recreate the great

Ragnarok, fighting against *Odin* and *Thor* in their final moments before they perished? Or maybe we are to fight unarmed against rabid mountain lions. Could he want us to battle one another in a duel to the death? What if—"

"Please, stop," Varan begged. "This is hard for me. Please don't make it any harder by making jokes about his intentions."

Caleb allowed his smile to fade and he leaned forward. "Well, what is it?"

He took a breath to steady himself. "The Commerce Guild has decided that there may be only one champion."

"Oh, is that all?" Caleb answered dismissively. "In truth, I was wondering what was taking them so long. Dual champions are unprecedented—and inconvenient."

"It's not as simple as making one of us the champion, it's—"

"Brother, do you enjoy this life?" Caleb asked, cutting him off.

"What?" The question confused him.

"Do you enjoy your life?" Caleb repeated. "Being caged like an animal, brought out to parade before the crowds and then kill other men for their enjoyment. Once the fight is over, getting locked away, back in your cage to fuck whomever has paid to become impregnated by the gladiator—" He leaned out and looked toward Freya. "Sorry, present company excluded. What I mean, Vengeance, is this what you want to do for the rest of your days until you are cut down on the sands of the arena one day?"

"I haven't—"

"It's not what I want," Caleb said, cutting him off once again. "I tire of this life, Varan." He held up his hands. "No, don't tell me to call you 'Vengeance' in the presence of others. I know the game we created to help deal with our family's betrayal, but I want you to know that I'm done.

"I'm glad the Guild has decided that there will be only one champion. You deserve it so much more than me. You've worked hard, and dragged me along with you, but I'm done. I just want to retire, possibly work in the office until I can buy my freedom. Maybe settle down with—"

"Dammit, *Caleb*, that's not the way it's to be. The Guild intends that you and I fight to the death. Whoever wins is the champion, the loser becomes nutrients for the soil... There is no buying your freedom."

A momentary expression of confusion crossed Caleb's face before he recovered and hid his feelings. "I will refuse to fight. The Guild will look like fools for putting a man into the arena who won't do anything."

"They will shoot you—and me," Varan countered. "They have thought of this. I said the same to Lucas and he threatened a fight with the Primus from Crescent City."

"The cannibal?" Caleb asked in alarm.

"The very same. What are we to do, Brother?"

Caleb unfolded his legs, then stood and walked over to the cell door. He rested his elbows on the crossbeam and placed his face in his shackled hands. The older of the two men stayed in that position for several minutes. Varan's eyes inadvertently wandered over to Freya. Her cheeks were glistening.

Who is this woman who weeps for us, without knowing much about me?

"Brother, do you truly believe in Fólkvangr?" Caleb asked, his voice a harsh croak as it echoed across the hallway. Several men gasped in alarm at his blasphemy.

"Yes, of course I do."

"No. Do you *truly* believe that there is an afterlife for us? That if we die a noble death in battle, then we'll go to Freyja*'s* fields to live in peace for all eternity?"

"With all of my heart, Chaos," he replied.

"What of the followers of Odin? Did they believe with all of their heart that he'd lead them from *Valhalla*?" Caleb continued. "Odin was destroyed by the Ragnarok. The mightiest warrior in our history and he couldn't withstand the forces of this world. How did Freyja survive?"

"I do not know. But she did and she tends the fields until the warriors come home. Týr has promised the faithful, and the gallant, our place with him in heaven."

"How do we know that's true?" Caleb pressed. "We've been fed this information about Fólkvangr from the moment we arrived here, but I never remember the Traxx family talking about it. I was thirteen when the slavers took us, so I would have remembered. They never talked of any deities; they relied on themselves to get things done."

Varan frowned at his brother's outright sacrilege against the teachings of the warrior priests. When he'd gone to sleep last night with Freya in his arms, everything was right with the world. It had all changed the moment Cooper woke him this morning. He'd been asked to kill his brother, burdened with a woman whom he knew nothing about and now, Caleb was questioning their religion, the rock-solid foundation that their lives were built upon.

"Chaos… Caleb, you must stop thinking like this. The gods will hear you and punish you for speaking out against them. You've heard the sermons; Niflhel is not where you want to go, ever."

"Shouldn't there be a better reason for wanting to be a good warrior other than fear of going to Niflhel? I no longer feel the passion in my heart like I once did, Brother. I feel… I feel dead inside, like none of this matters."

"What doesn't matter? Our lives? The promise of Freyja and the fields of Fólkvangr?"

"All of it, Varan. I'm glad that the Commerce Guild has decided that there can be only one champion. I'm… I'm ready."

"Ready for what?" Varan asked angrily. He already knew what Caleb wanted, but he needed to hear the man say it.

"I'm ready to die."

"We all are. That is what we do."

"No, I don't mean ready to die like we say in the Warrior's Pledge," Caleb said. "I'm ready to leave this world, whether that's in the arena or some other way, I no longer care. I'm ready to see what the next stage holds for me."

"The way you're talking, that may well be Niflhel."

"Then so be it. You are the Primus, the best of us. You deserve to be the single champion, Varan." Caleb turned back from the hallway and looked at him. "I want you to be the one who sends me to the afterlife."

Varan's vision began to get blurry. He tried to hold back the tears, but they flowed on their own, refusing to listen to his silent demands to stop.

Caleb smiled. "Brother, these are my own terms. I would rather die as I wish, propelled into Freyja's waiting arms in Fólkvangr by you, than to be killed in some backwater arena by an opponent who means nothing to me. Do me this honor."

Varan wiped roughly at his eyes before staggering to where Caleb stood. He wrapped his handcuffed arms awkwardly around the older man's neck and placed his forehead against Caleb's. "I will do this, Brother. You will forever be remembered as the greater of the two of us."

Caleb nodded, their skin rubbing roughly together. "Thank you. When is the fight?"

Varan wondered if Lucas had mentioned it, but he hadn't heard him because of the grief, which threatened to consume him at the time. "I don't know," he answered honestly.

FIVE

Tanya rubbed her stomach absentmindedly as the baby squirmed and moved inside of her. She'd developed the habit over the last several months as the baby grew, threatening to unbalance her completely. She felt like her abdomen had grown beyond any of the other pregnant women that she'd seen. Her mother, the queen, agreed that she was large, but laughed at her assertion that she was the biggest one ever.

Her cart jerked hard to the left, causing her to clutch her stomach in shock as she screamed, "*Eep!*"

"What are you doing?" Frederick demanded beside her.

"Sorry, missus," the porter called over his shoulder without missing a step and ignoring Frederick's comment. "There was a pothole that I didn't see until the last second, ma'am. The wheel would have hit it and jostled you good."

"Thank you for your concern," Tanya replied, smacking her lover's knee quietly for his outburst. "I'm glad we were able to avoid it."

"These old roads take a beating when the water freezes in the cracks. It breaks up the old pavement," the porter continued. "Before the end of winter, we've got another pothole that needs filling."

"I'll be sure to tell my father that the roads need more gravel in some places."

"That would be much appreciated, ma'am. Your father is a generous king."

Tanya laughed. "How would we know? He's the only one you've seen, right?"

"That he is, ma'am. But he usually gives us what we need—when it's reasonable of course—and his army keeps us safe. Homelake is better off with him as our ruler than that damn, penny-pinching council."

"Well, thank you, sir," Tanya answered politely. It was better to keep her own feelings on the council to herself than be baited into a discussion with the taxi driver, whom she only knew in passing.

She settled back against the cab's seat and stared off to the side. The sound of the porter's feet crunching against the gravel filled her ears as the old rubber wheels on the cart passed rapidly over the hard-packed ground. The porter was correct; the roads had really taken a beating this winter. The old world pavement was almost completely concealed by gravel these days, layer upon layer of the small rock covered one of the many marvels of the past that the city's engineers could no longer recreate.

Her hand started absently rubbing on her stomach again. The baby's movements inside of her caused her to smile as she waved to the townsfolk milling about on the side of the road. Winter was beginning to wind down and everyone was venturing out of their homes, some possibly for the first time in months. Shopkeepers cleaned away debris, long hidden under snow and ice in front of their stores. Woodsmen offered discounts on split wood, knowing that their trade would go into a period of disuse for five or six months. Here and there, old friends reunited. Homelake was waking after its winter slumber.

The Keep's doctor assured Tanya that she'd go into labor soon and since most women were laid up for a week or two after giving birth, she was headed down to the lake market before the delivery to find something special for the baby. She began listing everything in her head that needed done before he or she came and was quickly overwhelmed with the seemingly never-ending list of preparations for bringing a baby into the world.

Her father had given her two entire suites on the sixth floor of The Keep. One of them would be her personal chamber, which included a crib in the room if she chose to sleep with the baby, and workers transformed the second room into a nursery. Garrett had the old door reinforced with multiple ways of locking from the inside and the windows bricked over, except for small portholes near the top to allow fresh air into the room. The engineers stated that the windows were safe, incapable for a child to fall out of or an intruder getting through the barricade.

Tanya hated that the nursery was so dark, but her father insisted that it was for the best. The years had passed rapidly after the Seers' proclamation that the Vultures were coming for the Traxx family with no evidence that they were correct. The Guard and militia constantly expanded and improved upon the town's defenses, but she felt like it was a waste of time and resources.

Her mood turned dark as she thought about the hours spent in conversation with her father about the city's fortifications. Hadn't her family learned that walls, no matter how big or how well defended, weren't the best solution? Walls had surrounded the old compound where slavers attacked and kidnapped her cousins. Walls had defended the city of San Angelo in Aeric Traxx's time as well and the Vultures rolled over them with their big war machines. While the king admitted that the fortifications of their ancestors had failed, he refused to be swayed from building higher and more defensible walls around Homelake.

She didn't know what the alternative was, though. That was the problem with her arguments. She felt it involved a series of political deals, cooperating with the other towns for mutual protection. Her father was a fervent economist, establishing trading partnerships with every community that they knew of, but he continued to be an isolationist when it came to military matters. He preferred to handle things himself and pushed the militia in their battle drills.

Thinking about the single-mindedness of her father always gave her a headache. Her mother and Dr. Ephraim both agreed that getting worked up about things that were beyond her control was not good for her or the baby. No one could sway the king's belief that the Vultures were coming for them, so the city continued to be fortified for war.

The taxi came to a stop in front of a brick building with a sign above the door proclaiming that it was "**Burrell's Toy Store**." Tanya had picked this store because of the owner's widespread trading network. The general stores simply didn't have the selection of old world toys like this one did.

She'd visited the toy store before, but hadn't been able to find something that she felt the baby would like. The princess hoped that Mr. Burrell had been able to find new items since the last time she'd been to his establishment. It was a long shot, though. The winter months were harsh across the foothills and not many travelers risked the dangers of the land between the wastes and the various pockets of humanity.

"We're here, Princess," Frederick stated.

"Hmm? Oh, right. Sorry, I was thinking about the walls and then about the last time I came to the toy store for the baby."

"You don't have to explain yourself to me," he countered. "We've rented the taxi for the day, so you could sit here until the dinner bells call us home if you'd like. Or until the little prince or princess decides to make an appearance and I have to catch him before he falls out of the carriage and learns to ice skate early."

Tanya laughed at his attempt at humor. He was *so* awkward around her when they were in public, which was as different as the night from the day when they were alone. "We have time; don't worry, Frederick. Dr. Ephraim said there are still at least two months until the baby will come. Just yesterday, he cleared me to leave The Keep on my errands. We have nothing to worry about, okay? Now, please help me down."

She leaned forward, scooting her butt to the edge of the seat to make the point that she was ready to go inside the store. Frederick slapped comically at the door handle in his haste to exit the carriage, causing her to giggle once again. *Gods, I love that boy.*

"Hold on, my lad—*aaaeeeii!*" he cried out as he slipped on the ice in his haste to come around to her side of the carriage.

She slid over to the opposite side of the taxi's bench quickly, jostling her stomach uncomfortably. "Frederick! Fredrick, are you alright?"

"*Ungh…*" The sound of his groan drifted from far below her. She tried to lean out over the door to see him, but her stomach pushed up against the side of the carriage and wouldn't allow her to see.

"I'm fine, your highness. Luckily, I bounce well, so only my pride is damaged."

"Oh, thank goodness! I couldn't bear to see you hurt," she called down.

His hand appeared, startling her as he gripped the side to pull himself up. When she saw him, she had to place a hand over her mouth to smother the giggle that burst forth. "You, ah… You've got something stuck in your hair there, Frederick."

"What?" he asked in alarm as he let go of the taxi with one hand and reached up to feel his hair. The Guard came away with the watery remains of an old broadside, whatever ink had been left in the old newspaper was now transferred onto the side of his face. "Oh, this is totally undignified for a member of the Traxx Guard," he muttered as he flung the newspaper away and reached for his handkerchief.

Tanya's giggle erupted into a full, roaring laugh when she read the backward print stamped across his cheek. Of all the different broadsides printed over the long winter, what were the odds that it was *this* particular paper—known for their love of all things scandalous—that found its way into the street and lay in wait to ambush them?

"What's so funny now?" Frederick asked, hurt by her reaction.

"Oh, gods! You have... You have..." She took a moment to breathe and compose herself. Then, she continued, "That newspaper was about us."

"Huh?" he asked in confusion.

"Remember the article that *The Truth* ran a few months ago, the one about you and me?"

"Of course. How could I forget?"

"Well..." She dabbed at the corner of her eyes with her own handkerchief. "You have the headline stamped across your cheek..."

"What?" he gasped.

Tanya burst out laughing again when he darted around her to peer into the carriage's back windscreen.

"What the?" Frederick scrubbed vigorously with his handkerchief, but the words '**Stud For Hire**,' emblazoned on the side of his face, wouldn't budge. He stopped and looked back at his reflection. "Oh, no..." He spit onto the fabric and scoured his skin roughly with it.

"Stop it, Frederick. You look like a fool!"

"More so than being branded as the royal stud?" he asked, one eyebrow arched upward as his grimace caused him to squint.

"Okay, maybe not," the princess conceded. "But your face is as red as a beet."

He rubbed his cheek a few more times and gave up. "We must return to The Keep. I can't be seen in public like this. Can you imagine what the papers would say next?"

"*I'm* the princess, Frederick. *You* don't have to worry about the newspapers following your every move and being publicly embarrassed all the time."

"That may be what you think, *Princess*, but I am in the spotlight because of our relationship."

He has a point, she thought. Her lover was in the public eye as much as she was. *Maybe I need to start considering his feelings; he didn't ask for this. He didn't even know who I was when we first met.*

She placed a gloved hand on his shoulder and smiled, even though it hurt her cheeks after laughing so much—both at his initial clumsiness and then at the words imprinted across his cheek. "It's almost gone," she lied. "No one will notice. I promise."

Frederick swiped once more at his face in futility and then crammed the handkerchief into his pocket. "What do they use for the ink on those broadsides?"

"They use acids from an oak apple and iron filings."

"How on *earth* do you know that?"

"Before you met me, I worked as an apprentice in a news shop. I learned how to make ink while I worked there," she replied.

"It seems like you tell me about some other occupation you've had every day. What else have you done?"

"My father wasn't always the king, you know. We had to scrape by and help out wherever we could, so I had several jobs when I was younger."

He shook his head, "You will never cease to amaze me, Princess."

Her hand still lingered on his shoulder, so she let it drop slightly down to his back and shoved him playfully toward the store. "Come on. Let's go inside, I'm freezing."

"Yes, ma'am. Let's see what Burrell has managed to find this winter and then return to The Keep as soon as we can."

Tanya repressed her urge to grin once again as her rosy-cheeked *stud* led the way to the toyshop. As he opened the door for her, he called out, "Her Royal Highness, Princess Tanya of the House of Traxx."

She hated that the members of the Traxx Guard were required to do that every time one of the Traxx family entered a building, but Nicholas insisted that his soldiers do it. He said the routine helped to establish them as the royal family among the residents of Homelake—something Tanya thought was rather silly since all of the Traxx, except for her mother and aunt, held regular positions within the community. She wondered if her younger cousin Brandt's coworkers tired of his personal guard telling them that he'd arrived for the day to throw wood into the blacksmiths' fire.

The shopkeeper, a burly, hairy-armed man named Doug Burrell, came around his counter and met her just inside the doorway. "Princess Traxx, what a lovely surprise. Would you like to see our new baby toys or are you here for something else?"

The baby inside of her pushed its foot or fist out hard and Tanya grimaced, catching her breath painfully. She held up a finger and leaned into the doorjamb to adjust the baby's position. Her hand drifted to her stomach and she could feel a rock-hard little body part pressed outward and then it pulled back, only to push out from another area on the opposite side. *The little one is moving a lot now.* Normally the baby waited until after she'd eaten to become so active.

The baby's foot pressed out impossibly far, causing her skin to stretch. For a moment, she panicked, remembering the dream that she'd had a few nights ago. In it, the baby had been moving, much like it was now, and four large claws burst through her abdomen as the demonbroc that grew inside of her clawed its way out of her stomach, covered in blood and gore.

Tanya blinked away the vision that her overactive imagination gave her and bent over, placing her hands upon her knees to relieve the increased pain in her lower back. The baby kicked her in the kidney and she shot upward, regretting the sudden movement because of the lightheaded feeling that followed. She felt like the little one was beating her from the inside. *Is this how the next couple of months are going to be?* she wondered miserably.

"Is everything all right, Your Highness?" Frederick asked.

Tanya struggled to get a breath and to stay upright. "Chair," she gasped.

The shopkeeper appeared with a sturdy metal folding chair and she sat heavily onto it. The throbbing in her lower back eased slightly, replaced by an uncontrollable urge to use the restroom. Was that what was the matter with her all of a sudden? Were the contents of her bowels crowding the baby? *I feel silly asking for this.*

"Um… I'm sorry, Mr. Burrell. Do you have a bathroom?" she asked tentatively.

"Of course, Princess. I have one in the back of the shop. Let me show you."

Tanya accepted Frederick's hand under her arm as he helped her to her feet. "This baby is trying to beat me up today," she muttered.

The shopkeeper pointed out a few items on the shelves that were new as they walked toward the far end of his store. Tanya took note of several things, especially those still in the original packaging. The cardboard boxes and backings on most of the products were yellowed with age, but the clear plastic was still as pristine as the day it was produced, possibly meaning the toys inside were radiation-free.

"Here you are," Burrell indicated a small, dark room. "Let me light the lamp." He struck a match and ignited an oil lamp inside the bathroom before stepping out of her way.

Tanya went inside and closed the door. The acrid scent of the lamp's burning wick made her nose crinkle—although she was thankful for the small relief from the odor of the bathroom itself. It needed a good cleaning and she eyed the toilet warily, and then gagged at the stench. It couldn't be helped, she *had* to go, badly.

She covered her nose and sat on the seat. Once again, sitting helped to ease the pain in her lower back, but she wasn't able to relieve the pressure from her intestines. She tried pushing gently, remembering Dr. Ephraim's warning about pushing too hard and hurting herself. Nothing worked; she didn't need to do anything except urinate. *What's all the pressure down there, then?*

She pulled her pants up and fiddled with the elastic closure that The Keep's seamstress put onto her larger maternity clothes. Then she closed the lid with her foot and pressed the lever to flush away the contents of the bowl. She politely refilled the water tank from the bucket of melted snow under the sink for the next user.

The men stood near the center of the store when she emerged from the foul-smelling restroom. Frederick held a small box containing a rattle of some kind from the old world.

"Ah, all better, Princess?" her guardian asked.

"Yes, much better," she lied. The pressure had eased somewhat, but she didn't feel normal.

"I was just telling your, um…" The shopkeeper paused uncomfortably for a moment until he settled on the correct term. "I was telling the baby's father that my suppliers were active this winter. They brought in a lot of new toys from across the wastes."

"Are you sure there's no radiation on the toys?" Tanya asked.

"Yes, ma'am. The warehouses that my suppliers target are outside of the fallout zones. Regardless, each package has been thoroughly examined for radiation particles."

Tanya hunched her back slightly to relieve some of the pressure on her abdomen. "I didn't know that you could see radiation particles, Mr. Burrell."

"You, ah...no, ma'am, you can't see them. They are taken from places that were never exposed to the drifting ash—which, as you know, is the most dangerous of the long-term radiation—and the supplier guarantees that there's no harmful radiation remaining on the packaging. He has the most wonderful device that detects the pollution."

She'd heard of such devices from the old world. Although there was the rare exception—like the music machine that the magicians used at the festival—most of the things from that time no longer worked. A machine that could tell where the areas affected by radiation were would benefit everyone, not just a merchant. Children were taught to avoid areas where radiation is obvious, such as sickly vegetation in an otherwise healthy environment or the total lack of vegetation. However, everyone also knew that radiation particles could drift for hundreds of miles from where the detonations occurred and the signs weren't obvious.

Tanya wanted to think about the radiation-finding device more; maybe she'd mention it to her father when he returned from his trade negotiations. "Alright," Tanya replied. "I see Frederick found a rattle, what else do you—" She sucked in a painful breath.

Frederick tried to touch her elbow, but she pulled it away from him. "I need a moment," she told him.

"Are you okay, Princess?"

"I need a minute," she repeated. Her back throbbed in pain and the pressure in her backside increased. She felt like she'd eaten an entire meal of only meat and everything had settled down low in her stomach. She also felt like she was going to have an accident in the toy store. The broadsides would *love* that. She could picture the headline now, "*Princess Poops Her Pants in Public.*"

That wasn't going to happen. "Frederick, we need to return to The Keep."

"At once, ma'am," he stated and put the rattle down, then rushed toward the door to ensure that the taxi was still present.

"I'm sorry, Mr. Burrell. I felt fine this morning, but now I'm feeling ill. I need to go home."

"Of course, Your Highness." He picked up the rattle once more and pressed it into her hand. "Please, take this. You can settle up the account when you return."

"Thank you. I just need to lie down."

She trailed after Frederick. The shopkeeper said something that she didn't understand. Something about taking care of the baby. *Of course I'll take care of the baby*, she thought, annoyed but not sure why she was so irritated at him. He was only trying to be nice.

The carriage ride back to The Keep was a blur. The driver seemed to hit every pothole along the way, regardless of his earlier statement that he tried to avoid them to keep her comfortable. Frederick assured her that they made it back much faster than the trip out had been, but she didn't believe him. The ride took *forever* and she was about to defecate in the taxi.

Several of the Traxx Guard helped her down from the carriage. Her feet never touched the ground as they carried her down the walkway and through the gates of The Keep. Behind her, she heard the taxi driver apologizing profusely about the length of trip and all the bumps in the road. Frederick ran ahead, shouting for people to move out of the way and to bring Dr. Ephraim to the princess' chambers.

Tanya struggled against the men carrying her. Regardless of how much she acted like a tomboy, she was still the princess and it simply wasn't dignified to be carried like a child. "Put me down!" she ordered.

The two Guards reluctantly set her down and she walked haltingly between them, allowing one to keep a hand on her elbow. She lifted her chin and pulled away, walking faster—which lasted for only a hundred feet before the pain in her lower back flared once more, causing her to gasp and double over in pain.

Her sluggish mind finally began to wonder if she was going into labor. The thought terrified her. She was only seven months pregnant; it was far too early for the baby to come. *What if he does?* Could the doctor save a baby born prematurely?

All doubts that she was going into labor ceased when something leaked out of her. It wasn't enough to be noticeable, but the warm, sticky fluid in her crotch meant that her bag of waters had burst. She muttered an unladylike curse word that she'd learned from the soldiers on the parade field and did her best to continue walking.

By the time she made it to the front doors, Dr. Ephraim was there with his assistants. They took charge of her from the Guards and helped her to the old elevator shaft inside The Keep. The doctor pulled hard on the rope dangling from a hole drilled in the ceiling. Far above, a bell chimed one time to tell the porter to lower the platform to the first floor.

As the platform lowered from above, a member of the household staff used a crank to open the elevator's sliding doors. Once the heavy wooden platform settled even with the floor, he pulled a flimsy mesh contraption out of the way to allow the princess, her lover and the doctor into the elevator. All of the others rushed for the stairwell.

Dr. Ephraim helped Tanya onto the platform and told the bellman outside, "Sixth floor, please."

"Damn you, Tony, you know which floor we're going to," Frederick admonished the bellman. "Just get us there."

"Frederick, stop it!" Tanya ordered. She was stressed enough, and didn't need him yelling at everyone for trying to do their job. He glanced at her and nodded silently, properly rebuked.

The sound of the bell ringing six times above them was much louder inside the elevator shaft than it had been in the lobby. Tanya normally took the stairs. She hated the elevator and rarely took it because the strange upward motion followed by a pause as the porter readjusted his grip on the rope to pull more of it through the pulley was nauseating. She was in so much pain now, though, that she didn't protest the doctor's decision to take the elevator to her quarters on the sixth floor.

They arrived after a few minutes and the doctor's assistants met them outside of the elevator. He thanked the burly porter who'd pulled the platform up the elevator shaft and guided Tanya gently toward her suite. She muttered something that might have been a thank you to the porter, but she wasn't entirely sure that her mouth formed the words correctly.

Her back throbbed in pain and the pressure down low was incredible. If she didn't have the baby soon, she felt as if she'd burst. It was a strange mixture of emotions for her because she didn't want to have the baby so early, but she *wanted* the pain to end—which meant she had to go through an even greater pain of giving birth.

Tanya's mother, Queen Peyton, met them at the entrance to her rooms. "Are you alright, Tanya? What happened?"

"I think… I think my bag of waters broke," she replied.

"She's going into labor, Your Highness," Dr. Ephraim stated grimly.

"Labor!" the queen gasped. "She's only seven months along."

"It can't be helped. The baby is coming," he replied.

Tanya accepted a hug from her mother. "We'll be fine. The little one is strong," she whispered into the queen's dark hair before disappearing into her quarters.

*****

Peyton Traxx sat in a plush chair in the hallway outside of her daughter's suite. She'd been inside the room for hours with Tanya, but the doctor finally demanded that either she or Frederick leave the room. Between the two of them, they were causing undue stress on the princess and her baby. The queen took the high road and allowed the father to remain for the birth of his child.

Peyton had the chair and an ancient book that she'd been reading brought to her so she'd have something to do while she waited. Now that winter was almost over, Garrett was off negotiating terms with the mayor of some town or other, trying to gain some cattle for the kingdom, so she was alone in her vigil.

Heavy breathing, interspersed with brief screams of pain, was her constant companion as she sat by herself, the book resting unread beside her. She'd briefly considered going into the room once again, but decided against it. The doctor knew what he was doing and having the queen peering over his shoulder wouldn't help him.

Peyton worried about Tanya and the baby. She should have had several more months of pregnancy. Given how large the girl was, though, maybe her estimation of her last menstrual cycle wasn't correct and she was further along than they thought. She prayed to the gods that her daughter was really eight or even nine months pregnant.

The noises from inside Tanya's suite stopped and one prolonged shriek of pain carried into the hallway. Even though she'd grown accustomed to the sounds, Peyton jumped in response to the sudden scream from her daughter. Then, the cries of a baby permeated The Keep and she smiled. She had a grandson or granddaughter.

A man shouted inside the room. She stood up rapidly, feeling lightheaded at the sudden movement after sitting so long in her chair. The baby's wail was answered by Tanya's brief cries of pain before she fell silent once again.

Then, the wails of the baby became frantic and almost nonstop without pausing for a breath. Peyton rushed to the door, the sound wasn't the normal sound of a baby crying. *Is there something wrong with the baby? Did Tanya survive the birth? A lot of women don't make it—had that hack of a doctor cut the baby from the princess's lifeless body?*

Peyton's mind raced as she thought of all the things that could go wrong with the birthing of a baby. She'd come close to dying when she gave birth to Tanya. The midwife had been unable to stop the bleeding for several hours. By the time she was stable enough for Tanya to suckle at her breast, she was addicted to the powdered mother's milk fed through the plastic bottles and rubber nipples that Garrett had scavenged. The girl never fed from her and their relationship hadn't been as strong as it should have been between a mother and daughter.

The minutes passed quickly, each moment adding to her unease. Finally, Dr. Ephraim burst from the room, hands and arms covered in blood. He smiled, and then shouted, "The princess has given birth to twins, Your Highness!"

Beyond the doorway, between several of the women who'd gone into the birthing room with her daughter, Peyton glimpsed Tanya holding two babies against her bare chest. *Twins!*

SIX

Varan and Caleb stood together behind crosshatched iron bars, staring out at the sands of the arena. Brothers, both by blood and by experience, they'd prepared themselves for what was to come next. For months, they'd planned for the fight that the Commerce Guild forced upon them.

Winter storms blowing off the coast delayed Lucas' timeline for the fight from December into late February. During that time, the brothers discussed their options for the upcoming fight. The first idea was to walk to the center of the arena and have Varan simply kill Caleb outright, providing no satisfaction for the crowd—or the Guild. Both agreed immediately that it wasn't a true option; the gods would not look upon Caleb favorably for giving away his life so cheaply.

The next idea was to script the fight from their initial entry into the arena until the final, climactic ending with Caleb's death. They tried for several days to choreograph the fight properly, but the other gladiators agreed with them that it didn't look natural. While they fought and hit each other's shields with the passion of trained swordsmen, it still looked scripted.

In the end, they'd given up and decided that they would fight as true warriors. No preplanned moves, no rehearsals, and no quarter given—that is what their god Týr demanded of his faithful. Access to Fólkvangr was not granted to those who pretended to fight, like actors at a festival. They would fight against each other as men, to the death.

The gate keeping them locked under the viewing stands rose slowly and they walked out together, hand-in-hand. The announcer called out their names and the crowd roared for the fight to begin. The cheers and cries of excitement slowly faded and Varan smiled. He could feel the savagery of the crowd shrivel away like a grape left too long in the sun.

This wasn't the way a fight to the death was supposed to happen. Opponents entered the arena from opposite sides, not through the same gate, as equals.

The first shouts of displeasure and the *boos* from the crowd spread and by the time they'd made their way to the center of the arena the entire stadium shouted for their deaths. The mob wanted to see blood and hatred, not civility and companionship. They marched past the halfway point, the sand already covered in blood from earlier matches, and made directly for the Guild's reviewing booth.

Varan placed a restraining hand across Caleb's chest when they were only twenty paces from the wall underneath the booth. "We are here to fight for the honor of champion," Varan called out, his voice echoing across the stadium.

A fat man wearing nicely made old world clothing shrugged a woman off each arm and struggled to his feet. "You are the brothers, Chaos and Vengeance, are you not?"

"Yes. Co-champions of the arena for the last four years," Varan agreed.

"Do you agree to the Commerce Guild's decision that there will be only one champion? That you two will fight one another to the death?" The man's chins quivered and shook as he talked. *Clearly, the members of the Commerce Guild weren't hurting for food.*

"We agree," Caleb replied, allowing his voice to carry as well. "The warrior gods demand a fair battle. We will give them their due."

The fat merchant clapped his hands, first in front of him, then raising them above his head for all to see. It worked. Soon, the entire stadium was clapping and calling out the name of their chosen warrior while the bookmakers scrambled from row to row, taking bets on the fight. Varan was the odds-on favorite to win.

"You may begin," the Guild member shouted above the clamor.

Caleb and Varan placed their hands to their hearts and bowed to the reviewing booth, then turned to face one another. "Farewell, Brother," Varan stated.

"If you send me to Fólkvangr this afternoon, I will save a spot for you beside our lovely goddess Freyja," Caleb replied.

"And I will do the same for you if you are the victor."

They each placed a hand on the other's shoulder, keeping the one holding their weapon loose at their side. Varan rested his forehead against his brother's, it was something that they'd always done and it would be their last gesture of brotherly love. He hated the system that required him to fight against his only remaining family member.

For a moment, Varan had doubts that he'd be able to fight. He didn't want to do this, no matter what the Guild required.

"Promise me that you will escape," Caleb said suddenly.

Escape? "What do you mean?" Varan gasped.

The capricious crowd began to jeer and call out; their display of affection was boring. They wanted blood. Caleb looked to the stands and then back to Varan. "Promise me that you will find a way to escape and become a free man."

"Caleb, I—"

"I need to know this," his older brother interrupted.

"We are locked in like dogs every night. What do you want me to do?"

"I had a dream last night," Caleb answered. "You *must* go north, with Freya. You'll find a forest and the true path will be revealed to you."

"I don't—"

"Promise it, Brother!"

Varan thought for a moment of how he could escape. The gladiators were under constant scrutiny, barely able to piss without a guard standing over them. As the Primus, he *did* enjoy more liberties than the others, but it wasn't enough to allow him an opportunity to escape.

"I promise," he replied flatly. *By gods, I'll find a way.*

"Remember, go north. You have a destiny to fulfill. All will be revealed to you then, *Vengeance*," Caleb promised, shoving him roughly away. He brought the sword up from low to high and Varan thought that Caleb was going to salute him, but his brother stabbed outward rapidly, toward his midsection.

The move was a dirty trick, used to score a quick wound when a fighter knew that their opponent was much better than they were. Vengeance only had a moment to sidestep and deflect the sword thrust with the head of his adze. The war axe, once the former champion Balroth's weapon, was now his. He allowed the weight of the blade to carry the adze past the block and then reversed its course, hacking toward Chaos's leg.

The older man jumped back and slashed at Vengeance's shoulder. He twisted, further exposing his back to Chaos' attack. He continued to turn, whipping his head around to keep an eye on his brother as his body rotated. The adze came up, slashing from low to high at an angle as he whirled around.

Chaos was ready for the attack and hacked downward with his sword. It clanked loudly against the metal vambrace on Vengeance's forearm, knocking his hand roughly against his thigh. The crowd roared in approval.

They fought for what seemed like hours, both seeking an advantage over the other, but neither gaining any ground. While the bookmakers acknowledged that Vengeance was the better warrior, Chaos was having the fight of his life. Neither man seemed able to make it past the other's guard to do any real damage until Chaos stumbled. He recovered quickly and then attacked wildly, forcing Vengeance back.

Chaos slashed across his body, his sword leveled at Vengeance's ribs. The Primus blocked his brother's swing with the axe and stepped forward, delivering a devastating cross punch to Chaos' cheekbone. The jolting impact went all the way up his arm as his knuckles crushed the bone, caving it inward.

Chaos dropped to one knee and flung the tip of his blade out wildly, catching him in the side. The blade slid along the arc of Vengeance's lower ribs as he stepped backward out of the reach of the flailing sword. Unpredictable, wounded fighters were extremely dangerous.

His brother's cheek was visibly sunken inward; the bone had collapsed, giving Chaos a lopsided appearance. The swollen, fluid-filled skin around his eye made it so he had to turn his head at an odd angle to see what Vengeance was doing.

The Primus stepped closer to his brother and said, "Are you ready to yield, Chaos? You've fought well today; we could end this right now. You are too injured to continue to fight and I am the victor. The Guild will get its way and you will be allowed to live."

"Good one, Brother," Chaos spat. The words practically fell from his mouth. "Death is the only way to guarantee an eternity in heaven. You know that."

The crowd began to *boo* once more in response to the lack of action. "It doesn't need to be this way," Vengeance shouted to be heard over the noise.

Chaos turned his good eye over his shoulder to look at the stands and then back to Vengeance. He smiled sadly and lunged forward with his sword.

Vengeance stepped sideways and brought his adze down on the base of his brother's neck. The weight of the blade helped to carry it through the soft tissue and vertebrae, burying the blade in the arena floor as Caleb's body shuddered against the handle. His head bounced once and then rolled to a stop in the soft sand.

Once again, the crowd roared their approval and the champion wept.

*****

The scraping of boots outside of the room that Freya shared with Vengeance woke her. *How long have I been asleep?* she wondered. The Primus and his brother had left hours ago to prepare for their fight, leaving her alone in the gloom of the cell with no way of determining the time of day. She'd heard the roar of the crowds above, but they soon became a near-constant buzz that became difficult to differentiate between fights, lulling her to sleep.

She started, realizing that the crowd noise had quieted down, only the occasional shout drifted through the old concrete bleachers.

The cell that she and Vengeance shared boasted a large window in the door, which did little to allow light into the underground room. Cooper called the place an *office*, something that the people of the past used when a different type of sport was played in the arena. Freya thought that a place of work inside a bathhouse room was a stupid idea. Why was the office in the bathhouse? Did the workers watch the warriors bathe?

A small rectangle of light became visible as someone opened the outer door. Two shadows darkened the doorway and Freya's breath caught in her throat. *Who is with the jailer?*

A third shadow appeared and he lit a candle with an old lighter. The sharp angles of Vengeance's face appeared in a soft orange glow. Her heart leapt for joy that the Primus lived, while it filled with remorse at the probable outcome for Chaos. The brothers had prepared for this fight for months, ordered to battle one another on the same day that Freya was given to Vengeance exclusively.

"Stand back from the door, whore," Cooper's rough voiced ordered.

She edged away from the opening and rested her back against the cool concrete wall. Outside, locks twisted open and the door swung slowly into the cramped space. Cooper ducked out from under Vengeance's shoulder and the man collapsed onto the floor.

"Make him feel better. Fuck him or do whatever you need to do. He has an appointment to speak to Minister Thaynes tonight."

"Yes, sir," she muttered. She hated Cooper more than she hated all of the other guards combined. The man enjoyed causing pain and humiliation; and he excelled at being an ass.

He closed the door and locked each of the locks before setting the candle on one of the metal benches in the bathhouse room. The two guards secured the outer door, plunging the room into near darkness once again. The only light in the office came through the small window, casting odd shadows across the walls.

Freya turned to see Vengeance sitting on the pallet, knees drawn up against his chest. A dark stain covered his side. He'd been hurt.

"Primus, are you… Is it over?" Freya asked.

He dropped his head into his hands. "He's gone. I killed him."

"It's what he wanted."

"He was a fool."

She frowned and tried another approach. "Vengeance, I—"

"Don't call me that," he muttered.

"I—ah, Primus?"

"Vengeance died beside Chaos. My given name is Varan," he confided. "Never call me Vengeance again, understand?"

"Yes, of course," she lied. His sudden admission shocked her. She'd been his mate for several months, taken in the late summer and through the winter, and she'd never known his real name. She'd asked him time and again and he'd always told her that only his family—and Lucas and Cooper apparently—knew the name that his parents gave him.

"My brother's name was Caleb. They forced me to kill my only family."

She knelt beside him. "I'm sorry… Varan. Your brother died a warrior, like he wanted."

"Don't," he warned. "I don't need your sympathy."

"Well I don't need you moping around like a lost child either. Err—" she realized her error too late and cringed, waiting for the blow. She'd been beaten many times over the years for saying the wrong thing to lesser men. Men liked to be told that they were always right and without flaw. They didn't take kindly to a *woman* telling them differently. So far, the Primus had treated her kindly and never harmed her, but she'd hadn't been so bold as to say something about his personality before.

To her surprise, Varan laughed. "I *am* a lost child, Freya. We both were. Kidnapped and then abandoned by our family. They never came for us."

She eased down beside him, placing an arm over his shoulder. He'd alluded to his past before, but like every slave, it didn't matter how they'd ended up where they were. She'd never pressed; if he wanted to tell her about his past, then he would. "He knew what the outcome would be, Pri— I mean, Varan," she said tentatively, testing out the word.

"I know. We talked of this day for so long, I just can't believe that it's over."

Freya sighed. "It's not over. Lucas wants to parade you around as the sole champion of the Contest."

"You're right. It will never be over," he mumbled. "Not as long as we're slaves."

"It's our role in life."

"No, it's not," Varan replied. "Men weren't born to serve other men. We were born to be free. We could leave, tonight, and go north…"

"What? Primus, you know Lucas would never let you buy your freedom. You're his biggest moneymaker."

"I don't intend to buy my—our—freedom," he replied, his voice stronger than it was a moment before. "I plan to escape. I want you to come with me."

Her heart skipped a beat. *Does he really plan to escape and take me with him?* "How do you intend to do this?"

"I haven't thought through the details yet. I don't think it would be hard. We're only ever guarded by two or three men at a time and they have to transport us to the minister somehow."

"Its…intriguing," she said cautiously. They were lovers and she knew the Primus—*Varan!*—better than she'd ever known any other man before. Lucas had gifted her to him and relieved her of all her other duties, but she wasn't ready to commit her secret desires to him. Slaves did strange things to win the favor of their owners. What if he was in league with Lucas and made up the idea of an escape to trap her? Life was hard, but there was no reason to make it harder by trusting the wrong person.

"It will be dangerous," he stated, interrupting her thoughts. "Are you willing to try?"

"Are you really going to try to *escape?*" she asked, whispering the last word like someone may overhear her.

"Yes. Caleb made me promise him before the fight that I would escape. He had a vision that told me I should escape with you and head north. We'd find a forest and that was where I'd learn the truth of things."

Freya blanched. "Your brother had a vision about me?"

"Yes. He said that the two of us would escape to the forest and find the true path—whatever that means."

She nodded her head slowly as she searched her memories for the word 'forest.' She knew that it had something to do with a lot of trees, but she wasn't sure why another word was needed for describing trees. She *did* know that going north meant a colder winter; she wasn't sure that she could handle any colder than Trinity had been this past winter.

"Is this 'forest' someplace where we can be safe? Where we'll never have to worry about Cooper or the Contest ever again?" Each time he stepped into the arena—even for practice—she was worried that he wouldn't come back to their small little world and she'd be made a whore, passed around the guards and gladiators, once again.

Varan shrugged out from under her arm and cupped her face lightly. "I don't know if we'll be safe, but the Contest will be behind us. I'm done killing for those bastards' pleasure."

She remained silent, willing him to continue so as not to give away her intentions. "I allowed myself to become comfortable," he began. "When we were children, Caleb and I swore that we would escape. Over time, the desire to leave lessened as we learned to be warriors and once I became Primus, I forgot about it. Then, I became champion and didn't *want* to leave.

"Caleb knew that his fate was sealed, that's why he wanted me to send him to Fólkvangr. I have done this for him. Now I want to leave this place and become a free man… Hopefully with you beside me."

She considered her words carefully and then said, "If you are certain that *you* want to leave to find this place that your brother told you about, then I will go with you."

*****

The next few hours were a blur as they roughed out a plan to escape during the transfer between the arena and the minister's home. Once they worked out what they could, which was very little, they made love and then cleaned themselves, taking advantage of the fresh water provided. If all went well and they were able to escape, they'd be on the road for a long time and wouldn't be able to bathe.

Finally, Cooper returned with another guard. "Are you in a better mood now, Primus? I heard you rutting into your woman earlier, so you should be. Minister Thaynes is expecting you at his compound in an hour."

"Just me?" Varan asked.

"Yes, just you. Lucas is already there," Cooper replied. He threw in a set of clothing. "Here, put these on and make yourself presentable."

Freya watched as Varan separated the pile. There was an expensive pair of old world pants and a shirt with buttons down the front. Along the collar, some extra material folded over, giving it the appearance of throat armor, but it was soft.

"What is this?" he asked.

"Those are nice clothes, Primus. You are meeting with a minister of the Commerce Guild; you can't hardly go there in your underwear."

"Is there anything like these, the 'nice' clothes, for Freya to wear?"

"You want to bring your whore to mingle with the elite of society?" Cooper guffawed.

Varan chuckled along with him, but the veins in his neck told Freya that his anger raged inside. "I think she is a very pretty thing, is she not?" he asked. "It would look good for me to have such a beautiful woman on my arm."

Cooper stared hard at him for a moment, then at her. His eyes drifted down to her breasts and he licked his lips. "Yeah, you're right. The woman would make a good addition to the crowd." He turned to the second guard and said, "Go find a dress. The household slaves will have something that'll make her appear presentable, even if she is in the company of an animal."

As he stepped back and locked the door, Cooper continued to stare at her through the window.

Freya turned her head so the curls of deep red hair fell over her face. "I don't like him," she whispered. "And I don't trust him."

Varan nodded silently, continuing to stare at the cell keeper. Cooper finally looked away and sat on one of the benches outside while he waited for the other man to return.

It wasn't long before the guard returned. Freya thought his name was Mark, but wasn't sure since he was new to the House of Miller. She hadn't interacted with many of the guards after Lucas decreed that no one else but Varan would touch her. He was little more than a boy, but if he escorted them this night, he would die.

She felt bad for him since she didn't know if he was like the others, but given enough time, he'd be just like them. Belittling. Beating. Raping. They were all horrible human beings. *Good riddance.*

To prove her thoughts, Mark watched eagerly as Freya undressed, removing the plain dress that she wore daily. The bastard's eyes seemed to bore into her, so she turned away to slide the nicer, well-cut gown that the household women wore on special occasions over her head. He was still staring when she turned around.

"Get enough of an eyeful, guard?"

"Give me a few minutes and you'd get much more," he sneered, grabbing his cock.

"Back off, Mark," Cooper interrupted. "Lucas made it plain that she belongs to the Primus. Anyone who tries to violate her will become a practice partner for the gladiators."

Mark stepped away from the window, mumbling. "That's a waste of a perfectly good piece of ass. Why does the fucking slave get his own woman?"

"Because he's the champion and Lucas wants to keep him happy, which brings in the money," the cell keeper replied and then unlocked the door. "Hands, Primus."

Varan obediently stuck his hands out and then pulled them back. "Come on, Coop. Am I going to be handcuffed the entire time at the minister's house?"

"I don't know what Minister Thaynes' security at the house will do once we're there. But, I know that you aren't leaving that room without these cuffs on."

Varan allowed the jailer to put the shackles around his wrist and then stepped into the bathhouse room beyond where Mark waited. "Come on, Freya."

She held out her hands and Cooper laughed at her. "We don't need to handcuff a *woman*. I know exactly what to do to make you obey me. Who knows, you might like it."

Freya smiled, "I wouldn't think of disobeying. I was being kind to the Primus, to show him that we both would be restrained."

"The Primus is an animal," Cooper replied. "You, however, are a delicate flower." His face twisted into a scowl. "I'd crush you under my boot if you tried anything. Let's go; searching for that dress took too long and we're running late."

She walked dutifully beside Varan down a long, poorly lit corridor underneath the seats of the arena. The two guards followed close behind.

After a few hundred feet, they came to a door, which Cooper unlocked from a key he produced from his pocket.

Outside, the night air was crisp against Freya's exposed skin. The dress may have looked nice, but it did little to protect her against the elements. Goosebumps erupted across her arms and she hugged herself tight for warmth.

"How far is it to the minister's home?" she asked.

"Cold?" Mark snickered.

"Yes, I am." There was no sense lying about it.

"We have a carriage," Cooper replied. "It'll be warmer in there out of the wind."

The jailer talked to the guards at the fence and they opened the gate, passing them through to the freedom of the city. The carriage waited a few feet away and they hustled to the open door. It took her a few tries to climb the steps in the long dress she wore, but she was finally able to make it with a little help from Varan.

Freya scooted across the interior to the far side while the Primus sat beside her. Cooper and Mark sat on the bench opposite them. The cell keeper banged loudly on the roof with the pommel of his dagger and the carriage lurched to a start as the unseen driver flicked the horses into movement.

"How far is it?" she asked once again, following the branch plan that they'd developed in the office. They hadn't known whether they would walk to the minister's home or if they'd be transported by carriage. Now they did, and that narrowed down their different plans.

"It's about an hour," Cooper replied. "Maybe less if the streets aren't clogged with people."

"Oh, then I'll close my eyes and try to sleep. Please let me know when we're close so I can clear away the redness in them."

"Sure. You go to sleep," Mark hissed. "We'll keep an eye on this killer."

She leaned over into Varan's shoulder and pretended to rest just as they'd planned.

The carriage rocked back and forth as they travelled down the rutted road. It wasn't long before Freya started to get sleepy. She fought it; she was supposed to *pretend* to be asleep, not to actually fall asleep, but the cold outside and the sudden warmth of the carriage conspired against her, aided by the motion. Soon, she drifted off to sleep.

*****

Something hard poked Freya in the ribs and her eyes jerked open. *Where am I?* she wondered momentarily before realizing that she'd fallen asleep in the carriage. *How long have I been out? Is it time?*

Varan was supposed to nudge her when he decided that they'd traveled a sufficient distance from the stadium and all of the guards there. As they'd hoped, there were only the two men across from them and the driver above, who would be of little help to the occupants unless he stopped the carriage.

Freya hoped that she could be as violent as she needed to be. All she had was the element of surprise and a hint of desperation. *This might be my only shot to escape captivity.* She clutched at that idea and used it to fuel her anger. Why was she a slave while other women walked around freely without worry? What had she done to deserve being taken away from her family? *Nothing.*

She peered through the tangle of her hair. Mark sat directly across from her. He stared out the window, obviously bored with the assignment of transporting the two luckiest slaves in the House of Miller. Varan and Freya were allowed the most freedoms of any of the slaves. He probably thought that they wouldn't do anything to ruin their good fortune.

Cooper sat across from Varan. His bare knife rested on his leg, the tip pointing toward the outside of the carriage. He was not bored with his task. He stared intently at the Primus, waiting for him to make a move. Varan had predicted this as well. He knew that if Cooper was present, their chances of surprise lessened considerably.

This is it. This is the moment. Tentatively, she extended her index finger and pushed lightly into Varan's ribs. It was a quick, furtive movement, meant to pass on the information that she was ready without being seen.

"Hey, Coop," Varan said, startling her. "How long have we been together?"

"Hmm? I don't know, Primus. I was only a guard when Lucas bought you, so it's been a long time."

Varan nodded his head. "Yeah, that's what I remember. I was just a boy when I came to the House of Miller."

"And now look at you. You're the most powerful slave in California," Cooper mocked. "You even get your own woman."

The Primus shrugged, intending to look like he was careful not to wake her. "She's alright. Remember the lessons that you taught me about a slave's place in this world?"

"Remember those, do you? They served you well, you've been a model slave for Lucas. Don't cause much trouble, not like some of the others."

Varan shifted slightly beside her. "It would be hard to forget an adult entering your cell in the middle of the night. Being too weak to do anything about it. Begging for the pain to stop."

Cooper chuckled nervously and glanced at Mark. "Well, you know. The past is the past, right, Primus?"

Freya felt the muscles in Varan's legs tense and then he was gone. She sprung forward, hitting Mark across the bridge of his nose with her elbow and then used her other hand to claw roughly across his face. He screamed and lashed out with a foot, catching her in the shin. Her leg flew backward and she fell into him.

She didn't know where she landed, but she bit down hard onto whatever part of Mark was in front of her. He shrieked again and she was thrown into the side of the carriage by the struggle of the two men beside them.

Mark brought his elbow down heavily into her back and her eyes watered in pain, but she refused to unclench her teeth from his flesh. He hit her again and she almost blacked out from the agony of his desperate blows. She steeled herself; she'd been beaten by men before, although never this severely. Her entire life depended on staying awake.

Freya knew that if she allowed him to get a swing at her head, she was finished. She pushed forward, ramming the top of her head into his gut, the flap of skin from his leg tore loose in her mouth. She bit down in a new location and held on as the carriage bounced down the road, their struggle unheeded by the driver.

Her hand climbed along Mark's thigh and she found the intersection of his legs. She grabbed his testicles and squeezed with every ounce of strength she could muster. The pounding on her back became frantic and she pulled him toward her as she squeezed. Then she swung her other fist in an awkward punch, lashing out blindly above her head.

She rained punches into Mark's upper body and face. Over and over, she punched and he was forced to throw up his hands to protect himself. Finally, she opened her mouth to release his leg and wrapped the hand she'd been punching him with around the fist that grasped the guard's testicles. Then she fell backward, using her bodyweight to add to the fight.

Mark tried to scramble backward, his feet sliding along the floor, trying to gain a foothold. First one, and then the second testicle ruptured inside the soft skin she held in her hands. For a moment, she was suspended in the air and then she fell hard to the bottom of the carriage as the shriveled flesh passed through her grasp.

Freya didn't let her advantage slip. She jumped back on top of Mark and punched rapidly into the protrusion on his throat, collapsing his windpipe.

Beside her, Varan and Cooper continued to struggle. The older man had the advantage of fighting from his back, where Varan struggled against gravity to hold the knife away from him and punch with his opposite hand.

Freya didn't think; she just reacted. Her fingers, hooked like claws, dug into Cooper's eye socket and came away with a soft, gelatinous mass. She yanked hard, severing the connective tissue and flung the eyeball away.

It was all the help that Varan needed. He took the knife from Cooper and plunged it into the man's gut. Then again. "We were just boys, you sick fuck," Varan sobbed as he stabbed the blade into the cell keeper repeatedly.

Cooper stopped struggling against Varan and he handed her the knife. Freya used it to slash Mark's throat. The man writhed weakly against her weight, but couldn't take in any air. The damaged tissue across his neck was surprisingly easy to cut and blood bubbled out, covering her hand in the warm fluid.

"What do we do?" she asked.

"Take their clothes, money, weapons—whatever they have on them. Then we jump."

They stripped the bodies quickly as blood and the rising odor of severed intestines made Freya gag. She knew that they'd be thankful for the clothing once they were exposed to the cold night once again. She gathered everything in her arms and looked to her lover.

"Ready?" Varan asked, unlatching the carriage door.

She nodded, shuffling over to him. They were on a dark, tree-lined road in the middle of nowhere. The ground sped past them as the driver continued on, unaware of the violent deaths that his companions had suffered in the carriage below. Weeds and the detritus of a lost society choked the open area between the road and the trees. If she aimed for the larger bushes, Freya thought she might have a chance of not breaking her neck.

It's now or never. Either we jump and run for our lives or we'll be caught with the dead guards when the carriage pulls up to the Guild minister's house.

Freya wrapped her arms in Mark's bloody clothing and jumped into the wind.

SEVEN

The air fogged with Darci's breath. *Winter isn't ready to release its hold just yet.* She scanned the valley from her perch beside the chimney, thankful for the warmth radiating off the stone. In the way that chilly mornings seemed to do, it was exceptionally quiet across the Seer's valley.

Along the ridge, nothing moved. No animals slunk from tree to tree or boldly tempted fate by exposing themselves. She wondered for a moment if an invading army surrounded the valley, scaring away the wildlife—or was it simply a cold morning when the previous week had been warm and everything was curled up in its den?

Since she'd been working for the Seers, the valley had come under frequent attack, often by three or four man teams who'd heard of their "wealth," but the women always seemed to know about it and gave plenty of warning to the security forces. Each attack was a bloodbath, but they'd lost many of the old explosives and didn't have a way to replace them. Darci wondered if they could make explosives or build traps around the valley. *I'll have to look into that. Maybe I'll send Garth to Creede and dig around the old library.*

She watched the valley intently for several more minutes before deciding that it was nothing. Her back was nice and warm from leaning against the chimney, but her front was freezing so she stood and turned around. She opened her long coat, exposing the thick clothing underneath, and pressed herself snugly against the rock. Warmth flooded through her and she smiled. It was a beautiful morning; the only thing that would make it better would be—

"Darci," a male voice called from below. "I've got some coffee for you."

"Thank you, Ryan. I was just thinking about getting coffee."

The chief of security for the Valley Lodge scanned the perimeter rapidly once again and then climbed down the metal rungs that the builders had skillfully hidden among the chimney stone. Darci accepted the steaming mug with a nod of thanks and continued to stare out at the snow.

"It's quiet this morning," she stated.

"Probably the cold, ma'am," Ryan replied. "I know if you gave me the morning off, I'd be curled up, back in bed."

She smirked. "Well, you're not getting the day off. The weather seems to have taken a turn for the worse, but that doesn't mean we should let our guard down." She thought about everything that she'd seen in these mountains, the deviousness of people who were too lazy to work for their own food and wanted to take from the Seers. "Ryan, tell the men to get ready for a perimeter walk. I want to ensure that everything is as it seems."

"Yes, ma'am."

Darci didn't turn to watch the guard go. All of her men were good soldiers and followed orders well. Besides, the crunching of his boots across the snow, hardened by the cold, told her that he did as directed.

She raised the mug to her lips and paused as she saw a thick bubble of blood come up in the center of her coffee. It spread across the surface, then the half-full cup began to fill with the blood until her mug overflowed. The dark, steaming fluid cascaded over her fist and down her arm. It fell in a constant stream to the ground, splattering against the white snow, staining it a deep crimson.

There is to be another war.

The thoughts came unbidden as she watched the blood flowing from her coffee mug. She'd had visions of death her entire life; she was used to this. It would pass soon and she'd finish her coffee. Darci knew that she had a touch of the Gift, but not enough to be a Seer. Trying to understand her visions was one of the reasons that she'd accepted the offer to become the chief of security.

Crch. Crch. Crch. Boots crunched in the snow behind her.

In front of her, the snow melted rapidly where the blood fell and thick, green-leafed bushes sprang up. Movement across the valley made her look away from the bushes. Giant trees, taller than any she'd seen before, filled the space where she knew there was none. Mist swirled between their trunks, spreading over more of the same type of bushes that had sprung up at her feet.

"Darci, the Mistress wants to see you."

She didn't take her eyes off the forest before her. "I'll be right in."

As the guard retreated, the landscape continued to take shape in her vision. The trees were some type of pine tree, or maybe cedar, similar to those that grew in the mountain valleys surrounding the lodge. In the mist, men moved silently, their movements quieted by the long, pointed pine needles covering the forest floor.

Shadows covered the men's faces, disguising their features. The closest of them looked up, startling her. The eyes. The man's eyes were yellow, the color of fresh corn. He grinned at her and the vision ended. The trees disappeared and snow returned to the valley. The vibrant green bushes at her feet vanished and the blood along her arm faded to nothingness.

She'd had visions of people before, but none of them had *ever* interacted with her. That man, with those strange eyes, had seen her. He'd acknowledged that she was there; that was odd.

Darci glanced into her mug, half-expecting to see the remnants of blood along the surface of her coffee. Nothing remained. She took a sip; it was cold. *How long have I been like this?* she wondered. The frozen stiffness in her legs as she turned to see what the Mistress wanted indicated that she'd been standing there in the snow for a long time. She flung the contents of the cup out into the snow and walked around the building to the front entrance.

The woman stumped up the steps and across the porch, knocking the snow from her boots as she went. The vision bothered her. What did those men in the forest have to do with the war that she predicted when she saw the blood? She'd have to think about it, but for now, she had to answer the Mistress' call.

The inside of the massive hunting lodge hadn't changed at all since she'd been working there, the furniture likely sitting where it sat when the building was first built. She could almost imagine the place filled with people before the radiation killed so many. Two couches sat opposite each other near the fireplace that warmed her outside; blankets covered their worn, old world fabrics. In the old days, families and friends must have gathered to read stories near the fire. Several sets of armchairs with side tables made little islands of conversation where friends who wanted to chat could still be social, but be by themselves to discuss private matters. The bar would have been full with men and women drinking, attempting to erase the troubles of a long day's work or looking to find a mate for the evening. It must have been exhilarating to see the place back in the day. Now, the ghosts of the past competed with the terrors of the present.

The Mistress liked cleanliness, familiarity and routine—all things that contributed to the Valley Lodge remaining unchanged over the years. The young Seer acolytes spent half of their time just cleaning the large building. The remainder of their time, they assisted with preparing the hallucinogens and aromatics for the rituals and attended the full-fledged Seers' needs. To Darci, it seemed like a dull life for the girls, and that was coming from someone who spent most of her time perched on the roof staring at the ridgelines.

Diane sat in one of the armchairs by the fire. Arielle and Candace weren't present. *So, this is to be a private conversation then.*

"Good morning, Diane. I hope you slept well," Darci said in greeting as she walked over to the Mistress.

"I did, thank you. You and your men keep us safe and allow us to dream peacefully." The older woman's deep, abrasive voice, the lifelong gift from her bastard father, echoed across the open common area. She smiled and indicated the seat beside her. "Would you like some coffee?"

The vision of blood flowing from her cup flashed in her mind. "No, thank you, Mistress."

Diane shrugged. "I've asked to see you because I want you to begin training your replacement."

Darcie blanched. Of all the things that she would have thought the Mistress wanted to talk to her about, it certainly wasn't the termination of her employment. "I…ah, am I no longer the chief of your security?"

"No, sorry, that's not what I meant," Diane replied quickly. "I've had a vision, in my sleep, away from the sanctum—which is rare these days.

"Before I came here, I used to be terrified of going to sleep because that was when my visions would come to me," the Mistress continued. "I was exhausted all the time and went through life in a daze, unable to function or do my daily chores. Then, I came here. As you know, we use the Calamus to invoke the visions during a ritual, but one of the side benefits is that it eases the burden on us when we're trying to go about our daily lives."

"I didn't know that the Sweet Flag helped you outside of the sanctum, Mistress. I will ensure our gatherers bring in much more of it."

"That would be appreciated. It's always in high demand and we have the space to store much more than we already do," Diane acknowledged.

"Last night, I dreamt of the future. Humanity will have peace and families will not have to worry about their children going to war or suffering from radiation sickness… But that is in the future. To get there, we must endure much hardship, sadness and death." The Mistress paused for a moment before continuing. "Do you remember Garrett Traxx, the king of Homelake?"

"Yes, of course."

"Good, I wasn't sure since it's been a few years since he was here. During his prophecy, we saw that he would have to fight against an enemy that has plagued his family since his great grandfather's time and he has prepared for this. Somehow, your fate is intertwined with the Traxx, but I don't know how. I dreamed that they came to us for help and of you fighting alongside them."

"Is the lodge in danger?"

"I did not see that," Diane stated. "But when the time comes, there will be no hesitation, you must go with them or they will fail."

"And the Traxx were fighting against this enemy?" Darci asked.

"Yes. I still don't understand how you figure into their war, but without you, the peace of the future will not come to be."

The Mistress' words filled her with an overwhelming sense of responsibility, more than she already had as the chief of the Seers' security. "So, I'm supposed to wait for them to come here and then go with them? Wouldn't it be better suited if I went to them now?"

"The future in our visions is not a perfect picture and can be affected by what we do in the present. The gods allow us to choose our path to reach their destination." The Mistress paused while Darci thought about her words. "I don't know *when* my vision will occur. It could be a week or it could be twenty years. The choice of leaving is up to you, but sometimes being too proactive can have its drawbacks. Did you know that the Traxx family has a history with Seers?"

"I know that the king has visited twice for counsel, both before he was crowned as their king."

Diane smiled. "Yes, Garrett Traxx has been a good and generous friend to the Valley Lodge. Before him, when *his* father was still a child, the family's patriarch received information from a Seer. The Seers back then were just learning of their powers. Raw, unrefined talent often led to wild outbursts in public, causing our kind to become shunned by the society that struggled to come to grips with its own survival when so many perished around them. Traxx took the young Seer's vision and tried to preempt it by attacking the Vultures to kill their leader."

Darci's head snapped upward and she blinked hard. "The band of wild men and the Vultures are the same group?"

Diane nodded. "There's a long history between the two, most of it either kept secret within the family or lost to time. If the elder Traxx had remained in the city to lead the defense, they might have had a chance against the Vultures. Instead, he was off trying to stop the vision from happening and stuck his arm into a demonbroc nest. In the end, he still ended up in the city where he should have been all along."

"So, we just wait until they come asking for help?" Darci asked. "What if a lot of people die because of our inaction?"

"It's not our place to try and change the future. The gods allow us the free will to act within the boundaries they've set—how we get there is the point of being alive—but the endgame is predetermined."

She knew better than to ask the Mistress about religion, she wasn't a priestess. Creed, the town at the beginning of the trail, sent their priests and any who would hear them, to discuss religion with the Seers every two weeks. "Then what's the point of any of this if our end is already predetermined?"

"Well, we can't give up. That would guarantee us a spot in Hell."

Darci wasn't religious like most of the others at the Valley Lodge, but she knew enough to understand what the Mistress meant. "So, I'm supposed to train my replacement for the future, when the Traxx family will come to us for help against the Vultures, but I can't go to them and help now?"

"In my vision, you are here in the lodge, not in Homelake, when the time to assist the Traxx comes."

The missing piece fell into place in Darci's mind. She'd been confused about why she needed to stay here and that final part of Diane's dream made her understand. The Traxx patriarch had gone off and done all of those things to stop the attack on his city, but in the end, he'd returned to find it unprepared for the attack that he may have instigated. It didn't matter if she left to go to Homelake, because she was preordained to be here, at the lodge when the Traxx needed her. She was better off using her time to train a replacement and ensuring that the valley was secure against raiders after she was gone. The concept made sense to her now.

"I guess I'll stay here, then. Who will be the new head of security?"

"You will remain the head of security while you're here. Garth will be your eventual replacement. When you return, the position will be yours once again."

"Okay," she sighed. "We'll begin training immediately so when the time comes, the valley won't be caught unprepared."

*****

"Where have those two gotten off to?" Tanya muttered.

"They were just right there," Frederick replied as he pointed at the outcropping of bare rock where they'd last seen the children. "They couldn't have gotten far."

Tanya cupped her hands around her mouth and called out, "Jade! Jensen! Come on you two. Time for desert!" *That'll bring them running.*

She watched for a moment and then slowly stood up. "What's wrong?" Frederick asked.

"Come on," Tanya answered. "Let's go get the kids; it's time to go back anyways."

Her little family had enjoyed an entire afternoon together free of distractions, but now it was time to return to reality. Frederick had to return for his shift on the city gate and Tanya was supposed to attend a dinner with several of the most influential merchants in Homelake.

Frederick folded the blanket that they'd been sitting on, while she called for the children once more, "Jensen, it's time to go back! Jade... Where are they?"

Before she could blink, everything was stowed quickly in Frederick's daypack with his typical military proficiency. She smiled at him, still unconcerned with the children's whereabouts. When they'd first begun dating so long ago, he'd been an awkward youth. In the years since the twins were born, he'd blossomed into a confident, capable father and soldier. He was now a sergeant in the Traxx Guard, responsible for an entire formation in battle and Tanya couldn't have been more proud of him.

She gripped his hand as they walked to where they'd last seen the twins a moment before. The lake was far behind them and the children had been playing on the side closest to town, so she wasn't too worried about any them. They hadn't seen a demonbroc in Colorado in years and the snake population was likely still hibernating, the two had just wandered off out of earshot—or they were purposely ignoring her because they were busy getting into trouble.

Tanya loved being a mother. Although the twins had been a surprise because that bumbling idiot, Dr. Ephraim, didn't know how to recognize that a woman had *two* babies inside of her, they'd been an absolute blessing from the gods. Her mother called them the "two-for-one special" and all of The Keep staff seemed to genuinely adore the children. Of course, they were only two years old, so it was hard to find fault with their antics.

The twins were currently figuring out how to try their mother's patience, though. Lately, it seemed like all they wanted to do was get in trouble and find ways to make a mess of everything. Clarissa, the children's nursemaid, assured Tanya that the behavior was perfectly normal for children their age, even if she was the recipient of most of their mischief.

Tanya peeked around the corner of a small rock outcropping. "Boo!" she said, laughing. The children weren't there.

"Jade! Jensen! Where are you?" she yelled again, her voice echoing between the exposed rocks that jutted randomly from the soft grass.

"Mama!" one of the twins cried. The echo distorted the voice, making it so she couldn't tell which of them it was.

"Jade?" Frederick added his voice to the mix.

"Papa!"

"This way," he stated, pushing past the princess.

They searched frantically, calling out and using their child's voice to locate the children. "How'd they get so far away?" Tanya asked in frustration, not expecting him to answer.

Frederick found the twins near the edge of the road leading into the mountains. Jensen cried out when he saw his mother and began to run to her, but stopped. He turned slowly back to where he'd been crouched when they found them.

"Papa. Sissy," the boy said, pointed at his sister lying still on her back near another of the exposed rocks.

"Oh, gods!" Tanya shrieked and ran toward her children.

Frederick reached them first, picking up Jade. Her body was limp in his arms.

The princess scooped up Jensen as she ran, stopping only a foot from Frederick. "Is she... Is she..." She couldn't bring herself to say the words.

"She's breathing," Frederick answered. He set her down and began to feel around her head. "There's no bumps or blood."

"Check for a snake bite," Tanya directed.

He pulled her pants down and turned the child gently. Seeing no injuries, he pulled up her shirt and then rolled her onto her side to examine her back. "I don't see anything."

Jensen squirmed in her arms, crying for his sister. "Then what—"

She stopped as the toddler began to mumble. The words were incoherent, childish murmurings.

"Jade, baby. Baby, what's wrong?" Tanya asked as she transferred Jensen into Frederick's arms and knelt beside her daughter.

Jade's eyes opened and she struggled to sit up, pushing her chubby body with her hands. Tanya helped her into a sitting position and the girl stared toward the mountains.

She lifted her little arm and pointed. Tanya turned to see what she pointed at, but only saw the mountains, still covered in snow. Jade began to babble again, the words difficult to understand.

Two words stood out clearly, though. The girl said, "Murder" and, "kidnap." Both were words she was certain that her children had never heard before.

EIGHT

The terrain was rough, made worse by the ill-fitting shoes of a dead man she wore. Blisters had long since torn away from the joints where Freya's toes met her feet, causing each step to become an exercise in courage and a lesson in pain as she wandered northward. *Ever northward.*

They'd been on the run from the Guild, from Lucas and the Contest for almost four weeks, avoiding the small settlements scattered along their path and staying in the trees. Despite his recent faults, Varan had become quite adept at raiding hamlets for scraps of food, often returning covered in blood. Freya knew that on those occasions, he'd likely murdered guards or anyone who happened upon him in the darkness, but chose to look the other way. They were starving.

The constant threat of violence made her sick to her stomach and she had an uncomfortable burn that seemed to come from her intestines, spreading all the way up to her throat, making her want to either cough or catch her breath. Neither worked. Eventually the pain would subside when she didn't allow herself to think about their situation or interact with Varan.

While neither of them saw evidence of pursuit, every new sound caused Freya's heart to leap from her chest. The trip toward the forest of Caleb's vision may have been physically and mentally tormenting for the young woman, but by gods, she was free and she knew that she could never go back to that kind of life. She'd rather die in the wild than be turned into a slave once again.

If Freya was rattled, she believed that Varan was truly haunted. The poor man had trouble sleeping and was increasingly paranoid. Since their escape, he'd awoken constantly, interrupting her sleep. He gave half-hearted apologies and told her that the images of his brother's headless body twitching at his feet kept him from rest. Added to the lack of sleep, Varan often forced them to move after they'd already made camp, fleeing from imagined pursuers, adding to the stress they already felt.

Every time she tried to talk to him, it seemed like the man was on the verge of scratching his own eyes out and then strangling her. Freya finally stopped talking to him four days ago, keeping communication to the essentials, like food and rest. It was a precarious situation for her. The man she'd latched herself to—and gambled her life with—was rapidly going insane, haunted by the things he'd been forced to do in the service of the Guild. She wasn't quite ready to abandon him and strike out on her own just yet, but it wouldn't take too much more to push her over the edge.

Even though the issues with Varan made her wary, Freya was truly glad to be free of her life of servitude. When she allowed herself to forget about the constant pain in her feet, borderline starvation, her traveling companion's ever-loosening grip on sanity, and the fear of being hunted down and tortured for murdering two of Lucas' men, she marveled at the outside world's wonders. The land they traveled through in their never-ending journey north toward the forest was beautiful.

The giant trees that grew along their route dwarfed the ones that she was used to seeing around Trinity. When she first saw them, she'd been frightened that they'd topple over and crush her; surely, there was no way something so large could remain upright. But they'd passed that small stand of trees with no problems and now they were truly in what Varan called a forest, following a path that wound between the massive tree trunks.

They'd learned after they entered the shade of the forest that the soft, damp earth made for poor sleeping ground—which added to Varan's inability to rest. The constant wetness soaked past their thin clothing and into their skin, chilling them to the bone in the early spring evenings. They'd thought to use the giant mounds of earth and pine needles as a way to get up off the ground, but those ended up being nests for millions of massive, angry black ants, so they settled for sleeping on the ground.

She was in the lead of their little group now. Varan stumbled along, often talking to himself and he'd forget where they were going, so she'd been forced to take charge, leading them northward. Freya learned how to determine their direction of travel based on the position of the sun and the prevailing winds that blew from left to right across their route.

"Top of this hill and we'll rest," she mumbled, no longer caring if Varan understood her and not sure if she would have minded if he continued without her.

The hill took them half an hour to traverse. As Freya crested the ridge, a wide valley spread out below them, bisected by a large river. *How are we ever going to cross that?* She glanced at Varan to see if he recognized anything or if he was just as clueless as he'd been the last few days.

"Hey," she said, snapping her fingers in front of the gladiator's eyes. Freya watched him focus on her fingers, then trail to her hand, next her arm and finally to her face. "Do you recognize what Chaos—what your brother, Caleb, told you?"

"Go north. Find a forest and all will be revealed to you."

Freya sighed. He'd said the same thing repeatedly since the Contest, except back then, she'd thought that he had a plan besides 'go north.' She gestured toward a rock and ordered him to sit so she could reach their supplies in his pack. Calling it a pack was an overstatement. It was really a long-sleeved shirt with the holes tied off that they'd filled with a few vegetables and salted meat that Varan took from farms along the way.

She built a ring of rocks and then lit a few pieces of wood on fire. High up on the ridge, the smoke would be visible for miles, but the soggy twigs and leaves in the valleys were too wet to burn, so they had no choice except to set up their cooking fires where they could be seen—if anyone were looking. It was a risk she was willing to take to avoid getting worms from the meat.

Whatever it was that Varan stole this last time was a red meat of some kind, not the white of birds and chickens that they'd occasionally been lucky enough to snatch alive. The raw, salted meat went onto a stick and she propped it low over the fire before moving out of the smoke to sit on a boulder.

The river was a major obstacle. Even from as far away as they were, she could tell that it was wide. Given the time of year and height of the mountains around it, the damn thing was probably fast too. "Can you swim?"

Varan's head snapped around from where he'd been staring blankly northward. "What?"

"Can you swim?" she repeated. He tilted his head in confusion and she sighed. "The water down there in the valley will be deeper than you can touch and the snowmelt will mean that it's fast. Do you know how to swim?"

"Uh, no. I never learned."

"Figures," she muttered under her breath. Before the slavers took her, she'd learned how to swim and spear fish for food. Although, it had been years, maybe even more than a decade, since she'd been in water deeper than a bath.

Varan was going to be a problem. *Is it time to leave him and head out on my own?* She could easily escape him by swimming across the river and then find a town somewhere that she could stay... *And do what? I don't have any skills besides cleaning and keeping men entertained. What else could I do?*

She thought about it for a few moments and then wandered over to the fire to turn the meat. Cleaning a rich man's home was an option, but one that she doubted would need to be filled by someone who wasn't a slave. And she certainly wasn't going back into the business of keeping men entertained, so what other options did she have besides sticking with Varan until something came along?

"I think we're close."

She looked up in alarm. Varan's words startled her; he'd only responded to her questions in recent days, not volunteering anything himself. "What did you say?"

Freya watched her travel companion and former lover closely for any indication that he'd say something coherent once more, but the moment passed. He stared down into the valley, frown lines crinkling across his forehead.

"Ugh," she grunted in frustration and pulled a hunk of meat from the stick, thrusting it into the air in front of Varan's face. "Eat."

He took the meat and she waited until he started cramming pieces of it into his mouth before turning her back on him to eat in peace. Greasy fluid dripped down her chin as she took a bite of meat from the stick. She closed her eyes, savoring the taste.

Her mood began to lighten. The view from the ridgeline was beautiful and the ache in her legs seemed to diminish as she chewed. It was a pleasant afternoon, she was free and Varan stated that they were nearing their goal. The idea of stopping the constant movement definitely brought a smile to her face. She longed to find somewhere safe to settle down and possibly raise a family one day. *I hope the forest in Caleb's dream is that place.*

The food disappeared quickly and Freya allowed them a moment to rest before struggling to her throbbing feet. "Come on, Varan. It's time to go. I want to find a way across the river before nightfall."

He stood up wordlessly. *At least he can still follow simple instructions.* They eased their way down the hill, allowing gravity to carry them forward. It didn't take long before her legs were churning almost on their own as she stepped gingerly down toward the valley below.

The journey down from the heights took most of the afternoon. By the time they reached the banks of the river, most of the valley was shrouded in the shadows of western mountain peaks. She appraised the water and then looked to Varan.

It was easily thirty or forty feet to the far shore. Large tree limbs, bundles of sticks and various debris passed in front of them, carried on by the river's rapid current. There was no way he'd be able to wade across the river; they'd need to find an intact bridge or acquire a boat somehow.

"Wait here," she ordered and then walked to the river's edge where she knelt down and thrust her hand into the water. It was ice cold. *Snowmelt.*

The warmer weather that had helped to cheer her mood up on the ridge was the culprit of the obstacle before them. All the snow from the mountains' lower elevations was melting and making its way to the ocean somewhere far beyond their line of sight. It made the river wide and fast, but could also cause a flash flood, which would be the end of them.

She returned to where Varan waited. Recognition—and *fear?*— flickered across his face as she walked up to him. *Does he realize this is something he can't get past without help?*

"We can't cross here," she stated. "The water is too deep and moving too fast. I'm a strong swimmer and I wouldn't risk getting into that current. We've got to find another way."

He gestured weakly, as if unsure. "Go north. Find a forest and all will be revealed to you."

"I get it! We're *trying* to go north, but there's a big river in our way."

"We've got to go north."

"Dammit, Varan! I need you to come back to me." She let her emotions get the better of her as she grasped him by his shirt, shaking him wildly. *If he's going to lose it and attack me, this will be the time*. But she didn't care. She needed to get through to him.

Varan allowed her to shake him like a doll for a moment and then stiffened. "North. Go—"

Something inside of Freya snapped. She'd not been ready for the challenge of leading an invalid on a fool's errand. There probably wasn't even anything at this forest. It was too much for her. She released his shirt and slapped him across the face as hard as she could.

Her hand stung, but it felt good to release the tension. Varan had been a rock solid man only a few weeks before, until he slipped into depression and edged toward madness. She slapped him again. "Damn you, Varan. Snap out of this. I need your help."

Her actions were wild and reckless. He could easily break her neck and then drown himself trying to go north, but she had to try. She had to reach him somehow. Her open hand balled into a fist and she grabbed his shirt with her opposite hand once more. "I'm warning you, Varan. You're not going to like this. You need to come back to me."

He didn't respond, so she threw the punch, landing it squarely on his nose. Blood exploded from his nostrils, flowing over his lips and then dripping off his chin onto his chest. She pulled her arm back for another punch, relishing the feel of adrenaline that letting her frustrations out gave her.

"Don't," his voice rumbled from deep inside of his chest.

Too late, her arm carried forward and smashed into his ear.

"Don't punch me again," he warned, leaning his head to the side and pressing his battered ear against his shoulder. "I— I know that I've been crazy. I just…"

Freya released his shirt and took a step back from him. "Look, I get it. You were forced to kill your brother—and that's a disgusting tragedy that never should have happened—but you led us out here. You promised me freedom and a better life if we escaped, and we did. We killed Cooper and Mark, making sure that we could never go back and that we'd have a bounty on our heads."

"I know."

"This is *your* fault. I wasn't happy being a sex slave, but I sure as hell wasn't out wandering around in the wilderness on the verge of death. You've got to snap out of this."

"I'm— I'm sorry."

"Sorry doesn't cut it, Varan," she seethed. "You can take your apology and shove it up your ass. I need you to get well and help me. I can't carry you across this river; we'll both die. I need you to make decisions and think for yourself. We've got to find a bridge or steal a boat, or maybe even build a raft. All of those things require you to be coherent and operating under your own power."

She watched him puzzle through her words as the blood continued to ooze across his face. Whether it made her seem callous or not, the man needed to hear the truth. They would die on that river if he continued to stumble along without helping her. She let him think for a moment before dropping the final weight upon him. "Your brother is dead. There's nothing you can do about it; but you're not honoring his memory by acting like an imbecile."

"You're right," Varan sighed.

Freya allowed herself to soften. The man had meant so much to her mere weeks ago. Her feelings for him hadn't completely gone away. He was kind, polite and intelligent. She placed her hand on his cheek. "Varan, your mind is struggling to come to terms with what the Guild made you do. You'll probably have a hard time for months or years to come, but I *need* you to put those thoughts aside for right now. They could still be chasing us and the river is a major obstacle. If we can get across it, then we should be safer."

His lower lip trembled for a moment and Freya wondered if he would cry before it passed. "Okay," he said. "I'll try to put those thoughts aside." Varan paused and stared at the river before mumbling, "Let's get this over with."

Her hand lingered on his cheek for a second longer before she allowed it to drop and then she began walking upstream. "The farther downstream we go, the more water there's likely to be, so we're going to go toward the mountains. The closer to the source we get, the less water runoff there should be."

"It's okay. I trust you," he muttered.

They walked for an hour along the riverbank without finding anything useful. She wanted to put the barrier of the river between them and anyone who may be following, but it was almost full dark and it would be much too dangerous to attempt a crossing as they bumbled around in the night.

They made camp a few hundred feet away from the river. The wood in the area was too damp to burn so they rolled out the threadbare blankets that Varan had stolen and settled in for a long, cold night. Freya rolled onto her side away from Varan and closed her eyes.

The sweat from the day's journey chilled against her skin and Freya began to shiver. She wished for a fire to warm her, but it wasn't possible, so she'd just have to deal with it and hope she didn't get sick.

There was a rustling behind her and she felt Varan press up close against her. Warmth spread all along her back where his body touched hers.

"Varan, I… I can't be with you right now. I'm not sure how I feel about things."

He nodded into her hair. "I understand. My mind was gone for a while and you had to care for me like a child. Thank you for not leaving me. I'm not sure if I said that."

"The past is the past," she managed to say. "Just promise me that you'll stay away from that dark place."

He mumbled something that she couldn't understand, so she ignored it. "And promise that you'll stay next to me tonight, please," she said. "You're so warm."

He wrapped his arm around her and pressed his body closer. The journey's exhaustion overcame her and the hope that maybe the old Varan had returned filled her with relief. She fell asleep and slept peacefully for the first time since they'd left Trinity on the way to the last Contest.

*****

Birds whistled in the early morning light, waking Varan from his slumber. He slowly became aware of his hand under Freya's shirt, cupping her soft breast. The slight firmness of her nipple rested against his forefinger. He felt himself stirring, his body longing for the enjoyment that he hadn't experienced since they left the office after the Contest.

He resisted the urge to caress her skin, to feel the press of her nude body against him. It wasn't the right time. He'd just returned from a very bad place in his mind and needed to earn Freya's trust once again. He reluctantly released her breast, sliding his hand down to her waist and shaking gently.

"Wake up, Freya. It's morning."

"I know," she murmured. "I'm awake. I was just…enjoying the peacefulness of the morning."

They continued to lay with each other for a moment in silence before starting their search for a crossing. Varan wished for some of the meat in their packs, but the cold, uncooked meat would only get them sick, so they settled for a quick breakfast of raw tomatoes and a few gulps of water.

"Ready?" Freya asked once they'd put away their meager bedding.

"Yeah. Hey, listen, thank you for…for everything."

"Let's just keep it in the past and move forward. It's going to take both of us working together to get across that river."

They searched for several hours without finding an intact bridge or boat. Crossing the river began to seem like a more daunting task than they'd thought. Worse, they didn't possess any tools that they could use to cut down trees for a raft, let alone any rope to keep them together. The irrational desire to go north continued to pound into Varan's brain and the river blocked the way.

Midday came and went as their search stretched late into the afternoon. They were beginning to think about finding somewhere dry to sleep when Freya gave out a cry of alarm.

"Up ahead! It looks like someone's built a bridge."

Varan squinted to see what she did, but her eyesight was obviously better than his because he couldn't tell what she was talking about and said so.

"You don't see the concrete beams sticking out of the water right there?" she asked, pointing.

He followed her finger and then made out the gray pillars. They'd blended in with the river and the debris surrounding them completed their camouflage.

"It's just a bunch of river junk, not a bridge."

"No, all that stuff is up against the bridge and hasn't moved," she countered. "Come on."

As they got closer, two old bridge supports began to take shape. Three concrete pillars stood as evidence that at one time, a large bridge had stretched from bank to bank. Twisted metal reinforcing bars jutted from the top of each, giving the appearance of wild hairs sprouting from the concrete. Darkened stains on the supports told the story of what likely happened.

"Someone used explosives to blow up the bridge," he stated.

"What are explosives?"

He recalled the stories that his grandfather used to tell around the campfire about the days before the end of the old society. "They're a weapon from the old world. They could break concrete and allow attackers to go into places defenders thought secure—or bring down a bridge."

"Wow," Freya replied, wide eyed. "No wonder they almost killed everyone."

Varan shrugged. The weapon made perfect sense to him; without them armies would spend weeks or even months trying to breach a defender's fortifications. "I wonder why they used it to destroy the bridge."

"Isolation," she answered instantly. "Someone on this side—or that one—didn't want to be around others."

His mind took her idea and went in a different direction. "Or to keep someone away."

"True," she acknowledged. "But someone has built it back, see?"

Sure enough, trunks from several of the region's tall trees were placed upstream of the pillars and the current pressed them against the concrete, creating a floating footbridge of sorts. The trees also created a barrier for the detritus floating down the river in the snowmelt runoff. The debris field stretched upriver for a long ways; every so often, the current pushed some of it over the footbridge, causing the flotsam they'd seen downstream.

"You think that's safe to cross?" he asked, eyeing the structure questioningly.

"If someone took the time to make it, they must have intended to use it," Freya replied. "We haven't seen any boats or anything that we could make a raft out of—and we've been on this riverbank for almost twenty-four hours. We've gotta make it across this river to keep going north, so I say we go for it."

Dammit! he screamed at himself. *What if I fall in the water? I'll drown, that's what. Why isn't there an intact bridge anywhere on this stupid river?* Of course the people who'd destroyed the bridge wouldn't want a permanent structure. If there was trouble, they only had to cut away those tree trunks and they'd float down the river.

They had to go north to honor his brother's wishes. It was the last thing that Caleb wanted him to do. They *had* to get across the river and it didn't look like they were going to find any other options. "Okay," he sighed resignedly. "Let's do it."

Freya led the way to the logs and tentatively tested their buoyancy with one foot. "It looks safe enough," she stated. "If you fall in, don't panic. Keep your head above water and let the current take you. Try to angle toward whichever river bank that you're closer to and eventually, you'll be able to get out."

She stepped back onto the shore and went through a few moments of rapid instruction about how he could keep his head above the surface and how to swim. It took a lot of arm and leg movement and he was plenty strong enough, so in theory, it shouldn't be difficult if he accidentally fell in.

Varan had gotten everything he could out of her explanation. "Alright, I'm as ready as I'm going to be without a few days practice at swimming. Let's just get this over with."

Freya gave him a quick kiss on the cheek. "Good luck," she said and turned back to the logs.

He watched her step carefully along the floating bridge, arms held out wide to her sides for stabilization. Freya's feet splayed outwards at an angle to help her establish a wide base on the narrow platform and Varan made a note that he needed to do that as well. He'd practiced balance exercises for fighting his entire life, but there'd always been solid ground underneath him if he fell. This was something different.

When she made it to the first concrete pillar, Freya wrapped her arms around it and bent her legs a few times to stretch out the muscles. Presumably, the rocking of the log and the natural tendency of round wood to spin when it floated was giving her legs a workout. After a moment, she released the pillar and walked to the next.

It wasn't long before she stood on the far shore, waving for him to come over. It was time. *I was the Primus of the House of Miller. I am the champion of the Contest. I can walk across a damned log.* Varan stepped onto the bridge determinedly.

He wasn't prepared for the way the log sank under his weight and then bobbed back up as the far end sank back into the water. It almost caused him to fall into the icy water before he'd even begun the journey. He recovered, repeating the mantra of his accomplishments to himself as he spread his arms wide for balance like Freya had done. He took a tentative step forward, sliding his foot along the log until he planted it and slid his trail leg up next to that one.

The current of the river was strong, pushing against the log and threatening to sweep it out from under his feet. But, he continued forward, inch by inch until he was able to wrap his arms around the old bridge's support pillar. He looked over to Freya and she rewarded him with a smile.

Two more pillars to go and then it's the shore. Varan edged away from the pillar and continued onward. His pace slowed to a crawl as the stronger current in the middle of the river threatened to knock him loose. The log underneath his feet was much wetter than the first one had been as the current forced debris over the top of the bridge.

His balance started to leave him and he waved his arms in an effort to regain it. Somehow, his rear end forced its way outward over the water and he bent at the waist to compensate with his upper body. After a moment, he was able to right himself and quickly covered the last several feet to the middle column.

Varan smiled in relief, looking up to see Freya's reaction, but she wasn't watching him. She stared into the tree line behind her. He tried uselessly to see what she could see; it was no use. *Not anything good, I'll bet.*

He pushed off the concrete and stepped away, traveling only three steps before Freya screamed. Varan looked up from the log below him and had a moment to register several men running from the trees before he fell.

Icy water filled his nose and lungs. He sputtered, coughing out the fluid as he flapped his arms like a bird to get his head above the surface. Everything passed by quickly as the current carried him away from Freya.

As he swept by, he caught a glimpse of the men he'd seen before he fell. They surrounded Freya and there was nothing he could do to help her.

*****

Garrett Traxx poured over the map on the table in front of him. The gods-damned Vultures had attacked a small hamlet to the south two days ago, killing everyone except for one scared teenage girl. They'd sent her to Homelake as a means of psychological terror, letting the people know what waited for them.

When she arrived this morning, bruised and bloodied from her ordeal, the guards had dismissed her as a crazy person. Thankfully, Nicholas heard the commotion from his office and decided to investigate. Upon hearing her tale, he immediately dispatched a squad on horseback to determine the validity of her claims.

The girl claimed to have been in the field with her brother, spreading manure that they'd saved during the winter for use as fertilizer. The men, more beast than human if her memory of them was to be believed, attacked her hamlet just after lunch. They took the villagers by surprise. She said that her family was unable to defend themselves against the horde of men wearing the skins of dead animals. They butchered the farmers in the fields, and then went house to house slaughtering everyone they found.

The attackers beat her unconscious with a club. When she woke, they'd tied her to the hamlet's windmill. She said she witnessed the wild men cutting chunks of meat off the dead and grilling them. When they'd eaten their fill, a man came to her and told her that she'd been spared so she could take a message to the Traxx: *The Vultures knew where they'd hidden and they were coming.*

The riders Nicholas dispatched returned only an hour ago; confirming that the village had been wiped out. After the confirmation, the captain brought the girl to see Garrett. Her story sent chills down his spine as the Seers' prophecy began to unfold as they said it would.

The king ordered a mobilization of the militia and called in all of the workers in the field. After ensuring the girl was taken care of, Garrett called Nicholas into his office so they could examine the map to determine what their best course of action would be and how to deal with this new threat.

"Did she say how many of them there were?" Garrett asked his longtime friend.

"No. The girl said there was a 'horde' of them. She couldn't give an actual number, so it's best to prepare for the worst."

"You're right. Did the squad that you sent find any of them or was it only bodies?"

"They didn't find any of the bastards that did this," Nicholas sighed. "The girl's story of butchery is accurate. They found mutilated bodies with crushed skulls and missing limbs—most likely eaten, as she said."

The king turned back to the map. "How far away is that hamlet?"

"It's about twelve miles from here," Nicholas replied, placing a finger on the map. "If the Vultures wanted to come directly here, then they would have been here by now."

Garrett shook his head slightly and said, "I don't know this current crop of degenerates, but I know my family's dealings with them in the past. Whoever is leading them now is trying a different tactic than the frontal attack. He's trying to get into our heads and make us do something stupid."

He slammed his hand down on the map. "That's not going to happen, Captain. I want the Guard and two companies of militia to ride out and find these vermin. Find them and send them scurrying back to their holes. Then, I want to go to their lairs and annihilate them. They've been a thorn in the side of the Traxx family for too long. I want them eliminated so my grandchildren aren't dealing with their sick and twisted sense of revenge."

Nicholas inclined his head slightly, "As you wish…my lord."

Garrett heard the hesitation in his friend's voice. They'd remained close friends throughout his term as the king, never being formal with one another. Had that changed somehow?

"Nicholas, thank you. I know it's not an easy task that I'm giving you and I don't mean to be harsh toward you."

"It's okay. I know that you're under a lot of stress. We'll get rid of them like we've done with other raiders." Nicholas appeared to want to say more, but stopped.

"What is it, old friend?" Garrett asked.

He frowned before replying. "What of Frederick? After me, he's the best swordsman in the Guard."

"Ah…" the king trailed off. His daughter had put him in a tricky situation with the Guard. Frederick was sorely needed in the field, but he could also be of great benefit as the personal guard for Tanya and the twins. She was pregnant again and wouldn't be able to defend them if the Vultures took advantage of the large number of militiamen who would be away from the city. It was a leadership dilemma; did he send Frederick where he knew that he'd be of use or keep him at home to guard his family?

He let out his breath and seemed to deflate with the decision that he knew was the best for the city. "Take him with you. You need him and the combat experience will serve him well."

NINE

A piece of debris hit him hard in the back of the head and he sank beneath the surface for a moment. He twisted as a large tree branch floated over him on its way down the river. Varan grasped at the limbs, trying to find a way to climb on top of it, but it slipped away from his grasp. He flapped his arms and kicked his legs like Freya had shown him. It was no use; he was sinking. He knew that he was going to die on the river.

Two men loped alongside, keeping pace with him on the riverbank until one of them dove into the water. His head fell below the surface and the icy liquid filled his lungs. *This is how a champion dies*, he lamented as he sunk deeper into the murky water.

He'd given up hope when a pair of hands clamped onto the back of his neck and pulled him to the surface. Harsh breathing filled his ears as the man who'd jumped into the river pulled him toward the northern side of the river. He vomited water and partially digested tomatoes, watching it flow downstream, as the current washed it away.

Varan felt the muddy river bottom under his feet and scrabbled to get a foothold. "Stop," his rescuer ordered in a strange accent. "Let me carry you to shore."

He wanted to resist, to gain his footing and lash out at the man who'd been part of the group that attacked Freya, but his body wouldn't respond. The muscles in his arms seized first and then his legs as the combination of cold and the lack of oxygen sapped his strength. "Good," the man stated and continued pulling him toward the riverbank.

Dark, rough hands gripped his arms and pulled him from the water. They tried to have him stand, but he collapsed and began coughing uncontrollably as his body tried to expel the river water. *What do these bastards want? I'll never return to being a slave!*

He rolled to all fours, playing up the severity of his coughing. He planned to spring up and break whatever appeared before him. He could do it. He'd felt the urge to allow himself to go berserker before. Like the men of the church legends, he could release himself to the rage and take as many of them with him as he could before they killed him. He briefly wondered if his muscles would cooperate or if they'd betray him as they had when he tried to stand.

Varan tensed, preparing to strike. "Varan!" Freya shouted.

He looked up. She ran toward him, followed by the men he'd seen earlier. They wore dark green and brown clothing that allowed them to blend in to their surroundings. Something was wrong their faces...

"Oh, Varan!" Freya said again as she slid past his rescuers and knocked him over. "I thought the river had taken you."

"No," he groaned. "I'm still alive." He hugged her close to him, both as a gesture of his affection and to soak in some of her warmth.

"Stand behind me when I get up," he whispered into her ear.

"Varan, no—" she said.

"Come, Mother. We need to go," one of the men ordered. "There are too many normal men near the river."

Varan paused. *Normal men?* He pulled away from Freya to get a good look at the men surrounding them. Their faces and hands were completely covered in thick, brown scales. They didn't look human at all; they looked more like an upright lizard with a short snout.

"What... What *are* you?" he stammered.

The speaker looked at him; its glittering yellow reptile irises shocking him further into silence. "We are the People, from the Dominion. Come, we can explain on the way."

The cold had seeped into his flesh, chilling him more than when it had been on the surface. "We're not going anywhere with you," he replied.

"Varan, don't," Freya warned.

"We don't know who these *things* are," he countered. "I'm not about to become sidetracked from our mission."

"Your mission is over, *Primus*," the reptilian man stated, startling him. "You have brought the Mother to us. You are free to go where you want, but she is coming to the Dominion."

"How do you..." he trailed off. Freya had called him by his given name, not the term "Primus." How did these things know who he was?

"We have known of *Gaia's* coming for three decades. Our priests foretold her birth and we had a celebration when we learned that the physical embodiment of the Mother was born as a human child."

"Wait, what?" Freya asked. "I want to know what the hell is going on before we do anything."

"Yes, Mother," he replied bowing his head. He flicked his wrist at several of the others and they disappeared into the tree line. "Guards. We must keep watch against the normal men this far from the Dominion."

He made a noise, which sounded like a sigh to Varan, before continuing. "My name is Thistle. I am the Watcher of the Coven. We tried to reach Gaia when she was a child—"

"My name isn't Gaia, it's Freya."

"Yes, Mother," he agreed without truly acknowledging her statement "The distance was too far to travel to reach you; the great sand was too much for us and we had to turn back. We learned of the Mother's capture and bided our time until the moment was right. Before the last winter, our priests tried to communicate with you, Primus, but they couldn't reach you. Grobahn, our high priest, sent your brother a dream, which brought you and the Mother to us."

Varan *harrumphed* and wrapped his arms around himself in an effort to control the shaking that was beginning to take over. "Maybe that's why they couldn't talk to me then. Caleb was much more spiritual than I."

Freya held up her hands. "Wait, so Caleb's vision, the one that brought us north to find a forest, it was your people that sent it?"

"Yes, Mother. The place where you were held was still too far away for us to reach, so we sent the message to the other normal man so he could bring you to us. We were unaware that he was to die, but he passed the message and it turned out alright now that you are safe."

Varan's world seemed to drop out from under him. The idea that he was heading north to fulfill some great destiny faded away. He'd been used. He was simply a messenger delivering Freya to these creatures. *What if I hadn't decided to take her with me?*

He focused on what the creature was saying. He'd missed part of it trying to come to grips with the idea that he wasn't the reason for the quest.

"So, you see, Mother... *You* are the spirit of the earth, reborn in human form. *You* will help us to make the land whole again."

"S...s...so how is s...sh...she s...supposed t...to..." The shaking had now passed into his throat, making it impossible for him to get his question out.

Thistle tilted his head curiously. It was an animal-like gesture, which was much more unnerving to see than the human traits he'd previously shown. "What is wrong with him?"

"He's cold," Freya replied, wrapping her arms around him and rubbing vigorously. "He fell into the water and he can't warm up. We need a fire."

"No!" the creature hissed. "The normal men will find us for sure if we light a fire. We must leave this place. We have a camp where we waited for you. It's not far; much safer there."

"Okay. Take us there. Can you walk?"

Of course I can walk. I am the greatest warrior in all the land. Varan tried to speak, but no words could escape his lips. He felt pressure around his waist and the world spun as he was hoisted onto someone's shoulders before passing out.

*****

Frederick held the reins loosely in one hand as his horse, Ash, followed behind Nicholas at the head of the column of militiamen. Skirmishers beat their way through the brush alongside, trying to flush out any of the bastards that may be lurking about in the early morning fog.

The Guard and two companies of Homelake militia had been out searching for the Vultures for twelve days without an encounter. They'd found evidence of where they'd been, campsites and more burnt homesteads, but they didn't seem to be gaining any ground on their quarry. The force they tracked was much larger than their own, estimates went as high as a thousand men, but they were confident that the militia would be able to handle themselves against any untrained enemy in the phalanx formation.

Complacency and boredom were the real problems facing the Traxx Guard leadership. It was planting season and the men were already beginning to grumble that they'd been away from their crops and families too long. There was a narrow window of time between the last killing frost and the beginning of the rains to plant the fields. Otherwise, they'd miss out on all of that water and the crops wouldn't grow to maturity before the winter set in once more.

To be honest, Frederick was beginning to feel the pull toward Homelake himself. He missed Tanya and the children and had been shocked when Nicholas told him to kit up for the field. He didn't argue with his captain, but he thought that he'd be the most useful guarding The Keep against any of the Vultures who were so bold as to infiltrate the city.

"What are you brooding about?" Nicholas asked.

"Hmm? Oh, just thinking about where these vermin could be hiding," Frederick replied. He'd heard the king use the term "vermin" before and liked the way it sounded. He thought it made him sound more mature.

"Yeah, we're so close. I can feel it," Nicholas stated. "The coals from that last home were still warm."

The burnt homestead they'd come across that morning was still smoldering and the embers were barely darkened. At most, the fire had died three or four hours before they got there, but they had no way of knowing when the fire was set or how long before it burned out and the Vultures had left.

"Maybe we're catching up to them," the younger officer agreed.

"I think we'll catch up to them tomorrow night at the latest. They don't even know that they're being followed, so they're taking their time, killing at will." Nicholas paused and made a show of hammering his gloved fist into his open hand. "We will crush them; they won't know what hit them."

"Ah, sir. Is it wise for us to have left Homelake with so much of our force? What if the Vultures take the opportunity to attack while half of the militia is gone?"

Nicholas waved his hand dismissively. "They aren't that smart. You can see that we're chasing after a ragged bunch of savages."

They rode in silence for a while and Frederick considered his commander's words. *Were* they just a bunch of crazies living out in the woods or was that a ruse, meant to trick them into letting their guard down?

Somewhere, deep in the woods surrounding the road, something large fell. Frederick tried to make sense of the noise that he'd heard. Was it a tree falling in the forest, or a boulder dislodged from the mountain slopes? It sounded natural, not something that should concern him, but for some reason it did.

He glanced left and then right, ensuring that the skirmishers were still there. Dismounted men, carrying the militia spears and short swords stretched off into the distance. They were spaced ten or fifteen feet apart and had a second line of men offset behind them to ensure the first group didn't miss anything. The older, more experienced woodsmen seemed fine and not concerned with the noise, so he did his best to dismiss the sounds as well.

"I'm going to ride back in the column and check the troops," Frederick announced.

"Good idea," Nicholas answered. "We need to keep the militia tight. Their minds will begin to wander the longer we stay afield."

My mind is starting to wander, he thought sarcastically. "Okay, sir. I'll be back." He pulled gently on the reins to turn Ash toward the rear of their formation.

Frederick rode his dark grey horse slowly down the line of militiamen. They walked three abreast, shields strapped to their backs and spears resting on their shoulders. As they passed him by, several of the men and women called out to him and he waved back. They'd been training together during the city's mandatory drills for years and he liked to think that the troops respected, even liked him as a leader.

He'd passed the first company when a gruff voice called from up ahead, "Aye, Sergeant."

Frederick searched the group he was near until he recognized the squat figure of an older fisherman whom he'd become friends with over the years. "How are you, Rolf?"

He eased Ash back around in the direction that the column traveled and waited for his friend's row to catch up to him before flicking the reins softly. The horse began walking alongside the column, matching their pace down the overgrown road.

"I'm doing good, Sergeant. How's the princess?"

Rolf's question elicited several snickers from those in earshot, including someone who yelled out, "Must be givin' it to her right if she's keepin' ya 'round!"

Frederick let the statement slide. "Princess Tanya is doing well, thank you for asking. The children are growing and getting into more trouble every day."

The fisherman nodded his head and leaned over conspiratorially as they walked. "The lads was sayin' that yer daughter—Emerald, isn't it?"

"Jade."

"Ah, that's right, Jade. Anyways, the boys was sayin' that she's got a touch of the Gift. Is that true?"

He frowned. It was true; his daughter's visions had intensified recently. Some of The Keep's staff were terrified of the little girl and word had gotten out into the community it appeared. The only one who seemed comfortable at all times around her was their nursemaid, Clarissa. Before the Vultures appeared, the king had offered to take Jade to the Seers to see if they could ease the burden of her visions, but Tanya refused. She believed that if Jade went to the Seers, they would make her one of them, freaks and outcasts of society.

Frederick didn't think that the women at the Valley Lodge would try to steal the child. That seemed a little far-fetched. They were pariahs to most of the population, but that didn't mean that they were going to kidnap a child—regardless of Jade's frequent dreams of abduction. He'd sided with the king and argued that the Seers may be able to help their daughter, not hurt her.

Frederic forced himself to laugh. "Jade doesn't have the Gift, Rolf. She certainly has an overactive imagination, maybe that's what the city folk are all worked up about. You know how it is when you tell someone something. By the time the message has been passed four or five times, it's entirely different."

"I'm sure you're right, Sergeant," the fisherman answered unconvincingly. "But hey! I hear the princess is with child again. Is 'at true?"

"It is. The twins are excited and won't stop talking about the new baby."

"They's what? Four."

Frederick thought for a moment. Time had a way of slipping by without notice. "They turned five a couple months ago."

"Damn!" Rolf barked. "I remember when they was born. Don't seem that long ago."

"Believe me, I'm feeling those years," Frederick said. "You should have seen the mess they made in the—"

One of the skirmishers off to the right screamed, catching the words in his throat. He turned to see what it was and then the ringing of steel against steel echoed across the woods. They'd flushed someone out of hiding.

"Box formation!" Frederick shouted.

The men responded with the city's battle cry, "*Aaah Uhh!*" as he guided Ash inside the square of militiamen that began to form around him. Along the column, he could hear his order repeated as other Guardsmen called to their formations to do the same.

He dismounted and looked around at the men and women that he found himself amongst. Rolf's platoon was mostly fishermen and laborers from the poorer side of the city. Truth be told, even though it was purely coincidence, Frederick couldn't have picked a better group to fight with if it came to a battle in these woods.

Skirmishers streamed quickly back toward the road, filling in the ranks. Their tales of crazed half-men began to drift back to Frederick, who had to put an end to the rumors before they spread and softened the militia's minds. Then, the sounds of individual battle died away beyond his line of sight, replaced by guttural shouts and animal noises.

"What happened?" Frederick demanded as the last of the skirmishers came stumbling in, covered in blood.

"There's a whole bunch of crazies out there," the woman replied. "We interrupted them. They were cutting down trees to make battering rams."

The rams are to take down the city gates, he surmised. The hoots and whistles also began to come from behind them and Frederick saw the wild men emerge from both sides of the wood line. They were surrounded.

"Prepare yourselves," he told the troops.

"*Aaah Uhh!*" the men cried once more. The front row knelt behind their shields and tried to secure the end of their spears against the ground.

The pavement that had made travel through the countryside easier would work against the phalanx since there was no way to get the butts of their spears to bite into the ground. If the men couldn't use the ground to add to the stability of the weapon, then they'd quickly tire from holding the spear. Frederick's mind processed the information quickly and he calculated how far the closest enemies were. They had time, but it would be close.

"Phalanx, move off the road. Fifteen paces." He made an exaggerated gesture toward the direction that he wanted them to go so everyone could see.

The formation surged along the course that he'd indicated and then set themselves. The ends of the outer rank's spears buried in the dirt and the second rank settled their shields over their companions, sliding their spears along the shields of the first rank. The third rank fit their weapons where gaps in the wall allowed and the fourth rank prepared themselves to fill in if anyone fell or relieve those who needed a break.

Then the Vultures hit the bristling wall of Homelake's militia.

It was chaos. Spears bucked in their owners' hands as the wild men impaled themselves against the metal tips, driven mad by whatever drug they'd taken. Soon, the first rank's spears were loaded with corpses, too heavy for them to hold any more and they switched to the short swords, thrusting around their shields to cut deeply into anything that got within reach. The deeper ranks stabbed outward with their spears, hitting the attackers high in the face, neck and torso.

Frederick relied on his training to keep the phalanx together, rotating personnel in a controlled manner. Off to the side in his periphery vision, he saw several of the other boxes collapse. They'd stayed on the road, so their spears weren't held in place by the ground like those of the men in his formation. The enemy seemed to be everywhere, swarming over the other boxes and taking the superior weapons from the dead militiamen.

Spears began to appear in the hands of the Vultures fighting against his box as they jabbed inward awkwardly, unfamiliar with the Homelake spears. Frederick's men began to take casualties as blood from both the defenders and attackers mingled freely with the cries of the dying.

The savages who'd killed the rest of the militia renewed the attack against the side of Frederick's formation near the road, threatening to break his lines. The mêlée raged, each man fighting an impossible individual battle to the death, while at the same time relying on the person to his left, right, front and rear to defend him. The militia had spent hundreds of hours perfecting their carefully choreographed dance of death on Homelake's parade field.

Time became meaningless to Frederick. His single focus was controlling the troops to plug the gaps with men who were marginally healthier than the soldier they replaced. Even in the center of the phalanx, he wasn't immune to combat and had to surge forward to kill the Vultures seeking to break the formation on several occasions.

Frederick began to be dimly aware of a lessening of the battle around them until, finally, it ceased all together. Far away, near where Nicholas had been at the head of the column, one phalanx remained. "*Aaah Uhh!*" the other box cried in celebration of their victory as they broke up to sanitize the area around them.

The dead and dying lay scattered around his own box, hundreds deep. During the course of the battle, the formation's position had shifted several yards from where it had begun. They'd trampled across the dead and hadn't even realized it.

Frederick ordered Rolf, who'd miraculously survived, and his fellow militiamen to begin killing the wounded enemy—it was the only way they could be sure that they'd never have to fight these same men.

The militiamen spread out to follow his orders and he had a moment to relax, Frederick noticed the disgusting filth that filled his boots, leaving his feet slimy in places and sticky in others. The ground was a churned up mess of mud, created by the blood and gore from the battle. His boots sunk deep into it and the liquid seeped over the tops, filling them with the ghastly mixture. He retched and then vomited, adding to the filth on the battlefield.

The sergeant struggled to free himself from the mud and puke and made his way toward the other box.

"Thank the gods you survived," Nicholas called to him as he walked up.

"I'm glad I survived as well," he muttered and clasped hands with the Captain of the Traxx Guard.

Nicholas looked around forlornly. "I was dreading that I'd have to tell the king his daughter's love slave was dead."

Frederick folded his hands across his chest in mock anger. "I'm not a slave."

Nicholas laughed and clapped him on the shoulder. "Yes, you can't imprison the willing." His eyes hardened once again and he continued, "This was a terrible price to pay for our victory."

The younger Guard looked around, nodding. "They formed up on the road. Couldn't use the ground to hold their spears."

"I know. We did the same thing and when I saw you move I had my box do the same thing. It's the only thing that saved us."

"How many do you think we lost?" Frederick asked. His voice sounded distant and childlike to him.

"Too many," the captain appraised the men who methodically walked amongst the injured, every so often stabbing downward with their spears or swords. "We only have about fifty men left."

Frederick blanched. They'd set out from Homelake with more than two hundred militiamen. It was a terrible price to pay for their victory against the Vultures. "Surely, we've beaten the Vultures."

Nicholas shrugged. "We've beaten this group, but we don't have any way of knowing if that was every one of them." He paused and then, "What I *do* know is that we can't remain outside the walls. If there are more of them, this tiny force is done for. We're going back to Homelake."

*****

Smoke on the horizon near Homelake was the first indication that something had gone terribly wrong while they were out hunting the Vultures. Frederick stood in the stirrups in an attempt to see further.

"We need to hurry," he called to Nicholas. "The city is on fire."

"I can see it for myself," Nicholas sighed. "What do you want us to do about it? The men can't walk any faster and they sure as hell can't run— they're barely standing."

"Let me go on ahead then."

"And do what? Get yourself killed is what you'll do."

"I've got to do something. My family is in Homelake." Frederick snapped.

"Everyone's family is there, Frederick. We're going as fast as we can, but we're not going to stumble blindly into a trap."

"Then I'll see you there," he hissed as he dug his heels into Ash's flanks. The horse shot off quickly, opening the distance between the remaining militiamen and his commander.

"You won't be able to do anything by yourself," Nicholas shouted after him. "I'll have you hung for insubordination."

The miles disappeared quickly underneath his horse's hooves and the cloud of smoke billowing above his home city grew. As he got closer, he realized that the column of oily black filth pouring into the air came mainly from one giant fire. *The Keep!*

He kicked Ash harder and the horse surged ahead, threatening to unseat him. The sound of metal horseshoes hitting the ancient pavement echoed off the trees lining the road, pounding into his brain like a blacksmith's hammer. *Is The Keep gone? What of Tanya and the twins, did they escape?*

He reached the spot where the trees opened up to the farmland around the city of Homelake and pulled hard on the reins. Ash skidded to a halt, sending Frederick flying over his neck. He landed hard on his back and his head smacked against the road.

His vision began to go dark at the edges as he sat up to gaze across the fields. Several of the buildings outside the walls had been burned, but the city looked mostly intact. The sand-colored façade of The Keep rose high above everything, seemingly safe behind its own set of walls.

Several blocks off the main road, two lines of carts deposited their loads in a pile before returning for more of their cargo. The first of the lines stretched off toward the tree line, where they were loaded with wood for the massive fire burning *outside* of the city's walls. The second line of carts carried the bodies of the dead. Both were added to the flames that belched the dark, greasy smoke he'd seen from miles away.

Frederick groped blindly behind him for Ash's reins without luck. Finally, he tore his eyes from the scene around the walls to find his horse. Ash was only a few feet away. He rushed to him, climbing awkwardly into the saddle in his haste, and spurred his mount toward the city.

Up ahead, a pair of men stood beside the road holding spears. They were members of the militia and Frederick recognized the men's position. They were far away from the walls, just out of bowshot from the tree line, with horns that they could blow in warning to secure the gates. Ash thundered up to them and Frederick reined him in mere inches from bowling them over.

"What happened here?" Frederick demanded.

"Sergeant Hanson!" squeaked the man on the left, a merchant if he remembered correctly.

"I asked what happened here."

The merchant's partner recovered from the shock of seeing the Guard emerge from the woods by himself and answered, "The Vultures. They attacked when you and the captain were off searching for them…" His eyes drifted back up the path to where it disappeared in the trees.

"Nicholas is fine. We were ambushed by the Vultures, but we won the battle. He's about half a day's march behind me with the remainder of the militia. How many of them were there?"

"The Vultures, Sergeant?" the merchant asked.

Frederick decided that the man was entirely too stupid to be trusted with such an important task as being an outpost guard. "Yes. How many *Vultures* attacked Homelake while we were gone?"

The two men conferred with each other before the merchant replied. "It was a few thousand, Sergeant. We kicked their asses good though."

"Yeah, they came out of the woods four or five days after you left," the second soldier added. "They blocked the gates so we couldn't get out and shot thousands of arrows over the walls, killing a lot of people inside the city. They tried everything to get past the walls, but couldn't get through the gates, so it was a standoff."

"The battering rams!" Frederick exclaimed.

"Whazzat?" the merchant asked in a jumble of words.

"The savages we fought were cutting down trees for battering rams. They must have divided their forces."

"That explains the large group of them that left yesterday," the soldier surmised. "Once the big group was gone, only about five hundred of them remained so the king took advantage of the smaller group."

The dumb one nodded his head and continued, "The king ordered us to make a big distraction at the front gates and then the militia broke out through the back gates. One company went one way, the other company went the opposite way and the king himself led the way as we swept around the back side and crushed the savages between the two companies. Only a few stragglers got away."

"The king led the charge?" Frederick asked incredulously.

"Yup. The man is an animal! Your children have that same strong Traxx blood flowing in their veins." The two men slapped jovially at his leg since he was still mounted. If he'd been on the ground, they likely would have pulled him in for giant bear hugs.

Frederick ignored the comment about the Traxx family as he tried to do the mental calculations, the battlefield math. They weren't entirely sure how many of the wild men there'd been in the first place, but if they'd killed five hundred here and the phalanx had killed about a thousand of them in the woods, it was enough to put a major dent in any size formation. "How many men did we lose?"

The merchant and his companion grew serious. "We lost seventy-three men, Sergeant."

He worked the numbers for the militia. Seventy-three plus the hundred and fifty or so that died at the ambush point... That was almost three companies of militiamen gone, meaning there were only one, maybe two, companies left to defend Homelake if there were another attack. They needed to activate the Reserve immediately, if it hadn't already been done.

"What of the Reserve? Has it been called to duty?"

"Yes, Sergeant. The king ordered them up the moment the Vultures came out of the trees."

If the Reserve was active and the Traxx Guard still secured The Keep, then he could allow himself to relax slightly. The city was secure, now he could go make sure that his family was safe.

Frederick mounted Ash. "Thank you, gentlemen. Captain Nicholas will be along shortly with the remains of the militia force that we took out.

Keep up the good work out here and be sure to sound the alarm if you see anything out of the ordinary."

"Of course, Sergeant," the merchant called after him.

He thundered down the road toward Homelake, dodging uncollected bodies further out and then the carts he'd seen from afar as he got closer. The king had enlisted the help of everyone it seemed. Residents of all shapes and sizes pulled or pushed the carts of grisly remains to the fires. The sooner the dead were burned, the less likely it would be for disease to spread.

Frederick thought it was a smart move by Tanya's father. They could keep the soldiers on the perimeter for protection while the population helped clean up from the battle. The common experience would connect the citizens to the army, show them the sacrifices that the soldiers had made, and the savagery the enemy would bring if they were ever allowed inside the walls.

He continued through the gates of Homelake, racing past squads of soldiers cleaning weapons and impromptu aid stations where doctors and their assistants cleaned up from what appeared to be several days of hard work. Easily recognizable as the princess' lover from the broadsides and his position as a sergeant in the Traxx Guard, Frederick's return to the city was met with excitement. Men and women waved and a few of the militia even cheered as he rode by. He had to explain to people on multiple occasions that the rest of the militia would return by the end of the day to reinforce the city's thin defenses.

He finally made it to the gates of The Keep and was allowed to pass through quickly. Passing the reins off to one of the stable boys, he jogged toward the building and almost ran into the king and queen.

"Frederick! Oh, I'm so glad you're safe!" Peyton Traxx said, throwing her arms around him, regardless of the gore that covered his clothing.

He brought his arms up hesitantly and hugged her back. "Are the princess and the children okay?"

"Yes," she nodded into his shoulder. "She's been worried sick about you though. Hasn't eaten since those savages showed up. We feared... We feared that you and all the militiamen were dead when the Vultures appeared."

Frederick disengaged from the queen's embrace. "Sir, I have news to report," he told the king.

"Go ahead, then. Tell me quickly so you can go to Tanya."

"Yes, m'Lord. We were searching for the Vultures, as ordered, tracking them, but it always seemed like they were a few hours ahead of us—until this morning. We came across a group of them cutting down the large trees in the forest to the northwest to make battering rams."

"They couldn't get past our gates without those," Garrett said. "That's probably where the group that took off yesterday went. Once I saw the reduced army, I knew that I had to take the opportunity and counterattack before they joined together once again."

"That was a brilliant move, sir," Frederick agreed. "We were attacked this morning when we came across them. By our body count, it was a force of about a thousand men."

"Body count? So we were victorious, then."

"Yes, m'Lord. But fully three-quarters of our men are lying dead on the field as well. Nicholas is marching here with the remnants of the militia... Only fifty-six men survived the battle."

The king clasped Frederick's shoulders with both hands. "You listen to me, son. The militia did its job—what I'd asked of you. Your mission was to track down those savages and wipe them out, and you did that. I'm proud of you."

Frederic smiled. "Thank you, sir. That means a lot to me."

Garrett dipped his chin slightly and then grinned. "You say that old dog, Nicholas, made it through, huh?"

"Yes, sir. At the pace they were marching, he should be back a few hours after nightfall."

"Good. We'll prepare a feast in your honor and invite all the militiamen who fought with you."

"That's very generous of you, m'Lord. Thank you."

"No worries, Frederick. Now, I think it's time we quit talking and you go check on your family."

"Yes, please do. Tanya can't deal with any more stress in her condition," Peyton asserted, now that the talk of war was complete.

Frederick bid them farewell and began walking toward the entrance of The Keep. During those first few steps, his mind tugged at a string trailing from the storyline. It had registered when the sentries said the army split in two, but he'd overlooked it then and almost did again. He turned and strode back to where the Traxx's were still standing, talking softly.

"Frederick, what is it?" the king asked.

"You say that the Vulture army split in two *yesterday*?"

"Yes. That's why we attacked this morning. Why?"

"We've spent the last two weeks tracking the savages through the countryside, m'Lord. When we stumbled into the men cutting down those trees, we thought it was the men we'd been after."

"Hmm…" the king puzzled through the statement before glancing at Peyton and back to Frederick. "That means you either found the men you were looking for and the force that left here is still out there, or…"

"I think we stumbled on the force from here, sir. It makes sense. The group we'd been tracking wouldn't have known about the need for the battering rams to get past the gates."

Garrett Traxx came to the realization slowly as the elation of their victory faded. "How large was the force you were tracking?"

"Based on the size of their campsites and the clues left along the way, our scouts estimated it looked like about two thousand, sir."

He staggered slightly before recovering. "Garrett, are you alright?" the queen shouted, causing several of the Guard to come running their way.

"Yes, I'm fine. I was just... Just taken aback, that's all." The king held up a hand to tell the Guards that he was fine, but he gestured for one of them to continue over to them.

"Yes, My Lord?"

"I need you to tell Rylan that the danger isn't gone. We need to triple the sentries and keep the quarters open for families from outlying hamlets," Garrett told the Guard.

Rylan, the deputy commander of the Traxx Guard, was in charge while Nicholas was in the field and would likely shift the focus away from burning bodies to security. The dead would still need to be disposed of to avoid disease, but it would need to be accomplished almost exclusively by townspeople.

"Good work—again—on seeing the hidden danger, Frederick," the king told him. "Given our losses already, we have less than half the number of trained militia and Reserve forces as those lunatics out there. The city is still in danger."

Frederick agreed with the king, but they were forced to go on the defensive. The two battles had devastated the militia. The Reserve wasn't trained as well as the militia, so they couldn't afford to go out on a hunting expedition again. The king knew it as well.

"When Nicholas returns, we'll work up a plan to clear the Vultures from the countryside," Frederick said.

Garrett Traxx nodded his head in agreement. "We'll focus on defense and training until the time is right, then we'll get rid of them once and for all. Those bastards have been allowed to threaten this family for far too long."

"Yes, m'Lord," Frederick acknowledged.

"Now, go comfort my daughter. The time will come soon enough when you won't have time to do so."

Frederick left the king and queen, running into The Keep. He took the stairs two at a time, bounding upward until he reached Tanya's suites on the sixth floor. The Guard outside her door greeted him and knocked the special sequence they'd developed.

"Yes?" Clarissa asked from behind the locked door.

"It's Frederick. Open the door!"

The sound of the deadbolts twisting and security chains falling away filled the hallway. It meant that his family was still safe and that they would be together once again. Clarissa let him in and he gave her a quick peck on the cheek in greeting before continuing into the suite.

"Tanya! Tanya, I'm back."

"Frederick?" her voice called weakly from the bedroom.

He found her, lying in bed with the twins, who were napping. Piles of books lay on the nightstand, telling him that she hadn't left the room in days. Her skin was pale, so much so that he could see the blue veins underneath the skin in her neck and arms. She tried to sit up, but her expression told him that her stomach muscles weren't working, so he rushed to her.

She hugged him fiercely from her seated position and he let her hold him as long as she needed. Tanya cried into his shoulder for so long that his lower back began to tighten up from being bent awkwardly at the waist.

"I'm so glad you're okay. We feared the worst," she sobbed, wiping her eyes against his shirt.

He ran his fingers through her hair. It was dirty and unkempt. She hadn't bathed since he'd taken to the field. "I'm back. Safe and sound," he soothed. "You didn't need to worry so much about me."

She pulled back and tried to smile, but it came across as a frown, made macabre by the smeared blood on her face from his clothing. "My father never should have sent you. I don't know what I'd do without you."

"I'm fine," he tried to tell her, but she wouldn't hear it.

"You're not fine. You're covered in *blood*. I don't know if it's yours or someone else's, but you've obviously been in a fight and I can't take that. The baby can't take that," she amended, roughly patting her protruding stomach to emphasize her point.

"I'm sorry. I didn't mean to worry you."

"Well you did. I—" she stopped and fretted with the sheets around the children. "I was just worried about you," Tanya continued in a calmer tone. "I'm happy that you're back, I really am."

It was his turn to smile. "I know that. You were worried, I understand."

Ridges appeared along the bridge of her nose. "You smell horrible. Is that...poop?"

He glanced down at his pants where the dried brown mud from the battlefield reached almost to his knees. At one point, he had the intestines of a Vulture wrapped around his spear that he'd needed to unwrap, so it *was* shit on his clothing. "Probably. War is hell."

Tanya rolled her eyes. "Stop reading my books."

"It's not from—"

"Clarissa!" Tanya called in a practiced tone, meant to be heard by the maid, but allowing the children to sleep through it.

"Yes, My Lady?"

"Please have a bath drawn."

"Oh, thank the gods. Not bathing is unhealthy for the baby."

"Ugh... Okay, you're right. We'll do two. The first bath is for Frederick, though. He needs it far worse than I do and I don't want the twins catching some strange illness from his filth."

"At once. Does this mean that you'll eat as well?"

Tanya nodded and watched until Clarissa disappeared. "She's such a worrywart."

"She's right. You need to take better care of yourself. It's not good for you or the baby."

She pushed him lightly. "It's your fault I'm like this. If you could control yourself, I wouldn't be pregnant."

He leaned in and kissed her softly. "Then quit being so beautiful all the time and maybe I could do my job of being your bodyguard instead of your 'Stud for Hire'."

"Oh gods, not that again."

*****

The high priest sawed the athamé along his thigh, up underneath his robe where no one would be able to see it. The ceremonial blade had visited his skin often these past few years. "Why have you abandoned me?" Grobahn pleaded before the wooden statue of Gaia. "I have sacrificed my blood for you, what else must I do?"

The goddess hadn't spoken to Grobahn in several years. He faked it for the others, using his charisma and quick wit to keep the Coven's congregation believing he still communed with Her. Everything was going well until the acolytes began to have visions of that bitch, Freya, and the Mother's promise that she could help bring about the healing of the earth.

It was Grobahn who'd created the idea that she was the earthly incarnation of the Mother. What a ridiculous notion, but the People ate it up. Gods, they needed something to believe in and he'd given her to them. Pathetic.

He'd studied the notes of his predecessors, carefully recorded over the past two hundred years. The previous priests—especially the earlier ones—were scientists and they knew about the war and what had happened. By their estimates, it would take hundreds of years to restore the balance of nature after the damage that had been done by old world weaponry.

Somewhere along the way, the goddess began to speak to the priests, promising them that she would send help to the Dominion and heal the earth. Grobahn used to hear the singsong voice of the Mother, far back in the nether regions of his mind. With her help and guidance, he'd maneuvered himself into the top of the Coven's hierarchy.

In time, a different voice spoke to him, promising to elevate him to the highest position. He knew the new voice to be Gaia's stronger identity; the part of Her represented by Earth, not the Air. It wasn't the same soft, musical voice, this one was more harsh and directive, never speaking in full sentences, just snippets of words that he had to grasp for and derive the meaning of. With the sudden death of Harth—an *accidental* drowning at the baths—Grobahn was elected as the High Priest of the Coven. Once he'd been elevated to the position of high priest, the softer voice of Air stopped talking to him. At first, he thought she'd ceased speaking to everyone, but through careful questioning, he'd learned that Gaia still spoke to the others.

"Why have you abandoned me?" he repeated his mantra and made another cut as an offering to the goddess. Surely, the blood would make her hear him, surely—

"Is *that* it, Mother? Do you require more blood? What's that?" He cocked his head as the darker voice of Earth spoke to him.

He'd heard this voice before. It was Earth who'd told him how to kill the high priest before him and make it look like an accident so he could be elevated to the position. "More blood is the answer? That's what you need to heal the land?"

The mutterings intensified in the recesses of his mind, convincing him that it was the way to appease the goddess. She would come back to him. She'd been hurt so often by man that she needed retribution for their sins against her. The Mother demanded *blood* and sorrow from humanity and Grobahn knew how to achieve it.

"Grobahn!" the Summoner of the Coven shouted on the opposite side of the door to his chambers.

Goddess damn him. He was close to a breakthrough. The high priest wiped the athamé against the inside of his clothing to clean away the blood, and then placed it on the tabletop before pushing himself to his feet. He rearranged his robes to ensure that they hid the gash in his thigh before opening the door.

"Yes, Brahm? I am praying, what cannot wait until tomorrow?"

He bowed his head slightly to stare at Grobahn's bare feet. "Forgive me. I didn't mean to intrude on your reflections, but we have had a vision!"

"A vision? Of what? Who had it?"

He smiled at the high priest. "I did! Several of the other elders shared their same vision with me. Surely, you have had a vision just now as well."

"Yes, I did. I saw the way to heal the earth," Grobahn replied. It was only half-false.

The smile spread wider across Brahm's face. "Then you saw the girl?"

Girl? "Of course I saw the girl, *Summoner*. I have been having the visions of her for weeks, but you know that the laws of the Coven state that we can't act on one person's divinations alone—that's how cults are formed. We must take pride in the fact that we work together as a group."

"Yes, of course, Father. We must send the Watcher for her."

"The Watcher? Yes, Thistle must go on this quest immediately to find the girl." He twitched his leg involuntarily. The blood had begun to tickle his leg as gravity carried it toward the floor.

"So we are in agreement to send him to the Home of the Lakes to rescue her from the flesh eating birds?"

"Why do you question me, Brahm? Didn't I just say that we would send Thistle to rescue her?"

"Thank you, Grobahn." He grasped the high priest's sleeve and took a deep breath, holding it for a moment.

"Be careful of the sin of pride, my son," Grobahn cautioned.

The Summoner let out his breath. "You're right. Thank you for helping to keep me grounded. I'm just so excited that we've finally had a vision of how to heal the earth!"

"There is a long way to go, with many steps between here and there," Grobahn cautioned. "We must be careful we don't act alone without seeking counsel from one another."

"I would never do that, Father."

"Good. Now, send Thistle on his way. I must pray further on this matter."

"With bright blessings, Grobahn."

"With bright blessings," he responded and shut the door solidly behind the Summoner.

He turned slowly to the statue of Gaia. "What are you up to, Mother?"

INTERLUDE

The house was cold, causing the skin bumps to ripple along Scratch's arms. He'd need to get a fire started soon so he could warm up. The day's journey caused him to be chilled and he was through being cold, living like an animal in the dirt or occasional cave as they traveled the countryside to find the cursed Traxx.

Scratch turned to one of his slaves, who hovered on the periphery of his vision. "Fire."

The man nodded mutely. All of Scratch's slaves had their tongues cut out. He thought it helped to keep them in line since they couldn't communicate well with each other.

He sat on a rough, wooden chair that the previous occupant must have built out of wood from the forest surrounding the home. *Where had the owner gotten off to?* "Bring me the man who lived here," he ordered.

Another slave walked quickly out the door. As he opened it, Scratch glimpsed cooking fires already burning outside. The men deserved them. The day's movement had been excessively long as they tried to outdistance the pursuit. It turned out that they hadn't needed to go quite so far, though. Bear's forces had attacked the Traxx soldiers who'd pursued them.

His scouts hadn't been able to tell him who won the battle. But, the sheer number of dead meant that neither side really won. Add the defenders who'd likely died at the city and Bear's ill-advised, outright disobedience had taken a massive chunk out of the Traxx numbers.

Bear, the one-time second in command of the Vultures, had challenged Scratch's leadership by defying him and taking more than half of his people to attack the Traxx city before they were ready. Reports said that the men who'd followed Bear were now dead, jeopardizing his plans.

The Vultures had half-heartedly tried to track the Traxx family for almost seventy years and now they'd found them. Their destruction would be Scratch's legacy to the new world. His predecessor, Robert, had been one of Starr's original pupils before the group splintered and sent Sangelo, the city of the Vultures, into chaos.

Starr dedicated her entire life to trying to rebuild the losses suffered at the hands of the treacherous Traxx. By the time she died and Robert took over, there were enough warriors that they should have sought out and destroyed the Traxx. Robert delayed, content to allow them to exist and the Vultures broke up into rival, petty groups, fighting amongst themselves behind Sangelo's walls. His legacy was the elimination of the rival factions until there was only the one, true Vulture clan, which Scratch now led.

Eradication of the Traxx was one of the basic principles of the Vulture clan and Robert hadn't done anything to further the cause, allowing them to establish their city on the lakeshore. Scratch changed that, creating renewed fervor amongst the people and convinced them to leave the city of Sangelo to find the Traxx. Now they'd found them and Bear had almost destroyed his plans before he'd begun.

Scratch's plan was to eliminate the Traxx support network and make them tremble in fear. By destroying the small outlying villages and farms, the towns that supported the Traxx, it would cause a slow, inevitable panic to set in as the residents of the city realized that they were going to starve to death. Then, his forces were to surround the city and make them beg. They would have gladly given up the Traxx family in exchange for their lives and he could have finally wiped them off the face of the earth.

Now, with half of his force, including Bear, dead, Scratch's timeline would have to be extended. He still planned to continue the psychological assault, picking away a little at a time, but he'd have to take it slower than he'd promised his followers. For now, he knew that he still controlled them, but how long would that last if he didn't produce the results that he'd assured them?

A commotion at the door announced the arrival of the previous homeowner only seconds before Scratch's slave opened the door. The owner's massive shadow darkened the doorway for a moment before he was shoved through, landing hard on the floor. His hands, bound behind him, didn't stop him from hitting his head on the concrete. He cried out in pain and began to sob uncontrollably.

Scratch appraised the Traxx follower with scorn. He was easily double the size of most of the Vultures, a lifetime spent at hard labor on the farm had added slabs of raw muscle to his frame. Most of the men—and more than a few of the women—that they'd found out in the surrounding hamlets were built like the man cowering on the floor. By contrast, the Vultures were much thinner. They valued stealth, speed and skill with weapons over brute strength.

The differences in personality were just as stark as the physical differences between the Traxx and the Vultures. The residents they'd encountered so far were mentally weak. When the Vultures appeared, the people on the farms would try to hide or barricade themselves inside their homes—torches usually worked to bring them back outside. Very few of them tried to fight; they wanted to talk, or cried for mercy—like the worm on the floor now.

The clan's Teaching echoed in Scratch's mind as he stared in disgust at the waste of potential. He pushed himself up and sauntered over to the prisoner. Besides fighting, wrestling and swordsmanship, the Teaching was the only formal education that the Vultures' youth received.

Vultures are warriors. The land belongs to us. Your sworn enemy is the Traxx, they are the reason the land is sick, and they are the weak. You are not afraid.

Vultures are true men; all others are weak and seek to pass their weakness on to their children. A true man destroys the weak and fights until his dying breath. Your life is worthless if you do not fight for the clan. The future is ours for the taking. Vultures are warriors.

The Teaching continued to echo through Scratch's mind. "On your knees, you piece of shit," he ordered.

The man complied, pushing himself up awkwardly with his shoulder. He sat back on his lower legs, still almost as tall as Scratch, who stood in front of him.

The Vulture leaned in close, studying his enemy. His face was pockmarked, evidence that he'd survived some illness long ago. Tears streamed down over strong, prominent cheekbones. His shoulders bulged against the pressure of having his hands tied behind his back and his thick clavicles were exposed.

Scratch had learned that the bones of the Traxx *animals* were much harder to break than those of the Vulture warriors. He'd cracked them open, compared them to those of fallen Vultures; their bones were heavier and thicker than those of his people. It didn't make sense to him. How did an obviously weaker race like the Traxx have stronger bones than the righteous Vulture clan?

"Why are you so different than us, Traxx?"

"I… I'm not a Traxx!" the man sputtered.

"Yes, you are. Do not try to lie to me."

"I promise you. My surname is Anderson. The Traxx live in Homelake. I—"

Scratch cut him off, slamming the pommel of his dagger into the liar's temple. The Traxx collapsed onto the floor once more, knocked senseless. He untied the rope around his pants and pulled his dick out. His urine splashed across the Traxx's face.

"Wake up, worm. Wake up!"

The pathetic creature gagged and spat, turning his head to try to avoid the hot liquid streaming down onto him. His only respite came when Scratch ran out of piss.

"I'll ask you again, Traxx. Why are your people different than mine?"

He blinked away the remnants of the humiliation and looked around the room at the gathered Vultures. "Different?"

Scratch lashed out, kicking him violently in the stomach. He was tiring of this man's games. "I will explain it so even a simpleton could understand, which obviously you are. We are shorter, with ropes of muscle like old world steel. You and your kind are tall, often lumbering giants with large, useless muscles, and your bones are as hard as concrete. Why the difference?"

"I don't know!" the prisoner cried. "I'm as tall as my father was."

"So your Seers have nothing to do with making you this way?"

A look of confusion spread across his face. "I've heard of them, but I've never met a Seer before."

The man was worthless. Scratch smiled wickedly at him. "Did you see our cooking fires?"

"Uh…"

"Those are for you. See, you Traxx may be bigger, but that just means you provide more meat for the true warriors and masters of this land."

Scratch flicked his wrist at the Vultures who'd brought the prisoner inside and they grabbed him, pulling the struggling man roughly back toward the outside.

I hate them. I hate them all.

TEN

The Keep's hallways were cold and dark. *It shouldn't be this cold*, Tanya thought, pulling her robe tighter around her small frame. She clutched the hilt of the dagger that rested in its sheath inside her pocket. She always had a weapon of some type with her these days; the threat from the Vulture army outside the walls was too great to risk being unarmed. She'd found that the small knife was especially useful if she had to fight in close quarters, like the building's hallway.

She walked from her private chambers toward the nursery where her baby, Michael, slept. She'd been woken by a nightmare, a dream of her children being murdered when the Vultures attacked the city. The princess knew that her imagination tended to run into overdrive this time of year. It had been twenty years since slavers attacked the old Traxx compound in the middle of the night. In the attack, her cousins, Caleb and Varan, were abducted, her uncle Luke was killed and her grandfather's brother was killed by a demonbroc. It'd been a traumatic night for a seven year old girl.

Tanya arrived at the nursery. The heavy steel door was closed, as it should have been, and she contemplated not disturbing her children since the Guard was in place, but the feeling that something was amiss wouldn't leave her. She nodded to the man sitting beside the entrance and tried the handle. *Locked.*

A slight sigh of relief passed over her lips. The baby was still secure inside. She tapped gently on the doorframe, rewarded with the sounds of the nursemaid stirring inside.

Clarissa followed the protocols and asked, "Who is it? The prince is sleeping." She sounded annoyed at the late intrusion on her own sleep.

"Clarissa, it's Tanya. Something felt wrong, so I wanted to check on Michael."

"He's sleeping, My Lady. You're the only visitor that we've had tonight."

"No one has come to see you? Not even his brother or sister?" she clarified.

"No. Once we locked the door for the evening, there have been no disturbances. Do you want me to remove the locks?"

"No, thank you. Go back to sleep, my mind is just playing tricks on me."

"Yes, My Lady," Clarissa responded.

Tanya waited for a few more seconds and then turned down the hallway to go to the twins' room. They were six, which meant that they were loud at night as they protested their bedtime, so they'd been moved from the nursery once Michael was born. Otherwise, the baby would have never slept.

She peeked around the corner and saw the two Guards sitting attentively beside the door to the adjoining bedchambers.

"M'Lady!" the older of the two Guards whispered, jumping to his feet when he noticed her.

She placed a hand on his arm. "Good evening, Frederick. I had a strange feeling, so I wanted to check on our babies."

"They are secure inside. I wouldn't let anything happen to them."

"I know." *Am I being paranoid?* She hesitated, then after a moment's pause she said, "I wish to check on them."

"Of course," Frederick replied. "James, can you watch the doorway? Secure it behind us."

"Yes, Sergeant. Tap the code when you're ready to leave." Tanya nodded her approval of the Guard's protocol. Since the attacks by the Vultures, security of the Traxx family had increased even more than it had before. The Keep felt like a true fortress these days.

Once the door was secure behind them, Tanya grasped Frederick's hand and they walked side-by-side through the entryway to the twins' bedchambers. "What do you think is wrong?" Frederick asked.

"I don't know. I just have a feeling that something is."

He squeezed her hand lightly. "It's been twenty years, right?"

She nodded and wrinkled her nose at the sour smell in the twins' suite. She'd have to have the maintenance man examine their bathroom. The toilets in the building were still operational, flushed by pouring water into the reservoir behind the seat, but it was far from a perfect system. The refuse went into a gigantic underground tank far from The Keep that had overflowed before, causing a disgusting, smelly mess inside the building and out in the field. It had taken a crew of ten men several weeks to clean the filth out of the tank, using buckets and hauling the night soil off in carts to be used as fertilizer.

"Yes," she acknowledged, making a note to have the septic tank examined. "Twenty years ago today, my cousins were abducted and we've never known their fate. They're dead, in all likelihood, but I wish we knew for certain."

"It's just your mind playing tricks on you, then, dredging up memories of the past. The Keep is secure. See?" He gestured to the bricked-over window in Jensen's room. The small space at the top that wasn't sealed to allow in fresh air was firmly locked for the night. The boy slept soundly on the old, worn mattress, small noises escaping his lips when he breathed out.

She nodded in the darkness. "Looks like you're right. I guess I'm feeling nostalgic."

"It's okay; you're allowed to, Tanya."

Tanya bumped her shoulder into him, "Sorry to make you leave your card game."

"Mmm…hmm," he murmured, turning toward Jade's room "What's that smell?"

"I noticed it too," she answered, relieved that at least one of her senses wasn't going crazy. *Maybe I'm pregnant again*, she thought in a panic. Michael was only three months old. It was much too soon for her to have another child.

A thump in the next room made her jump. Frederick slowly drew his sword so as not to make more noise than necessary. "What is it?" she asked.

"Stay here," he ordered, taking charge of the situation as a trained Traxx Guard.

"I'm not staying here if something's the matter with my daughter," she hissed back at him, pulling the dagger from her pocket.

He sighed and his shadow moved away from her toward the shared bathroom that led into Jade's room. The smell of stale sweat, assaulted her nose when he opened the door. Frederick glanced back at her and motioned for her to stay once again. She shook her head furiously at his suggestion.

He pushed open the door into the second bedroom slowly, peeking around the corner. Tanya jumped when he yelled and charged into the room, sword lifted above his head. Tanya didn't understand what was happening. She heard the sound of metal hitting against something hard, like wood and then a loud crash.

She rushed into the room and stopped. The room was much too bright. Moonlight shone through the *open* window. Frederick lay bleeding from a wound to his head amongst the bricks that had once sealed the room from the outside world. A tall man with an oversized backpack stood with one leg on the windowsill, preparing to jump. In his arms, he held her daughter.

Tanya screamed, running at him with her own weapon held in front of her. He turned toward her and hissed.

What looked like scales of some type covered the man's face and he wore a type of close-fitting armor that was nothing like the Vultures wore. She had a moment to think that his yellow eyes looked much more snakelike than human, and then she was upon him.

Tanya thrust outward, attempting to come in low with the knife, under his guard, but he easily batted her arm away. She allowed the momentum from his defense to turn her around and crouched as she spun. He swung a brick at her head and she ducked under it, stepping inside his defense and burying her dagger deep into the man's leg.

He cried out in pain and almost dropped Jade, who somehow remained asleep through the ordeal.

Tanya's weapon was gone, stuck in the kidnapper's leg, so she dove to where Frederick's unconscious form lay, grabbing his sword before standing up. She wasn't as well trained with a sword as she was the dagger, but she was decent and could hold her own against most of the Guard.

"Put my daughter down."

He pulled the knife from his leg and it clattered to the floor. "You are doomed, but Gaia will protect this child from your war," he rasped, the words misshapen in his mouth.

The kidnapper pulled himself completely up on the windowsill and leapt into the night.

Tanya screamed and rushed to the window. They were six floors up; the fall would kill them. Far below, a set of triangular wings appeared above the man's back and the contraption caught the wind current, lifting them higher into the air.

The princess watched helplessly as her daughter disappeared into the night.

Near the walls, the alarms began to sound and her heart dropped in her chest. The Vultures surrounding the city had finally chosen to attack.

*****

"Prepare yourself. The time is near."

"Mistress?" Darci asked in confusion.

She'd been eating a biscuit and egg sandwich in the kitchen, preparing for her shift on the observation platform. Her coffee was strong and hot to keep her warm on the winter morning. The Vulture army plaguing the kingdom of Homelake hadn't ventured over the mountains yet, but Darci believed it was only a matter of time. As their attack continued to stall, they'd become interested in settlements further from the walled city. Vigilance was more important now than ever.

She'd had the cup of coffee to her lips, sipping lightly, when Diane glided into the kitchen silently, announcing that the time she'd prophesied so long ago was now at hand.

"Why now, after all these years?" Darci asked. "The Vultures have been fighting in and around Homelake for over a year with no luck."

"I don't know what's happened there. I only know that your services will be required before the next cycle of the moon."

Before the new moon? That meant that sometime in the next two weeks, Traxx would ask her to leave the Valley Lodge and go to Homelake. Her specialty was defensive tactics; did the king think that the Vultures would begin their assault once again? They'd failed miserably the last time they attempted to siege the city. *I can't leave the lodge now, with an army of madmen roaming the foothills.*

"Mistress, it isn't safe for me to leave anymore. You and the others will be vulnerable here."

"Did I not tell you many years ago to begin preparing yourself and Garth? Have you been doing as I directed?"

"Yes, of course," Darci replied hurriedly. "But—"

"There must be no hesitation. The time prophesied is upon us. Either you're prepared or you aren't."

She dropped her eyes in submission. Diane would not tolerate the statement that she'd almost uttered. *The Seers are blind to their own deaths. If I go, they will only have the small guard force—none of which have my natural talent at fighting from a distance.* They'd have to rely on the new defenses that'd she'd built. "Yes, Mistress. I will do as you command."

Diane's feet slid closer and she looked up into her eyes. "You have a great destiny to fulfill. I have seen it, Darci." The Mistress' hand rested heavily on her shoulder. "You have prepared us for what is to come. Garth is a competent leader and the men have trained hard in the defense of the lodge. We will be fine."

"Will I come back?" Darci asked in a rare moment of vulnerability. She genuinely liked living and working at the Valley Lodge.

"I don't know. The future isn't set in stone and is always changing. I have seen you return…and I have seen your death."

Darci nodded curtly. Death came quickly in this world and she was lucky to have made it this far. Every day beyond the plague that had wiped out her village as a child was another day granted by the gods.

She'd become an expert bowman and a competent swordsman over her lifetime, somehow knowing that her skills would be needed. She'd seen it, her own touch of the Gift that she kept locked away. Not that she'd had delusions of grandeur, but she'd always known that there would come a time when *someone* would take her on a journey of great importance.

Darci smiled sadly as this chapter in her life seemed to be coming to a close. "I'm ready, Mistress."

ELEVEN

"I'm not going to stay barricaded behind these walls while my child is out there," Tanya screeched, jabbing her finger toward the city's walls.

"Honey, please," Garrett soothed. "Screaming at everyone won't change things. We can't—"

"I don't want to hear about what we can't do, father. We need to go after that thing right now!"

"Princess, please," Nicholas said. "We all feel Jade's loss; but we must think of everyone's safety. I've seen firsthand what those savages are capable of doing; they'd butcher all of us without a moment's hesitation. There's too much risk in opening the gates right now."

"Then I'm going after that *creature* myself and I'm going to get my daughter back if the *men* from this city are too scared to go after it."

"Tanya, I forbid it," the king bellowed. "You aren't trained in fieldcraft; it would be like handing the Vultures a gift. The Guard will try to sneak a force out through the back gate."

The commander held up his hands. "Garrett, please. Listen to reason. If we open those gates during their attack, the enemy will pour through and then we've lost the city. *All* of your grandchildren—not only Jade— would be in terrible danger. The prudent thing to do would be to use archers to clear away the scum. After a few days, they'll retreat back to the tree line and we'll have room to maneuver our forces. We'll mount an expedition as soon as the siege is over."

"We've been under siege for *years!*" Tanya cried. "Are you really foolish enough to think it will end any time soon?"

"I mean this latest attack, Tanya. Don't—"

She cut Nicholas off. "No, you don't get to tell me what to do about my children. The last time I checked, I was a member of the royal family, not the other way around. I'm going after my daughter. That thing flew west, toward the mountains, so that's where I'm going."

"Tanya, listen to yourself," the king joined in. "The kidnapper *flew* over the Vulture army and went west. Even if you could make it past the fighting outside the walls—which you can't—you wouldn't have any way to track him because he was using mechanical wings! That means he's not leaving tracks for you to follow. And westward? We know that there is another half a continent 'west' of here. But what's left of it, no one knows."

He sighed and sat heavily in his desk chair. "Nicholas is right; we need to think of the safety of everyone in the city. We'll need time to search for Jade, we have no idea where to begin."

"That's why I'm going to the Seers," she replied.

"The *Seers*?" Nicholas scoffed. "Those crazy old ladies don't know anything about tracking a kidnapper. The Traxx Guard will go after your granddaughter as soon as we can clear some space around the back exit."

The king smiled resignedly. "Thank you, Nicholas. One week. I'll give the Guard one week to break this siege and send a search party to speak to the Seers—it's a better place to start than anywhere else we could think to look."

"Father, in one week, she could be dead!"

He attempted to reach for her, but she stepped away from him. Garrett sighed and said, "We can't just open the gates and charge out into the waiting arms of the entire Vulture army. The Guard will clear some room and—"

"You are all fools," Tanya spat. "My daughter—your *granddaughter*—was kidnapped by something right in front of our eyes."

"Yes. About that," Nicholas intervened once again. "How did the kidnapper slip past your guard, Frederick?"

Tanya glanced at her lover, who held a cloth full of ice against his bloody forehead. "Ah…erm. He didn't come past James or I at the front door, so he came from outside." He paused and then continued, "I think he flew into Homelake—with those mechanical wings—and then climbed the side of the building."

"Impossible, that room is six stories off the ground. There's no way a man could—"

"He wasn't a *man*!" Tanya snapped. "I mean, he was, but he wasn't like us. He had scales and eyes that glittered in the moonlight like a snake."

Nicholas crossed his arms over his chest and thrust his chin accusingly toward Frederick, ignoring Tanya. "And what of you? I placed you on guard of the royal grandchildren because of your skills with the sword. Why didn't you stop him if you saw him?"

"I tried. I hit him in the ribs; it should have cleaved him nearly in half, but my sword didn't even make it past his armor. Then he hit me with a brick."

"You know better than to attack the midsection of an armored opponent, Frederick. You've been taught better than that."

"It was the only opening he gave, so I took it, Captain," Frederick replied glumly. "The creature held Jade and I wasn't able to attack low or high. You weren't there."

"You're right, if I was there, I'd have made sure the exit was blocked before I tried to attack," Nicholas answered. "I knew placing you on this assignment was a bad idea. You should have thought with your head and not with your heart."

"You don't get to second-guess me about a situation that you weren't involved in. I did everything I could in the span of a few seconds."

"No, Frederick, you're wrong. I *do* get to second-guess you. I'm the commander of the Traxx Guard; you failed in your duty and I'm trying to determine why."

"Would you two shut up!" Tanya broke in, "I'm not leaving my daughter alone with that thing a moment longer. You can debate who did what after we kill that thing and get Jade back."

The Captain of the Traxx Guard looked like he wanted to say more, but instead, he inclined his head to the princess and then shot Frederick a look of disgust. Tanya wondered if the shaky friendship between Nicholas and Frederick had eroded entirely this night. Nicholas could make his life pure misery by assigning him to duties that were necessary, but dreadful— like guarding the sewers.

Garrett cleared his throat. "Tanya, go to bed. We'll figure out a way to get a force past the Vultures in the morning."

"Father, the longer we wait, the harder it will be to find them."

"I've been on search parties for missing youth in the middle of the night, Tanya," the king said, reminding her of the search for her cousins so long ago. "Even if we could get past the Vultures, searchers would likely miss clues in the darkness. I've given the Guard one week to clear an opening."

"Father, I disagree. I think—" She stopped herself. Arguing with him was pointless. He'd made up his mind that the Vultures were an impenetrable barrier in their way. She would have to do this on her own, without him knowing.

"But," Tanya started again, "I understand what you mean. We've got to take care of the Vultures first."

Frederick's eyes narrowed as he stared at her. She wouldn't give up the fight so easily and he knew it. Tanya shook her head slightly, warning him to remain silent.

"There," the king bobbed his chin, "We'll make a plan in the morning and rescue Jade. She'll have an interesting story to tell her own children one day."

"I know you're trying to cheer me up, but it won't work. The longer we leave her out there, the higher the odds that she'll die—like Varan and Caleb. We abandoned them to their fate as well." She spun on her heel, leaving her father with the sting of her words.

Behind her, she heard her father let out a frustrated breath before telling Frederick, "Go after her and make sure she doesn't do something stupid."

*****

"Ready?" Frederick whispered.

"As ready as I'll ever be," Tanya replied.

He nodded and disappeared into the darkness. She heard several soft *thuds* as his boots impacted against the wall. Finally, the rope went slack as he unlatched it from his harness somewhere below.

She turned to Brandt and told her cousin, "Your turn."

He nodded wordlessly, wrapping the rope around the carabiner on his harness. He turned and eased himself out, then pushed off, slipping into the black night below like Frederick had.

Brandt had surprised her and Frederick as they attempted to steal the rope from the town's supplies. He already had his own bag packed and held several coils of rope out for them. They'd argued quietly about his involvement in their plan, but ultimately the fact that he'd visited the Seers before and knew how to get to them won out. Now their search party equaled three.

The rope went slack once more and it was her turn to go over the wall and rappel into the unknown below. For all she knew, the Vultures could be waiting for her at the bottom. She took the rope and wrapped it through the ancient metal carabiner twice like Frederick had shown her before his own descent. She'd rappelled with the Guard before, but there'd always been someone who hooked her up, it was the first time that she'd done it herself. She double-checked the direction of the rope through the carabiner, if she passed it through the wrong direction, it would unravel and not arrest her fall.

Everything seemed to be correct. Tanya grasped the running end of the rope and wrapped it around her side, tucking her fist into the small of her back. She extended her legs and felt the pressure of the rope harness that Frederick had tied dig uncomfortably into her crotch and waist. The tightness of the seat was only slightly reassuring as she stood against Homelake's wall, thirty feet above the ground. The rope tightened around the carabiner and she breathed a sigh of relief.

With her free hand, she pulled her pack off the wall and fed the rope tied to it slowly through her hand until it dangled five feet below her. The weight of the pack added to her own and the rope harness dug even deeper into her hips. She grasped the rope that led from her carabiner to the anchor point inside the wall and prepared to rappel to the ground so she could find her daughter.

Then, she untucked her brake hand from behind her back and felt the oil-slicked rope slide through her gloves as she pushed out with her legs. For a terrifying moment, she was suspended in the air, weightless and then she slammed back into the wall.

The darkness was disorienting. Tanya had never rappelled at night before, or had a pack dangling below her—and it was always with a *dry* rope. They'd been forced to soak the rope in oil so they wouldn't leave a ready-made entry into the city if the Vultures discovered their escape route, but it added an immense degree of difficulty to the task.

There was no way to tell how far she'd gone on her initial bound in the darkness. It had been too far, she decided. If she wasn't careful, she'd end up flipping upside down, which was dangerous enough in the daylight, but she wouldn't have any way of knowing what to do if that happened in the night.

Tanya steadied herself for another bound and pushed with her legs against the wall, throwing her brake hand out at the same time. The rope slid through her gloves once again and her feet landed against the wall much sooner than the first time. She repeated the quick bounds until she felt her pack hit the ground, relieving some of the pressure against her waist.

She kicked out again, pushing off the wall. Her feet brushed against hands as someone grabbed her boots. They guided her to the frozen ground and her Frederick quietly urged her to hurry.

The rope harness came off after a few tries and she secured it, along with the carabiner, in her pack. They were ready to make a break for the woods surrounding Homelake.

"We're about four hundred feet from the tree line," Frederick whispered into her ear. "Once I light the rope, we're stuck out here."

"Understood."

He pulled off his glove and used a rusty old lighter to ignite the oil on the rope. It began to burn brightly, the oil slowly carrying the bright flame up the rope. The three of them shuffled off quietly into the night.

Behind them, shouts of alarm rang out from defender and attacker alike as the line of fire trailed up the rope along the city's wall.

*****

"Are you sure we're going the right way?" Tanya asked.

"No," her cousin replied truthfully. *I'm not sure if we're going the right way. I'm not sure about what's around the next bend. It's been three days since Jade was abducted; I'm not sure about our chances of success at all.*

Instead of voicing his thoughts, Brandt restated what he'd told them several times, "I remember an old world bridge just before a town at the base of the trail to the Valley Lodge. It took us two days to get to the town when I went with the king—and we were on horseback. Once we got to the town, we had to leave them because the path was too treacherous."

Tanya sighed resignedly. "Okay, I just thought we were closer to them than this."

Brandt searched his memories, but couldn't find any other useful information. "That merchant we ran into said if we keep traveling down the road we're on, we'd find the town of Creede just after a river crossing with an intact bridge. That's got to be the town from my memories."

"So you don't really know how far it is to Creede then?" Frederick asked, stomping hard on the shallow layer of snow that covered the road.

"We're going about the same speed—maybe faster—than we did back then. Uncle Garrett went in the dead of winter and the horses had a hard time with snowdrifts."

"So…are we going the right way?" Tanya repeated.

"I don't know," he threw up his hands, finally admitting the truth. "It was a long time ago, Tanya."

"Oh, gods. What if we're lost?" she asked.

"I swear, Brandt, if you led us astray and we've lost three days, I'll rip you to shreds."

"You can't talk to me like that," Brandt countered. "I'm a Traxx."

"And I'm a really mean asshole when it comes to people messing with my children, regardless of who they are. And, the princess, is *my* charge, so I'd be within the Code of the Guard to defend her."

Brandt started to debate the truthfulness of his statement, but decided against it. Arguing with the two of them wasn't helpful. He understood their frustration; their daughter was missing. He could cut the Guard a little slack. "Look guys, let's just get to this Creede place and ask around. At the very least, we're still going west."

They both grumbled unintelligibly and he put his head down, concentrating on putting one foot in front of the other. The wind swept off the plains behind them, driving them forward, which was better than the alternative. The snow had even abated, so it was just cold and windy, instead of cold, windy *and* wet.

The knot in his stomach made Brandt wish for the hundredth time they would have had the time to properly provision themselves before sneaking out of The Keep. They'd been fighting against the coming morning and didn't want to lose an entire day waiting for the next night. Normally, the small villages and hamlets along the way could have offered some assistance, but the ones they'd ran across had all been ransacked or burned by the Vulture army. Between the three of them, all they'd been able to scrounge up before they left was a loaf of bread and a small wheel of cheese.

The hours passed in mind-numbing boredom as they walked endlessly towards their presumed destination. Brandt's mind wandered and he often found himself falling behind the two. Once, he had to run to catch up to them. *By gods, they'd just leave me out here.* It was enough to convince him to not become separated from his cousin and her protector.

They came around a bend in the road where it curved around a finger coming down off the mountains. "Hold on," Frederick said, causing Brandt to stop. "What's that up ahead?"

The younger man squinted against the glare of the snow. "Is that the bridge?" He shielded his eyes with his hand. "Yes! That's it. The town is about a mile or so after the bridge. We'll be able to get final instructions about how to get to the lodge from the people there."

Before long, they shuffled past the bridge, dipping into their nearly depleted energy reserves for the final push into town. If they didn't get some real food soon, they weren't going to be able to go much farther.

A pair of armed men met them at the road when they were about a quarter of a mile from Creede. In the distance, workers emplaced long tree trunks into pits and secured them to one another before other laborers buried the base. They were building a wall around the town.

"What business do you have, travelers?"

"We're going to the Valley Lodge," Tanya replied.

"Goin' to see the witches, eh?" the guard replied casually.

"We…ah, yes. The Seers have helped my family before and we need their advice again."

"What do you have as payment for them?" the second guard asked, staring intently at Brandt's backpack. The attention made the young man feel uncomfortable, so he shifted his stance, putting his body between him and the man.

"We don't have anything of value," Tanya admitted. "We were forced to leave Homelake quickly and only had time to grab a few things."

"Homelake?" the two guards asked in unison.

"Yeah," Frederick joined in. "We've been under siege for a long time and we're coming to the Seers for help."

Brandt nodded his head. They'd decided that they would keep their identities and the real nature of their quest a secret from everyone except the Seers. They didn't know much about anyone outside of their city and had no way of knowing who could or couldn't be trusted, but in order to get directions to the Valley Lodge, they had to let a little bit of information slip.

"The mayor will want to see you, then," the guard who'd been interested in Brandt's backpack said.

"Please, we have urgent business with the Seers," Tanya pleaded.

From the corner of his eye, Brandt saw Frederick uncross his arms and drop a hand casually to the hilt of his sword as he set the other on his belt. It was a gesture meant to resemble the swordsman relaxing and showing mild boredom, but Traxx knew better. He placed a restraining hand on the Guard's chest and stepped forward.

"I'm afraid all we have to offer is information," Brandt said. "We can spare a few minutes to speak with your mayor."

"Nobody goes past Creede unless the mayor says they're allowed," the guard stated. "Wait here."

The two men returned to the little three-walled shack they'd been sitting in and one of them picked up a bow. He lit the end of an arrow from their fire and launched it toward the town. Within minutes, a heavily bundled horseman rode up the road from town. He conferred with the guards for a moment before spurring the horse toward Brandt and his companions.

"Welcome to Creede," he said. His muffled voice was difficult to understand beneath the thick scarf he wore over his mouth.

"Thank you," Tanya replied. "We're going to the Valley Lodge and need to pass through your town to get there."

"Aye. You do. If the mayor says it's okay, we'll let you through. First, you need to give the mayor any information you can about that army over your way."

Brandt understood the activity now. They were worried about the Vultures as well. That's why they were erecting the wall and had the increased security—although, he had no idea what they thought two men could do to stop an army of crazed lunatics.

"Of course," Tanya answered. "We can provide any information that we have."

"Good, follow me," the horseman stated. He turned his horse toward Creede and began walking slowly down the cracked and pitted old road so they could keep pace with him.

They went past the construction site, wisely situated far enough from the town to allow for expansion in the future as well as standoff distance for weaponry fired over the fence. The townspeople used the terrain to their advantage, tying the ends of their fence to the natural barrier of the mountain slopes that rose around Creede.

"This is a good first step," Frederick remarked, breaking the silence. "After this fence is built, you'll want to construct a legitimate wall that can withstand battering rams and fire; something that can be defended."

The horseman nodded. "We're going to do that. We should have built walls decades ago, but we relied on our isolation to defend us. It took what's happened to all those isolated villages around Homelake to spur us into action."

"Hopefully it's not too late," Frederick said, effectively killing the conversation he'd started.

The mayor's office was an old, crumbling stucco building with a tattered rectangle of faded cloth flying from a pole out front. "I've seen that before," Brandt stated. "What is it?"

The horseman looked around and finally followed his finger to the top of the pole. "You mean the flag?"

Brandt shrugged. "I don't know. If that's what it's called, sure. What's it used for?"

Muffled laughter billowed out from the horseman. "That's the American flag, son. That's the symbol of our nation."

Brandt wasn't sure about that. The region was named Colorado. He was from Homelake and this town was called Creede. What was this place that he spoke of? "So you're in alliance with American?" he asked hesitantly.

The man guffawed again. "It's called *America*. And no, we aren't in alliance with them—well, actually, maybe we are... We're all a part of America. That flag was the symbol of our nation back in the old world."

He pointed to the flag and continued, "You can't even see them anymore, but there used to be red and white stripes on the flag and fifty stars that meant there were fifty states. Colorado, where we live, was just one of them fifty states."

Brandt's eyes grew wide. He knew about Texas and Colorado, but had no clue about the others. "Are there many people living in the other states?"

The horseman dismounted. He was much shorter than Brandt once he was off the horse. "Your guess is as good as mine, son. We know about a few settlements over the mountains—not many, but there are a few—and there's a bunch out your way, but what else is left?" he shrugged, "No idea. The war destroyed most of the major population centers and the ones that didn't get wiped out instantly killed themselves off within a few months or years afterward."

"Like Austin, where my family came from?" Brandt asked.

"No clue. That was in Texas, right?" He waited until the younger Traxx nodded before continuing. "I've never been outside of Colorado myself, but if your family says the people of Austin survived the war and then fought amongst themselves afterward, then they probably did."

The horseman tied the reins of his horse to a post near the entrance and went inside, holding the door open behind himself to allow the three travelers through. He unwrapped the scarf and took off the heavy coats that he'd layered on, revealing a balding brown head, and walked over to the fireplace to stoke it. "Have a seat; I'll be with you in a moment."

Brandt watched the man as he placed another log on the fire and adjusted its location with a poker before standing upright and rubbing at his lower back. He felt like he'd been here before, with his uncle when they came so long ago, but he couldn't be sure. The king had dragged him to so many meetings over the years that few of them stood out in his mind; the ritual with the Seers being the exception.

"Ahh… Sorry, I just can't stand the cold," the small horseman stated.

"It's only the beginning of winter," Frederick stated. "What are you going to do when it actually gets cold?"

"I'll put on more coats," he said as he walked around behind a giant wooden desk. "Luckily, I live here where I work, so most of the time, I don't have to go outside."

"Are *you* the mayor?" Tanya asked.

He smiled, revealing a set of coffee-stained teeth. "Yes, ma'am, I am. Name's Craig. Josh Craig."

He reached across and shook their hands firmly. Brandt noticed that his hands were soft, like a merchant's hands or like the hands of both of the seamstresses that he'd been able to bed. It made him embarrassed by his own rough, calloused hands, abused by years of apprentice work in the blacksmith's shop and countless hours spent holding his sword during the Traxx Guard's fighting lessons.

Tanya and Brandt sat in the two chairs in front of the desk while Frederick stood near the doorway. The mayor's eyes lingered on the warrior for a moment, likely assessing his role in the group, before he sat down himself.

"Nice to meet you, Mr. Craig. My name is Tanya, this is my cousin Brandt and our friend Frederick."

"Nice to meet you, too," the mayor replied. "Jim said you were in a rush to go up and talk to the Seers. Not that I can blame you, the weather is just going to get worse from here, but we've got a deal with Ms. Diane to screen anyone who wants to see them."

"That's understandable," Tanya replied. "People's lives depend on us talking to them soon, though. So, can we please hurry this along?"

"Quick and to the point. I can respect that. Is this because of the army of madmen that surround Homelake?"

"Yes."

He inclined his chin. "Knew it. I'm not gonna lie to you folks, they have us real scared all the way over here in Creede too."

"You should be scared," Brandt exclaimed. "They can't get to us for now, but it's only a matter of time before they figure out some way to do it."

"There was reports of a big battle last spring, about halfway between here and there—that's what prompted us to get off our hind ends and begin building that fence. Do you know anything about that?"

Frederick cleared his throat. "I was at that battle. They'd split their forces, part of the army stayed at the city and the rest went out to cut trees to use as rams or ladders to get past the walls. We killed almost a thousand of the savages in that fight."

The mayor waited until Frederick finished speaking and then said, "You're one of those special protectors, aren't you?"

"I'm not sure I—"

"Yes," Tanya cut in. "Frederick is a member of the Traxx Guard, our elite fighting force."

"That's right," Mr. Craig said, slapping the desk with his open palm. "The Traxx Guard, men and women who've dedicated their lives to war and fighting. Homelake is lucky that they have enough resources to allow people to be soldiers full time."

"We've been fortunate," Tanya acknowledged. "The climate in the foothills helps our farmers to produce a surplus of crops, which we freely trade with our neighbors."

The mayor leaned back, holding his hands out. "Oh, I know. I didn't mean to send the wrong message. We've benefitted greatly from Homelake's generosity. But, with those lunatics out there murdering everyone they see, I'm more than a little jealous of your Traxx Guard. I wish we had something like that here. We just don't have the population to support it…"

The mayor paused, waiting to see if Tanya would add anything to her statement. When she didn't, he continued, "So, why do you wish to speak to the Seers?"

"We seek their advice on an extremely urgent matter," Tanya replied, keeping her voice steady. Brandt knew that she wanted to shake the little man senseless until he let them pass, but she was being diplomatic, like her father.

"That's it? You're not going to tell me how the three of you, including a Traxx Guard, slipped past the savages? More importantly, why?"

"How we got past them is our business," Tanya stated.

"Aren't we allies?" the mayor asked.

"We are. But with a marauding army on your doorstep, you could be convinced to give up secrets about our city to save your own."

"Or forced to tell them as they disembowel you in front of your family," Frederick expanded.

The mayor chuckled nervously. "Well, there is that. Okay, you're correct, how you got out of the city and past the army isn't my concern.

Now that you're here, I'm still the gatekeeper for my *primary* allies, the Seers. Why do you wish to speak to them?"

Tanya took a deep breath before she answered his question. "Something was stolen from Homelake three nights ago and we don't know where to start looking."

"Something?"

"It's not your concern, but it's very important to the king—which is why Frederick is here."

"I see. The savages took it?"

"We... We don't know," she admitted. "This is going to sound strange..."

"I work with the Seers, I'm used to strange."

She smiled. "I'll give you that. Okay, I saw the man who took the thing. Only, he wasn't fully a man."

"How so?"

"He walked upright—and spoke—but, he was covered in scales and had eyes like a snake. He also leapt from the sixth floor of the Traxx Keep, and then opened a set of mechanical wings to soar off into the night, flying westward the last time it was seen."

Tanya paused to allow their host the opportunity to digest the information. After a moment, he said, "Well, that's a new one."

"Frederick hit the creature in the ribs with his sword and it didn't seem to affect him at all, he batted away the best swordsman in Homelake like he was a child...and I'll never forget those eyes."

The silence in the room stretched toward becoming uncomfortable when the mayor finally spoke. "I simply don't know what to say. Since Creede lies along one of only two routes open through the mountains, we get a lot of information from travelers going east or west seeking a better life. We've heard of giant, hairy beasts that stalk travelers in the mountain snow, man-eating fish in the lakes north of here and creatures that build elaborate tunnel systems to trap their prey out on the prairies beyond Homelake, but I have never heard of flying lizard-men."

"I know it sounds far-fetched, Mr. Craig. If I hadn't seen it myself, I'd have a hard time believing it; which is why we seek the aid of the Seers. They may be able to help us."

The mayor's eyes wandered the group before settling on Brandt. "And you, what's your role in this?"

"Tanya is my cousin. I couldn't let her go alone."

He seemed to accept the statement and stared out the tiny window at the snowflakes that had begun to fall since they came inside. "Let's see," the mayor finally muttered. "We have a Traxx Guard, a woman who saw a flying lizard that stole an artifact, and her cousin, who seems content to be along for the ride. The three of you left your walled city somehow, evaded an army of savages on foot, and are now sitting at the base of the trail, which leads to the famed Valley Lodge. Is that right?"

"Yes, sir," Tanya replied.

Mr. Craig tapped his finger along his jawline. "Something doesn't quite add up... Something..." he trailed off, working through the details of their story.

"Does the king know you've left?" he asked.

"I, uh... I'm sure he does now," she stumbled.

"There's a piece of it," the mayor jabbed his finger toward her. "So you weren't authorized to leave, which means either this artifact that was stolen wasn't *that* important—"

"Believe me, it's the most precious thing in our kingdom," Tanya cut into his stream of consciousness.

"That means that *you* are too important to leave, then."

Damn, Brandt thought. *He's good.*

"You could have been elected the spokesman, but I see how the other two defer to you," the mayor continued. "Who are you really, Ms. Tanya?"

Brandt saw the muscles in Tanya's jaw flex several times as she stared at the mayor. He knew from experience that she did that unconsciously when she was deep in thought or struggling with an issue.

"Frederick is my body guard," she finally allowed herself to say.

"Hmm… Ahh. You *are* a Traxx." He turned to Brandt. "Which makes you one too. So, now that we have it in the open who everyone is, what was stolen?"

"I'd rather keep that private, Mr. Craig," Tanya replied coldly.

He considered her words further, causing Brandt to think that he wouldn't accept her answer. Finally, he acquiesced. "Fine, it's your business. Far be it from me to keep the *princess* from speaking with the Seers. You're granted access to the trail."

Tanya smiled and stood, quickly pushing the chair backward. "Thank you, Mr. Craig. You've been very helpful."

The mayor walked to the window and waved at someone outside. "I wish I could say the same," he stated. "Although, if the princess is seeking something in the mountains, it must be extremely important, so I wish you luck."

Once again, everyone shook hands and they shuffled outside into the biting wind. The mayor bid them a safe journey and closed the door tightly.

"So, we just head up into the mountains?" Frederick asked, staring pointedly at Brandt.

"Uh, yeah, sure." He turned in a circle out on the street. The paved road through town ended only a little ways from where the mayor's office sat, but a rocky trail picked up where the road left off. The lighter gray and brown trail clearly followed a draw higher into the surrounding mountains.

Brandt was out of his element. Just because he'd been somewhere when he was a child didn't mean that he knew how to get there now. His family needed him to be a leader right now. He remembered that the path led upward, ever upward, until a sharp crest and then a beautiful valley opened up before them—a valley laced with explosive devices and armed men. There was a woman....

"Ho, travelers," a female's voice called to them from the house across the street.

Brandt turned to see a woman in dark brown clothing standing on the porch. Her midnight black hair reminded him of the woman with the crossbow from the Valley Lodge.

"Hello," Tanya offered.

"Mr. Craig has talked to you?"

"Yes. He granted us passage into the mountains."

"That's good! Few make it past Mr. Craig."

"Do many people try to seek counsel from the Seers?" Tanya asked.

"More than you'd care to know. It keeps the mayor busy." She stepped off the porch and walked toward the remains of a picket fence bordering the yard. "Where are you from?"

Tanya glanced at her companions and said, "East of here."

"It's good to be cautious. Are you from Homelake?"

When it became obvious that Tanya wasn't going to respond, the woman pointed toward the building they'd left. "I can just go in and ask him, he'll tell me everything I need to know."

The woman's self-assured mannerisms reminded Brandt even more of the bowman he'd met all those years ago. She'd been in charge of the Seers' security detail and was a hell of a shot with her bow.

"Who are you?"

"I think I know her," Brandt stated. "You work for the Seers."

She shifted her attention from Tanya to him and smiled. "Traxxling. You've returned."

It *was* her, but he couldn't remember her name. "Aye, I've come back."

"The mistress sent me here to wait for you. She didn't want an entire day wasted on you stumbling through the mountains to find us and another spent coming back down the mountain, so she told me everything."

"I'm sorry, who are you?" Tanya asked in confusion.

"My name is Darci," she responded, stepping around the fence and sauntering up to their group. "I'm here to take you to your daughter."

TWELVE

"Mother," one of the young ladies bathing in a pond greeted her as Freya walked by on her way to check on the child.

"Daughter," she replied informally. Even though she knew the girl's name, Freya had taken to calling all of the People who lived in the Willamette Valley her children, regardless of their age.

The faith of the men and women who lived in the forest community had won her over. Their religion predated the fall of the old world and they believed that she was the earthly incarnation of Mother Gaia, sent here to help heal the environment after the damage by the war...and she was starting to believe it herself. Even Varan was coming around to the idea after living with them for more than a year.

The community's priests talked with him every day about his misguided devotion to the Norse gods of the gladiator society. Since the slavers sold her to Lucas as a child, the gladiator deities were all that Freya had known. The message of the forest People was one of hope and love, based on the interaction with nature, not about the desire for a glorious death. Varan still held to his hard-won beliefs of living amongst the gods in Fólkvangr during the afterlife if he died in battle, but he also admitted that the similarities between Freya and the goddess Freyja were simply too great to be a coincidence. While the two religions seemed to counter one another, Varan believed that both were real and complementary to one another. The light couldn't exist without the dark, and vice versa.

As to their new home in the Willamette, it was simply the most beautiful place that Freya had ever seen. Everything was green from the daily rains; the grass, the trees, the heavy underbrush between the trees...everything. Even the home she shared with Varan was green with moss and ivy.

At first, Freya had been frightened of the unusual men and women who lived in the Dominion, but she'd quickly learned of their history and discovered that they were just like her, only different. Before the war, people who devoted their lives to nature established the Dominion, choosing to live alone in the forest away from the problems of the old world. They'd been outcasts by people who believed the way to achieve peace was to have bigger and stronger weapons. They were the same ones who eventually ordered the destruction of their way of life.

The residents of the camp had been able to survive in the lush forest that provided for all of their needs. Over time, wanderers and other outcasts began to appear, cast out by the remaining men because they bore the scars of disfigurements from the wars that they'd begun. The new arrivals were welcomed with open arms to the overflowing love of the nature worshippers.

Then, something magical happened. The deformities that the new citizens brought with them turned out to be hereditary and the changes became more pronounced with each generation. Less than one in five of the residents who lived in the Dominion were changed, but those who were lived, worked and loved freely amongst the others. Everyone hoped to have a child with their special abilities, so they were sought out as mates.

Even as the unofficial head of the Coven, the Dominion's religious community, Freya didn't know everything that they could do. *All* of them seemed much more in tune with nature, that much was certain. Most were physically different. Some, like the men who rescued Varan from the river, had scales that grew over their bodies, others seemed to have no facial features at all, and there were a few men and women who had developed longer body hair, with vaguely wolf-like features. And then there were the priests, the religious leader who often showed no outward signs of change except for their eyes, but were able to do things with their minds—the ability to invade dreams being one of them.

All were welcome in the Dominion. No one was turned away unless they sought to harm others; there'd been a few over the years, Freya learned.

She was on her way to see the priests now. A messenger had been sent to rescue a special child from a war-torn land called the Home of the Lakes. He was due back this evening. Given her own past, Freya had been against the idea of taking the girl from her family at first. The priests convinced her of the dire need for the child, as she was the catalyst that would unlock Freya's abilities. How, they had no idea, but their visions told them that the girl was important.

As the chief of the Dominion's new security team, Varan was present at all the important meetings. He was vehemently opposed to the rescue attempt, calling it kidnapping, regardless of the fate that awaited the girl if she stayed. He'd argued that it wasn't their place to take the child from her family and if the girl was required, then the entire family should be given the choice to come to the Dominion freely, not taken in the middle of the night.

The priests argued that they'd seen the hearts of the men and women that the child lived with. They'd rather die in the battle at their gates than leave their lands behind them and they would never willingly allow one of their people to leave, so it was imperative that they take the girl to save her from the atrocities that would fall upon the people of the Home of the Lakes.

As a last-ditch, desperate bid to sway Freya, Varan brought up the fact that they'd both been abducted as children and made into slaves. It was an unnecessary reminder of the pain she'd experienced her entire life. Again, the priests argued that letting the outside world know about the People was lunacy. Normal men didn't understand them and they'd be slaughtered.

In the end, it wasn't the girl's abilities or Varan's urgings to leave her be that made up Freya's mind. It was her compassion. She couldn't allow a child who'd been thrust into the middle of a senseless war to die foolishly because some prideful man wouldn't leave his home. According to the priests' visions, the girl would be dead before the end of the winter as her family huddled behind the safety of their walls, unwilling to go forth and end the siege. It became a much easier choice to go against Varan after she knew what the future held for the girl and she authorized the rescue.

"Mother," another member of her flock greeted as she walked the forest path to the priests.

The forest was truly a magnificent place; and unlike anything that she'd ever seen before. Its remote location meant that it was spared the horrific fires and explosions that rocked the old world, leaving it mostly intact. The location, deep within the river valley, helped to keep the Dominion isolated from the problems of the new world as well.

Freya had become accustomed to the larger trees down south when they fled from the Commerce Guild. While not quite as large as those were, the trees of the Dominion were wide and varied by type. She hadn't even known that so many different kinds of trees existed.

The People taught her the names and uses of all the local varieties. The mighty maple, which produced a sweet sap used to flavor foods and offered as a treat to children. The Dominion was home to the wonderful-smelling fir trees that dropped their needles to provide bedding for animals. The cottonwood, whose wood was light, but strong, had bark that the People used to relieve pain when chewed. The buckthorn was used as a laxative to help relieve swollen bowels. White oak was the preferred fuel for fireplaces since the wood burned hot for hours. They used the ash to make hunting bows and the fighting staffs that the defenders carried. The willow, whose branches caressed the earth, became baskets and traps for fish. And finally, the mighty red cedar, which was used for just about everything that the People made of wood that would sit outside since it weathered well and didn't warp as badly as other types of wood once it was cut.

The forest was certainly a beautiful place and she'd thoroughly enjoyed living in the Dominion, but as she neared the priests' home, she couldn't help wondering if her time here was ending. Somehow, the little girl was supposed to unlock Freya's powers to heal the earth, which likely meant that she'd have to leave the pristine forest and travel to the awful places that bred sickness and decay.

"Freya! Freya, wait up!" Varan's voice carried between the trees.

She turned in time to see him emerge from the woods, running. "Varan," she replied in surprise. "What are you doing?"

"I missed you leaving this morning so I took a shortcut through the forest to catch you. Thistle is back, is he not?"

"He is." She'd tried to find him when she left that morning, but had been unable to do so. "Where were you this morning?"

"I was practicing with my sword. I was right there in the back yard."

"Mmm," she mumbled. "I've had a lot on my mind and just missed you. I'm sorry." It didn't help that tensions had been high between the two of them since she decided to go forward with the rescue. It had been easier to simply avoid Varan rather than get in another argument.

He accepted her apology and pointed toward the priests' house. "Well, let's get this over with."

"I don't want to cause a scene inside," Freya stated. "Can we just not fight in public about this? The girl has been rescued, she's here and there's no further discussion on it."

Varan's eyes narrowed for a moment and then he smiled. Freya knew it to be the same fake smile he would put on for the crowds during Contests and he wore it when he was around Lucas. She hated that he did it to her now as well. "Of course, *Mother*. I respect your wishes in all aspects of our life here in the Dominion."

"Dammit, Varan. You don't have to be a smartass."

"No, I'm serious. You are the leader of the People here and I'm just a fool messenger boy."

Here we go. He's in one of his moods again. "Don't start with me. You know damn well that I had nothing to do with those dreams. It was the priests who sent them to your brother, not me."

"And my brother died thinking there was some great destiny for me to fulfill. What a crock of shit."

She sighed. It was the same argument they'd had since coming to the Dominion. Varan still struggled to come to terms with the fact that the priests used him and Caleb. They'd purposefully misled the gladiators into believing that they had a purpose in life, which would be revealed when they got to their destination. In reality, they were just supposed to free her from captivity and bring her here.

Varan's lack of an identity in the Dominion was the main reason that she'd created his position as the head of security for the community. The position was both a boost to her lover's psyche and a needed correction in their defenses. Before they arrived, the People relied mainly on defending their own homes, which anyone who wasn't born and raised in the peaceful forest town knew was a bad idea. Attackers could eliminate one family at a time that way. Against the priests' wishes, Varan trained a fighting force that now stood a slight chance against a small group of raiders.

"Stop it. You've done wonders for this community and the defense force is getting better every day."

"We rely on isolation and our relationship with nature to keep us safe, not barbarism," Grobahn interrupted the pair.

"I've told you before, priest," Varan hissed, "I'm likely to cut your damn head off if you sneak up on me."

The religious leader inclined his head slightly, "My apologies, Defense Leader Varan. I am simply excited to finally bring the two parts of the prophecy together."

"The girl? Did Thistle find her?" Freya asked.

Grobahn blinked at her, his eyelids flicking rapidly over those strange yellow eyes that all of the priests had. "Was there ever any doubt, Mother?"

"No, I—"

"If you were worried that he would fail, why did you send him out into the world of normal men?"

"You've taken my question out of context," she answered in frustration. "I didn't mean that I thought Thistle would fail. What I meant was that I hadn't heard confirmation that he'd returned with the girl."

"Thistle was raised as a Watcher of the Coven," Grobahn said indignantly. The corners of his mouth turned upward in a sneer of derision at her lack of knowledge of their religion. "He would not return if he failed in his mission to rescue the child."

Most of the residents of the Dominion were calm and gentle, slow to action like a pond in midsummer, but the priests were intense and short-tempered, often confrontational for no reason. Grobahn, in particular, essentially bullied the congregation into following his orders. Freya often wondered at the strange juxtaposition of personalities between the leadership of the Coven and the rest of the People.

"Forgive me," she said through gritted teeth. "I am still learning the ways of the People."

He bowed lowly. "Of course, Mother. Those savages, the normal men, raised you in a land far away from our peaceful Willamette Valley. You will understand our ways over time."

She nodded in agreement. *Time.* She had plenty of time to think about things in the Dominion. "May we go see her?"

Grobahn stepped aside, sweeping his arms wide toward the priests' home. "You came all this way, it would be rude for me to refuse. Keep in mind, though, that Thistle had to constantly give the girl cottonwood bark to keep her asleep, so she is still tired."

"He drugged her?" Varan asked in shock.

The priest's laughter sounded like the rattling of dead leaves blown about by the wind. "It was necessary. Otherwise, she would have struggled and could have fallen to her death."

Freya placed a hand on Varan's forearm to calm him. "Let's just go meet her."

He jerked his arm away and stared at her. "Do you mean to tell me you approve of drugging a child?"

"No, of course not. But, it's done, there's nothing we can do about it now."

He jabbed a finger at the priest, who recoiled as if he'd been struck. "We can't let them do this. The more we turn a blind eye to the small things, and say that it's in the past and there's nothing we can do about it, then the worse things will become. Freya, I've seen this before, that's how Lucas' guards got so bad. It was incremental and each time they weren't reprimanded, it became an accepted practice. Then it got worse until… Well, you know how they were."

She nodded her head. "Of course I know how they were, Varan, and this is the second time in less than a week that you've reminded me of our past. That's not what's happening here. The People's goal is to heal the earth and that little girl is the final key to unlocking the puzzle of how to do that."

Grobahn smiled at her statement. As they walked past she saw him stare in open hatred at Varan. *So much for the People being forgiving and welcoming of all.*

*****

"Wow, I really like this stuff," Brandt said rapidly. "What did you say it's called?"

"Coffee," Darci answered. "Be careful and drink it slowly."

The youth drained his cup and held it out to her. "Can I have some more?"

"Are you joking?" Tanya asked, holding her cup with both hands to absorb the warmth. "She just said to take it easy. You're already jittery, just like you get when you drink beer—which, if I remember right, you don't do well with either."

Frederick laughed and raised his own mug in a mock toast to Brandt. "She's right. Remember the last fall harvest festival and that *lovely* girl, the baker's daughter?"

"Who'd clearly spent her entire life sampling her father's products," Tanya joined in.

"And that sheep. Oh gods, I can't—"

"Could you please stop discussing my dating mistakes in front of Darci?"

"Dating mistakes?" the archer asked with an upraised eyebrow. "Do you often make a habit of dating farm animals?"

"No!" The color rose in his cheeks, turning them red in embarrassment. "I was really drunk at harvest and mistook the sheep for the baker's daughter—who I actually *was* trying to sleep with that night."

Darci chuckled quietly, afraid of the noise that full laughter would produce. "She must have been lovely, as Frederick said if you confused her with a sheep."

Brandt hunched over to stare into the fire. "Well, it was very dark," he muttered, which caused the others to laugh again.

Tanya excused herself so she could go relieve the morning pressure on her bladder. She walked a short distance away and put a large rock between her and the others for decency. The princess could still hear them talking, so she would have preferred to go much farther away to do her business, but Darci had been adamant that the highlands were full of hungry creatures that would love to find a defenseless traveler with their pants around their ankles.

The trip had been uneventful so far. The Seers had given Darci a strange map, sketched by Mistress Diane when she was in the trance stage of her vision. It showed row upon row of mountains that they had to traverse as they cut northwest toward where Jade was taken. Their first target along the way was a giant lake. Then, after that, it was just a wide-open space with skulls drawn on the map. She'd drawn trees on the far side of the Skull Lands, as Tanya called the desert, with a few small humps for hills and written the word "River Valley" on the other side of the trees.

It was enough to get them close to where the Seer said Jade was. Once they got near the forest, Darci said she could determine the final location, but didn't tell Tanya how she planned to do it, so she just had to trust that the archer knew what she was doing.

As she finished relieving herself, a woman's scream pierced the morning air, echoing off the exposed red rock around her.

"Tanya!" Frederick cried from the campsite.

She pulled her drawers up quickly, cringing at the wetness that she hadn't had time to wipe away, and rushed back to camp.

"I'm fine," Tanya replied as she walked back into the perimeter. "What was that?"

"Mountain lion," Darci said. "Their screams have haunted mankind for millennia. We need to get moving."

"What's a millennia?" Brandt asked.

"A thousand years," the archer grunted as she poured the last of the coffee onto the fire.

"We've been around for a thousand years?" Tanya's cousin asked in disbelief.

"Humans have been around for a lot longer than that—and so have the animals that hunted them in the darkness. That's why our ancestors took away the night, flooding the world with false light."

The mountain lion's scream bounced off the rocks once again. Tanya turned slowly in a circle, trying to determine where the creature was, but couldn't get a bead on it. The acoustics of the cut they'd camped in made it impossible to determine the large cat's direction.

"If the lion doesn't want to be seen, then you won't see it," Darci instructed. "This far west, I don't know whether the cougars are the same as the ones around the Valley Lodge. Those are vicious hunters that will continue to track their prey until they catch it."

"Then shouldn't we wait for it and kill the damn thing when it comes close?" Frederick asked.

"No, we need to get moving. We don't know if it's hunting us or if it's on the trail of something else, so it's better to leave the area before it decides to reorder its shopping list."

"I'm not staying here longer than we need to," Tanya added. "Every minute we delay, the longer Jade is with those things, scared and missing her family."

They finished packing their bags quickly and threw them across the backs of the horses Darci had provided for them in Creede. They turned toward the west, putting the morning sun behind them, before spurring their mounts into a gentle trot.

THIRTEEN

"What did you just say your name is?" Varan asked menacingly.

The little girl looked from him over to Freya. "Why's he mad at me?" she asked, her lower lip quivering. She was on the verge of crying.

Freya physically pushed Varan back away from their guest. "I'm sorry, Jade. Varan gets excited and he doesn't know how to talk to little girls," she soothed. She leaned in close and put her hand up to shield her face from the warrior and Grobahn. "But don't let him fool you. He has a big, soft heart on the inside."

"I... I want my mommy."

"I'm sure she'll be here shortly," Freya lied, thinking it was better to try to keep her calm for as long as possible.

The girl started crying softly. She'd been trying to be brave, but the realization that she'd been taken from her family in the middle of the night got the better of her. Freya knelt and opened her arms for Jade, giving her the option to decide if she wanted to hug the stranger or not. After a moment, she threw her arms around the Mother.

Freya hugged the girl tightly and looked up at Grobahn. The bastard could have told them that the people in danger of being wiped out were the Traxx family. He knew of Varan's past and the issues he had with feeling abandoned by them. To bring this Traxx girl here with no warning was a slap in the face.

"Why didn't you tell us who she was?" Varan asked.

"Because it would have only increased your desire to sabotage the rescue," Grobahn retorted. "You've been against this from the beginning and—"

"He's scary," Jade whispered into Freya's ear, effectively saving her from hearing their argument.

Freya followed her gaze to where Thistle stood off to the side. "The People are just like you and me, sweetie. They just got sick and that happened to them."

"They look like snakes. Daddy says snakes are evil and that we need to stay away from them."

She hugged the girl tighter. "Well, don't worry. They're not bad. They were the ones who told us about you. We had to bring you here because of the war."

"The war?"

"All the fighting at the Home of the Lakes."

Jade nodded solemnly. "The Vultures. They're bad. They fight with our friends."

"The Vultures?" Varan seethed, hearing the girl's words. "After all this time, they're still fighting the Vultures?"

Freya waved her hand angrily, attempting to shut him up. "See, that's why we needed to get you and bring you here. It's dangerous back at your home."

"What about Jensen and Michael?"

Freya shook her head, "I'm sorry, I don't know who they are."

"They're my brothers. Jensen is my twin brother. I miss him."

She released the girl and stood, turning to where the priest argued with Varan. "She's a twin, and you separated her?"

"The boy is not important," Grobahn said. "The girl will help you unlock your powers to heal the damages done to the earth."

She shifted to place her body between the men and the girl. "And how is she supposed to do that, exactly? You keep saying that she's the final piece we need to unlock my powers, but you haven't told me how that works."

"I… I don't know," the priest admitted.

Varan threw up his hands in disgust. "So you found the Traxx family—*my* family—and decided to take one of their children, *another* of their children, I might add, and you don't know how her power works?"

"Our visions often come in stages. Now that the first stage is complete, we will soon learn what it is that needs to happen."

"Grobahn, if I may," the Summoner, Brahm, interjected. The high priest motioned for him to continue. "What if the child goes to stay with the Mother? Maybe developing a relationship between the two and the responsibilities of being a physical mother for the girl will unlock the spiritual power of being the Mother."

"I don't know about that," Grobahn said. "I'd planned on keeping her here in the rectory to have her close to assist with our visions."

Freya looked around the priests' sparse lodging. The common area was designed for functionality and durability, not comfort. Nothing in the room would even remotely interest a girl Jade's age and she would be miserable.

"I like Brahm's suggestion," Freya stated. "Jade should come stay with me and Varan."

"Whoa. Hold on," Varan said. "I don't want a *Traxx* anywhere near me."

"You are a Traxx, Varan! You need to come to terms with that."

"They abandoned me and Caleb a long time ago."

"Varan and Caleb?" Jade asked. "My mommy talks about you."

"What do you mean she talks about us?"

"She says that the family searched for a long time to find you, but there weren't any tracks to follow. It didn't stop grandad and Uncle Blake from looking for so long that mommy thought they'd gone missing too."

Freya saw the war of emotions battle across his face. He'd conditioned himself for so long to hate the Traxx family for abandoning him, but what if the girl spoke the truth? What if they tried to find the boys and they couldn't? Varan himself said that they traveled for weeks inside a cage on the back of a wagon, barely kept alive, until Lucas purchased them. The tracks could have easily been concealed if they traveled down a paved road.

"Who... Who's your mommy?" Varan asked, showing the first signs of vulnerability.

"Tanya. She's the princess."

"*Tanya!* Tanya is your mother? Little Tanya?" He fell to his knees and began crying.

Freya held her tongue and gave warning stares to the hovering priests. This was going to be good for him. He was a broken man and had almost fallen off the cliff into insanity after he killed his brother. Learning of his past and what had happened in his absence would go a long way toward healing his soul.

Varan wiped away the tears and reached out tentatively to place a hand on Jade's shoulder. "Little one, I know your mother. She was my cousin and we used to play together every day, training to fight against the Vultures that our fathers told us would return one day. I guess that means I'm your uncle."

*****

"Dammit, Nicholas. No more excuses," the king slammed his hand down on the map of Homelake. "I want to get a force outside of these walls. I gave you a week to get us outside and here we sit. Tanya and Brandt have been out there on their own this entire time."

"Garrett, we're trying. The Vultures have countered every move we try. Your daughter snuck off in the night over the wall and lit a beacon for the entire world to see as she left, effectively eliminating rappelling a force down the walls impossible."

Traxx clenched his fist. It was true, dammit. When Tanya and Brandt snuck out of the city, they burned the ropes they'd used to climb down. He knew that they did it to ensure they didn't leave a ready-made way for the Vultures to infiltrate the city, but it also eliminated that method as a way to get the search team outside the walls. The Vultures tightened their siege lines and lit fires every night that illuminated no-man's land at overlapping intervals.

"You've told me that your troops were capable of opening a hole in the Vulture lines. That we could force a bubble of safety around the back gates to get a mounted force through, but we've had zero progress."

"We've killed dozens of them this week with archers, My Lord," Lieutenant Rylan, the deputy commander of the Traxx Guard, stated.

The king turned on him. "We need to kill *hundreds*, Rylan, not dozens. My daughter and granddaughter are out there somewhere along with my nephew and that fool sergeant of yours. Every day we delay, the greater the peril they face."

"Yes, sir, but—"

"You've been out there," Garrett continued. "You know what it's like beyond the plains. Man is not the master of the wilds any more than he's welcomed in the wastes of the old cities. There are things out there that will easily kill such a small party. We need a breakout."

Nicholas cleared his throat. "We are setting the conditions for—"

"Shut up, Nicholas. We've been friends our entire lives and I owe you more than I could ever repay, but this is personal. We need—*I* need—a breakout from the city. The future of our people is out there, wandering around looking for clues about where that thing took my granddaughter."

Nicholas took a deep breath and then let it out slowly. "Garrett, this is personal for *all of us*, which is why we need to step back and look at it strategically." He held up his hands as the king began to protest. "No, hear me out. I love Tanya and Jade, and they *are* the future of Homelake, but if we attack the Vultures without proper planning to ensure ourselves a victory, then we risk opening up the city. If those animals get inside, we're done for."

He's right, you old fool, Garrett told himself. *I'm responsible for almost ten thousand residents, I can't let my heart overrule my mind. Be the king that the people need you to be, dammit!*

"Nicholas, you're right," the king said. "We can't allow the Vultures to get inside the city and they seem content to try and starve us out for now. But I also can't allow my family to be decimated out in the wilds."

He held up his hand to keep the commander and his lieutenant quiet as he worked through the problem. His thoughts turned to the books he'd read about the kings of old and how they led their people to victory—or to defeat. They'd been great warriors, and their subjects loved them for their sacrifices. Garrett didn't need the adulation of the people, but he did need their support. The answer came to him.

"Rylan, I need you to find my brother, Blake," Garrett ordered. "He's likely in the smithy, working on that giant crossbow design of his. That damned thing may save us one day, but for now, he needs to put it aside. I'm appointing him as Regent in my absence."

"Absence?" Nicholas asked in confusion.

"I can't allow the Vultures to get into the city, but I will not allow my family to be left alone in the wilds. I'm going to lead a force of fifty volunteers on a breakout from the back gates."

"My Lord, I—"

"It's decided, Nicholas. We will have an old-fashioned cavalry charge and smash through their lines. We'll keep riding west to the Seers and figure out where those witches sent my daughter."

FOURTEEN

"We need to stop for the night," Darci said as she slowed her horse to a slow walk.

"Are you sure?" Tanya asked. "I mean, you said that the mountain lion was still stalking us."

The archer looked up to the rock ledges surrounding them. The red and yellow cliffs held dozens of places for the animal to hide, but this was the most defensible spot on the ground that she'd seen for several miles. The light from the moon and stars barely reached the bottom of the canyon, so they couldn't risk stumbling around in the dark any longer. If one of the horses' legs broke before they crossed the Skull Lands, they were done for.

"I'm sure it still hunts us," Darci acknowledged. "It would do so if we went another ten miles, but it would have a much better chance of taking one of us in the darkness. It's best to make camp on our terms while we have a little bit of daylight left."

"Why don't we try to kill the damn thing, become the hunters ourselves?" Frederick said in frustration, swinging his leg over his horse's rump and stepping down to the ground.

The older woman smirked. "You're welcome to go up onto those ledges and attack it. Maybe you'll get lucky and it's a young cat, not a grizzled fifteen-year veteran of fighting in these canyons. Or, it could be old, slow and on the verge of death instead of a blur of motion that will eviscerate you with one swipe of its paw." She held up a finger. "Maybe it'll be a small, malnourished creature, barely able to open its mouth instead of a three hundred and fifty pound monster capable of crushing your skull in its massive jaws, just as sure on its feet up there on the ledge as if it were on the ground."

Frederick swallowed hard and looked around the space she'd picked as a campsite. "This looks like a good place to stay for the night."

Tanya laughed nervously and then dismounted as well, followed by Brandt. They began to unroll their blankets and the younger Traxx fussed with untying the string wrapped around his bedroll. His cousin took the blanket from him and untied the knot before handing it back to him. The boy was an enigma to Darci. She shook her head and chastised herself, *He's not a boy; he's twenty years old. Just because I'm starting to show my age doesn't mean I should consider him less capable than the other two.*

It was hard for her to think of him as an adult, though. She couldn't quite put her finger on it, inexperience mostly, but there was something else underlying his actions. Darci wasn't sure if it was privilege or arrogance, maybe a little of both. She'd learned a lot about the way of life in Homelake over the past week and decided that their lifestyle is what made Brandt seem so childish to her. By the time she was twenty, she'd already killed several men and was more than capable of handling herself in any situation. But Brandt, he was another story. The royals apparently still worked in their fields and shops like everyone else, but there was obviously a difference between the two Traxx in her company.

Brandt became part of the royal family when he was thirteen, whereas Tanya had been nineteen, already an adult capable of seeing after herself. Sure, his musculature told her that he spent hours each day loading wood into fires and pounding metal with a hammer at the blacksmith shop where he worked, but he often displayed an inability to do the simpler tasks for himself, like untying the knot just now. Darci hoped he wouldn't be a liability to the group's success.

"What are we having for dinner?" the youth asked, rubbing his belly.

"Hard biscuit and salted meat is all we have," Tanya said. "We haven't seen much wildlife for Darci to shoot."

That was her cue. The archer put aside her observations and closed the gap between them. "Just because we haven't seen it doesn't mean it's not here," she stated. "The high desert is teeming with wildlife; it just does a good job of hiding."

As if to emphasize her point, the mountain lion screamed. "Shit, that sounded close," Frederick said, sliding his sword from the scabbard at his waist. She appraised the way his stance changed and how natural the blade seemed in his hand. *Frederick is a fighter, what does Brandt offer?*

"You two, continue setting up camp," Darci told Frederick and Tanya. "Brandt, come with me."

He withdrew his own sword and fell into step slightly behind her, off to the side. "You know how to use that thing?" she asked.

"Everyone from Homelake is required to enter the militia when they turn seventeen and all men must participate in the reserve force for their entire life after they're released from compulsory service at twenty-three."

She glanced sidelong at him. "Okay, thank you for the rundown on the city's military, but I asked if you knew how to handle your sword. I don't need you accidentally gutting me when you get spooked."

"I'm much better in the phalanx, but I can hold my own with a sword. Frederick is the best swordsman in the entire kingdom—that's how he ended up getting assigned as Tanya's bodyguard before they began having children together. I've trained with him since I was a kid."

"I could tell that he knows how to handle his weapon." She paused as she knelt near a waist-high rock beside the old road. Darci began scanning the ledges through her crossbow's scope. The distance seemed to disappear in the lens.

She didn't like how close the mountain lion had gotten. It had been mildly interested in them earlier and she hadn't been too concerned with it, but now it was right on top of them, which meant it was more than interested in them now.

"What's a phalanx?" she asked to pass the time as she searched for the lion.

Brandt spent the better part of twenty minutes explaining the weapons and fighting techniques employed by the militia at Homelake and told her about the victory that Frederick had been part of last year against the overwhelming Vulture force. They'd won a battle of nearly three-to-one odds through their superior tactics.

Finally, Darci decided that the mountain lion wasn't going to show itself for an easy kill and they returned to the campsite where Tanya had unpacked some of their supplies for dinner. It was a cold and meager meal, composed of the rations purchased in Creede for their journey. She wished that she'd been able to shoot a rabbit or deer for fresh meat, but none presented themselves. The fresh meat would have been welcome and a deer carcass would have helped to get rid of the lion as well. As it was, they had to eat from their packs. That worried her. The map that the Mistress gave her showed that they were on the verge of the Skull Lands where water and food sources were nonexistent.

After dinner, Darci set the watch at two people awake at all times. They hadn't been able to find enough wood to make a fire, so they would just have to cope with the darkness and be vigilant when on watch. She took the first watch with Brandt so she could continue to keep an eye on him.

The night stretched on and a chill settled over the valley. Darci wondered what was on the other side of the giant water. She'd read about deserts and tried to prepare their supplies appropriately, but she knew that they would suffer, especially the horses.

Behind her, the soft snoring of Tanya and Frederick was distracting. *Is Brandt distracted by the noise?* Darci was used to hours of solitude on her perch, watching for trouble around the lodge, the boy wasn't.

She shifted to look at him and saw the white of his eyes practically glowing in the moonlight as he stared wide-eyed at her. "Everything alright?" she asked.

"I heard a popping noise. You know, like when your knee joint pops after sitting or standing for a long time."

She nodded and gently shook Frederick's boot. "Wake up. It's coming."

To his credit, the bodyguard rolled out of his blanket quickly, sword already in hand. "Where is it?" Frederick asked.

"Haven't seen it yet, but Brandt heard it approaching," she whispered. "Everyone stay still."

Frederick nodded and sank to the ground to wait. It didn't take long before the creature showed itself. Darci suppressed a gasp of surprise. Slinking from rock to rock, the lion was almost six feet tall at its shoulder and easily nine feet long. She'd seen them in the mountains near the lodge, but this beast was something different.

Besides the obvious size difference, its shoulder and hip joints seemed to work in odd angles from one another and the skin across its forehead was missing, exposing the dirty white skull underneath. She slowly rotated the focus on her scope and zoomed in. The injury was old, the ragged skin around the wound healed long ago, lending an evil appearance to the creature.

Each of the canines emerging from its mouth to frame its jaw was larger than a man's thumb. She'd seen big teeth before, but nothing like what this beast sported. They could probably pierce the light armor she wore with ease. The creature was something from her nightmares.

Slowly, Darci pulled two more crossbow arrows loose from the storage rack along the stock of the weapon and then lined up the crosshairs on the lion. She thought about trying for a shot through the eye, but quickly discarded the idea. There were too many variables to account for and any slight movement by the animal would cause her to miss. Besides, she wasn't entirely confident that her crossbow could pierce that thing's skull.

She shifted her aim point lower to the center of its chest and then slightly off to the side. If she was extremely lucky, she could get it through the heart, otherwise, it would penetrate the lion's lung and she'd be able to get another shot off before it closed the distance. The *twang* of her bowstring shattered the silence of the night.

The lion's scream told her that she hit it, but Darci didn't wait to see where the arrow went. She dropped the front of the bow to the ground and stepped through the handle on the end of it, then grasped the bowstring on either side of the stock, pulling it upward until the locking mechanism caught the string. In one, practiced motion, she slid her foot out of the handle, nocked one of the arrows that she'd pulled off and raised the crossbow toward the charging beast.

It was only fifteen feet from their campsite, too close for the scope, so she aimed along the fixed sights and squeezed the trigger. The arrow embedded into the lion's front shoulder and it shrieked its anger at her as it continued bounding forward.

Darci stood her ground and then dove to the side when it leapt. She felt a searing pain across her shoulder as the cat adjusted in midair, swiping one enormous paw down while it sailed overhead. Her face hit a split second before her body slammed into the rocky ground. She skidded for several feet before finally coming to a stop.

She rolled awkwardly to her side in time to see Frederick shout, "*Aaah Uhh!*" as he swung his sword, cleaving open the creature's neck. It turned its head and grasped the blade with its teeth, twisting the sword from his hand. The ringing of metal against the hard ground seemed to freeze in the air as the beast took ragged breaths.

Their horses cried in terror at the sight of the monster, pulling against their leads. Darci had a fleeting thought that if they broke free then the quest would be jeopardized, but they couldn't do anything until the threat from the lion was gone.

She snapped her eyes back to the beast. It still stood, so she jumped to her feet and pulled her dagger free. The creature swung its head listlessly toward her, causing her to freeze. The combination of Frederick's sword and her arrows may have severely wounded it, but the lion was still dangerous.

Brandt drew his sword and the animal turned its head back to the other three. It took a tentative step toward them and stumbled.

"Stay back from it," Darci warned. "It's not dead."

"Yeah, but shouldn't we just kill it and be done with it?" Brandt asked.

His voice reinvigorated the lion and it lunged forward. Tanya and Frederick moved out of the way, but Brandt fell backward, hitting his head on a rock and knocking himself unconscious.

"Shit," the archer muttered, dropping the dagger. She cocked her crossbow once more. The beast made several efforts to move forward, but the injuries to its shoulders limited its mobility, causing it to roll slightly onto its side, giving her the opportunity she needed. She aimed at the gaping wound in the lion's neck, hoping that the injury would allow her arrow to penetrate deep enough to reach its heart. The crossbow bucked up slightly as Darci pulled the trigger. Her eyes never left the target and she watched the arrow burrow into the lion nearly halfway up the shaft.

It wasn't a quick death, but it did the job.

No one moved for a few moments, everyone wanted to ensure that the beast was dead. Then, they all began moving at once. Tanya rushed to see if Brandt was alright and Frederick retrieved his sword. He pulled it quickly across the lion's throat to guarantee that it wouldn't attack them after they'd dismissed it as another lifeless carcass in the wastes.

Darci went over to the horses to soothe them. The appearance of the big cat had spooked them and even with her there, they continued to stare at the lion, pulling to the end of their reigns with their ears flattened in terror.

"We're going to have to move campsites," the archer announced. "The horses aren't going to calm down with the body of that lion so close."

Tanya looked up from where she knelt with Brandt. "He's still out," she said.

"Well, we need to wake him up or lash him to the back of a horse. If we lose one of these horses, we're in trouble. That desert on the Mistress' map will kill us if we're on foot."

Frederick, who'd wiped his blade clean on the lion's fur, agreed. "I don't relish sleeping near this thing either. The smell of blood will bring in other predators soon enough."

"We won't go far," Darci said. "Just about a mile or so to get away from it. That should be far enough to calm the horses, but not so far that we risk going near the edges of the cliffs."

"If Brandt's injured, we shouldn't move him," Tanya countered.

"We *can't* stay here, Tanya," Frederick said as he slid his sword into its scabbard. "She's right. If we lose the horses, then we decrease our chances of getting to Jade anytime soon."

"Okay," Tanya relented, looking over at Frederick. "I'll need a few moments to make sure we've got everything."

She follows his lead, Darci observed. She'd seen it in a few subtle examples, but this was an outright change of direction for Tanya. When it came to matters of fieldcraft or warfare, she clearly passed the responsibility over to him. *I need to continue to get Frederick to agree with me so I can steer this party where we need to go.*

It was useful information that she filed away for later.

They packed up their gear and tied the unconscious Brandt to his horse, then secured the reigns to Frederick's saddle. Right before they left, Darci recovered her first two arrows from the lion's carcass. The other was buried too deeply to pull out. *Never know when these will come in handy*, she told herself.

*****

"Uncle Garrett is the *king*?" Varan asked incredulously.

"Yup. Everybody in Homelake has to do what he says," Jade replied in between mouthfuls of food.

When they'd brought her to their house from the priests' rectory, Freya and Varan discovered that the girl was famished. The last meal she could remember eating was a dinner in remembrance of Varan and Caleb at the Traxx family home. She told them that she had shadowy memories of being given water on the journey from Homelake, but didn't remember much else.

Varan scratched his cheek in thought. *How did his uncle end up as a king in a place called Homelake?* They'd lived in a walled compound of about twenty or thirty homes in Texas when he was kidnapped and there wasn't a lake anywhere near there that he knew of. He'd already asked her where the town was located, but she was too young to know those sorts of details.

"Well, I'm sure he's a good king. It's been a long time, but Uncle Garrett was always a level-headed man with a kind heart."

She stared at him blankly, so he amended, "He was smart and nice."

"Oh… Yeah, Grandad is really smart. Everybody likes him."

"Okay, you two," Freya interrupted from the kitchen where she'd been washing the dinner dishes with water from the river. "It's very late and Jade needs to get some sleep."

"I'm not tired, ma'am," the little girl replied.

"You should be," Freya countered. "You've been taken from your family and carried halfway across the country over the last three days. There's no way you're not tired."

Jade held up her thumb and forefinger. "Maybe I'm a little bit tired."

"That's it," the Mother said, throwing her towel onto the counter. "Off to bed."

Varan watched as Freya led the girl to their second bedroom where she'd placed blankets on the couch there for her to keep warm. It was a strange set of circumstances that brought his cousin all the way out to the Willamette Valley and he was starting to believe—just a little bit—that maybe the Coven's religious crazies were in tune with some type of higher being.

It wasn't like his own beliefs that a woman tended a bunch of dead warriors in a beautiful field was any more sane. He *knew* that the goddess Freyja had spoken to him before, so why couldn't the priests commune with Gaia?

"She fell right to sleep," Freya said from behind him.

"Good," he replied. "She must be exhausted. I can't imagine that Thistle was gentle with her."

"That's why he drugged her," she responded before dropping into the seat beside him. She reached across and grabbed his hand. "Are you alright? I mean, this is more than a little odd that she's part of your family—your real family that you've spent your entire life trying to forget."

He waved his free hand dismissively. "I'm fine. The Traxx are dead to me."

She released her grip and leaned back, crossing her arms under her breasts. "Even with what Jade said about them looking for you for weeks?"

"What does she know? She wasn't around, that's just what they told her. They abandoned us."

"Then why do they hold a memorial each year on the anniversary of your kidnapping?"

"To appease their guilty consciences," he retorted.

"Varan, I rarely talk to you about your feelings, because it seems like each time we do, our relationship takes a step back, but this time, I think you're wrong. You need to open your mind and look at this objectively from an outside perspective. Your uncles didn't abandon you, they searched for so long that their own children thought they were dead. That sounds like they were pretty damn committed to finding you."

He sighed. *Maybe she's right.* "What does it matter anyways? You know the reason Grobahn wanted to retrieve her in the first place. The Vultures are going to wipe them off the face of the earth before the end of winter."

She shrugged. "There's nothing we can do about that. But, you can't dislike the girl because of who she is… Or because of who *you* are."

"I never said that I didn't like her. I'm just— I don't know. I'm just confused about my feelings right now. I spent almost twenty years hating the Traxx for abandoning me to a life in the arena, then that gorgeous little girl shows up and says that they tried finding us and our kidnapping is such a big deal to them that they have a memorial every year… That's a lot to put on somebody out of the blue."

"You're right. It is a lot, but you can handle it. We need to—"

"Um, excuse me, Miss Freya," Jade interrupted, startling them.

Freya placed her hand on her chest. "Oh my goodness, girl. You scared me!"

"I'm sorry. I was wondering…" She looked down at her feet. "Can I stay out here with you two? I don't like that strange man looking in my window."

Varan jumped up and grabbed his dagger from the table behind the couch where they sat. "Stay here," he ordered.

He slipped into the extra bedroom and edged along the wall until he stood next to the window. A quick glance told him that no one was directly outside, so he moved in front of it to see the full yard better. As he did so, the flowing cloak of a man disappeared around the corner at the front of the house.

The warrior burst from the room, nearly bowling over Freya and Jade, neither of whom had stayed where he told them to. "Someone was in the yard. By the time I got to Jade's window, they'd slipped around the front of the house."

Thud… Thud… THUD!

The front door shook under a heavy fist banging against it. Varan snapped the dagger's sheath onto his belt and picked up his sword from the table by the front door where he'd set it when he came home. He slid it out of the scabbard and held it in one hand as he slid aside the curtains on the small, vertical windows beside the door.

Grobahn stood outside frowning.

"It's the priest," he muttered, looking back at the girls.

"What in the gods' name does he want?" Freya asked. "It's late and we have a little one to worry about these days." She added the last part with an affectionate arm around the girl's chest, pulling her in tight against her body.

"I don't know." He turned and unlocked the door before pulling it open. "Grobahn. It's late, what is it that couldn't keep until morning."

The priest started to cross the threshold and thought better of it when he saw the sword in the warrior's hand. "Expecting trouble?"

Varan placed the sword back on the table and allowed the door to swing wide. He took a step back to give their visitor enough room to come inside. "It never hurts to be prepared, priest. What do you need?"

Grobahn's eyes wandered briefly around the candlelit room and settled on Freya and Jade. He sniffed through his flattened nose and said, "That seems to be a little rude for someone who stays free of charge in the Dominion."

"I stay with the Mother. She's the whole reason this place exists, remember?"

"Oh, I do indeed remember, outsider," he whispered. "I remember all too well."

Grobahn pushed past Varan toward the girls. "Mother. Daughter. How are you tonight?"

"We're getting ready to go to bed for the night," Freya answered.

"I'm sorry, Mother. I didn't mean to disturb you."

"Yes, you did," Varan interjected.

He ignored the comment and pressed on, "Mother, I have had a vision. I know how to unlock your powers."

"That was fast," the warrior muttered. While he may have been open to the prospect of Gaia being real, he absolutely didn't believe that Grobahn was legitimate. He smelled dirty and was nothing but a charlatan who'd convinced the People to put him in power.

"Yes," Grobahn answered, licking his lips. "It's as I suspected. Once the Daughter and the Mother were united, Gaia gave us the answers we sought."

"What do I need to do?" Freya asked.

"We must travel to a place where the earth opens up to a seemingly bottomless pit. My vision showed me the location and I've conferred with the others about what it means. We know where it is."

He paused for effect, which made Varan roll his eyes. "Keep in mind that the people of the Dominion have been in the Willamette Valley for centuries. They were drawn here originally by the freedom of oppression and the need to explore their spirituality. This place in my vision is known to us as a place of great power."

"So, we need to go there and do what?" Freya coaxed, rolling her hand to get the man to explain.

He continued on with his explanation, ignoring her question and obvious frustration, "It's known as The Devil's Hole. It was a closely guarded secret by the old government, before the fall of their society. My ancestors say that they used it for experiments with developing weapons of great power—which is why it was shut away from the world.

"Before the government took possession of the site, the legends say that men tried to find the bottom, but were never able to travel as far down as the opening went into the ground. Those who went into the Hole were changed men, often driven insane by the wonders of the pit. When dead animals were thrown into it, they would reappear weeks later, healthy and whole."

"That sounds like something that goes against nature. Against everything that humanity stands for," Varan stated. "Maybe the old government took control of it to protect the population."

The priest whirled to face him. "Does it? And what is your formal training on the ways of our planet, of the way that nature responds to us and what humans have done? Think about it for a moment—if you can comprehend this. Men once traveled to the moon and back; they could cure diseases and communicate with the other side of the world. They had all of those marvelous inventions and they couldn't find the bottom of a hole in the ground? Something is in there and now we know what it is."

Grobahn threw his arms wide and shouted, "Mother Gaia lives in The Devil's Hole!"

Jade jumped at his outburst and turned to hide her face against Freya's stomach. "Your vision showed you that Gaia is in the pit?" the woman asked.

"Yes. We leave in the morning."

"No, we don't," Freya said. "Jade is in no shape to travel. She's exhausted after her abduction. We need at least a week, possibly two to prepare."

"Mother, please. We've waited for one hundred and twenty years for this moment. You must allow us to leave in the morning."

Varan stepped closer to the priest. "If you've waited so long," he said menacingly, "what will waiting another week or two matter?"

"You don't understand!" Grobahn replied, practically crying in his desire to convince them to leave. "My vision showed us leaving. Everything must happen as soon as possible."

"What did your vision show you about our trip to The Devil's Hole?" Freya asked.

"I saw us leaving the Dominion with a party of thirteen in honor of the Wheel of the Year and the lunar cycle. We travel northwest for six nights, on the morning of the seventh we go into the pit. It is foretold."

Freya frowned. "You haven't told me that your vision actually told you *when* to begin the journey."

"Soon…" the priest answered in dismay.

"No. If your vision happened the way you described it, there's nothing telling us when we are to go."

"The earth needs to be healed!"

"If I can make it happen, then I will—" She stopped and a strange look crossed her face.

"Freya, are you okay?" Varan asked.

She didn't answer him. Instead, she blinked several times and then turned her head to look into the eyes of each person in the room. Varan did not see his lover reflected in the depths of those emerald greens.

"You will leave in four weeks to coincide with the Winter Solstice," Freya said. "The annual rebirth of the sun is the perfect time for the healing to begin."

"Mother, please," Grobahn pleaded. "We need to go as soon as possible. We can't wait all the way until Yule! The time is perfect now—"

"Fool. You know me not. You listen to the Taker, he has deceived you and led you astray."

Grobahn recoiled as if struck. "You can't talk to me like that. I am the High Priest of the Coven, *Freya*. It is I who had you brought to the Dominion."

"Silence!" the Mother barked. Varan pulled Jade toward him and slid her behind his body to protect her. The woman standing before him was definitely not Freya.

"I have made my decision and you will abide by it, priest," she continued. "The Winter Solstice is the turning point for the year; it will be the turning point for the entire planet."

"I... I don't understand," the high priest muttered. "We have waited so long, why wait any longer?"

"*You? You* have only waited forty years, Grobahn. *I* have waited the entire age of man. The end of the old world was a long time coming. Ever since man learned to produce electricity and weapons that could kill with no effort, the end was written."

Varan stared at Freya. Nothing she said made sense to him.

"When you get to the Hole, the healing of the world will begin. Fresh grasses and fruit trees will spring forth in the wastelands. The burning rain that plagues the plains will cease. Rivers and lakes that no longer support life will teem with fish. The lands far from here, separated by the big waters, will begin to return from the chaos. All of this will begin on the Winter Solstice."

She took a ragged breath. "Man must never forget that they have been given a second chance. There will not be a third."

Freya collapsed backward over the sofa table and Varan rushed to her side.

FIFTEEN

Garrett Traxx shifted in the saddle to ensure that it was seated properly on Champion's back. It seemed secure enough to carry him into battle. He was as ready as he could be for what he was about to lead his men into.

When the call went out for volunteers to attack the Vultures and break the lines so the king could rescue his daughter and granddaughter, more than five hundred men and women showed up. Garrett was shocked at how many people wanted to end this siege and help him reunite his family. They had to pare it down to only fifty mounted men, a small enough force to be able to fade into the mountains beyond Homelake, but large enough to have a fighting chance against the savages.

Garrett nodded to the boy holding his spear and accepted it from him. He held it aloft and shouted to the others in his small force, "We ride for the hills to the west. Kill every one of those bastards that gets in front of you. If you get separated, the rendezvous point is the Anderson farm."

The assembled men and women cheered for a moment and then he signaled the gatekeeper to open the gate. It creaked slowly as porters rotated the giant cogs that controlled the opening mechanism.

The gates creaked in protest, but finally broke apart. Garrett cursed at the engineers who'd designed the damn thing. He didn't remember it taking that long to open before the siege set in last winter. *They haven't been opened in over a year, no wonder so many people wanted the opportunity to attack the Vultures.*

Beyond the wall, he could already hear the shouts of the savages, alerted to the opportunity to get into the city through the opening gates. The king watched as Lieutenant Rylan's bowmen began firing from the walls. Several of them fell from the battlements with arrows protruding from their bodies as the Vultures shot back.

He glanced behind him to where Nicholas stood with the militia on the ground. Their job was to fill the gap in the gates after the cavalry charged through. They were the lynchpin to keeping the residents of the city safe. Without their shields and spears standing in the way, the Vultures could pour into the city—especially considering how slow the damn gates moved.

The bowman began screaming for more arrows and children scrambled up and down ladders all along the wall, resupplying them. Garrett wondered what in the hell was happening outside. He'd been up on the battlements twenty minutes ago, the plains surrounding Homelake seemed quiet. The only things breaking up the open area where his men would charge through were the skeletal remains of a few burned homes.

The gates cracked open a few more inches, allowing Garrett a view of the outside world through the sliver of light. A slight fog hung low to the ground that hadn't been there before. He knew that the fog would deepen as the sun warmed the ground and then eventually dissipate once the sun got high enough in the sky to burn it off.

The shadows from the buildings helped to hide most everything immediately in front of him and he couldn't tell what the archers were shooting at. It was maddening. Somehow, the Vultures had moved around to the back gates and it seemed they were waiting for them. Was he leading his men to a quick death?

Finally, something gave way in the gate mechanism and the two massive doors separated rapidly, as they'd been designed to do. They opened a full ten feet across and he spurred his horse forward. Behind him, the other horsemen screamed their battle cries and charged out behind him. The pent up frustration of being trapped behind the walls of the city poured forth.

Directly into a line of Vultures.

Garrett had a split second to register battering rams, ladders and siege towers that rested on their sides for concealment. It looked like this was the culmination of the attack that started a week ago on the night that Jade was taken. They'd used the cover of darkness and the growing fog to mass on the back gates. *Too many!* There was no way his archers could stop that many of them. They were going to breach the walls. He lowered his spear, bellowing his own rage at the animals that ringed his city and murdered his subjects.

The riders behind him adjusted and followed their king. The horses built up speed as the Vulture archers began to fire amongst the cavalrymen. The king didn't hesitate. He was supposed to sneak away into the hills, but this threat before him would destroy the city he loved. The remainder of his family lived behind those walls. After seeing what the Vultures had planned, he couldn't abandon them.

For now, Tanya's quest would need to be her own.

The riders spread out in a line on either side of him. They were well trained and knew what they had to do. The distance between the two groups closed impossibly fast and then the battle was upon them.

The cavalry smashed through the unprepared Vulture lines. Men and equipment went flying in every direction. The riders' spears grew heavy with the bodies of their enemy skewered upon them. Garrett had to drop his weapon because he couldn't hold the weight and risked being unhorsed amongst the savages.

In seconds, they were beyond the line of fighters and into the archers. The king pulled his sword free. He hacked into the neck of a woman on one side of his horse and then took the head off a man fumbling to pull a dagger from his belt on the other. The line of archers broke quickly and the horsemen rode them down, slaughtering them by the handful.

"Turn!" Garrett shouted to his riders.

They wheeled about and got on line, preparing for another charge. He allowed the horses a moment to breathe and checked his line. Of the fifty he'd left the city with, it seemed like there were less than thirty left. Down below, between the cavalry and the city, the Vultures were reforming.

Their lines had been broken, but they were far from beaten. Garrett tried to estimate how many of the savages were before him. It seemed like they hadn't done anything to thin their numbers, however, losing their archers would help turn the tide in favor of Homelake tremendously.

Garrett looked longingly toward the west. They were beyond the lines. They'd achieved their goal and could travel unhindered now. He could still go to the Seers and find his daughter and granddaughter, leave the fighting behind him… *And then what, old man? All the people of Homelake are your family, not just the Traxx.*

"Ready!" he called to his riders.

They responded in kind, shouting the battle cry of the city, "*Aaah Uhh!*"

Garrett nodded. They were ready. It was time to meet their destiny. These thirty men and women would sweep across the fields of Homelake and ride into legend. He raised his arm to signal the charge, but stopped.

A horn blasted from the walls and the call of the city's infantry echoed across to them. The Vultures turned in dismay as row upon row of dismounted militiamen poured forth from the gates. Nicholas marched forth with the army of Homelake.

"*Aaah Uhh!*"

The gates closed rapidly behind them and Garrett watched as they molded into the phalanx formation. Once they were set, they began moving forward. They would crush the wild men between the two forces.

"Charge!" the king shouted.

His men surged forward and the Vultures turned in fear toward them, exposing their backs to the archers from the city walls. Arrows fell among them and then stopped moments before the king's cavalry hit the savages.

He lost visibility of the larger battle, focusing on his own individual fight. Men and women appeared and then fell before him. Garrett was injured in multiple places, cuts and scrapes, a blade in his calf, nothing stopped him. His sword flashed up and across, terminating the animals who'd slaughtered his people.

Then the riders were through the enemy lines once again. "Right!" he roared, the bloodlust taking hold of him.

The remaining horsemen wheeled right. They would harass the edges of the enemy formation while the phalanx attacked the center. He spurred his horse faster to reach the far right where the Vultures were already beginning to break formation. The thundering of Champion's hooves rang loudly in his ears and drowned out the sound of the ensuing battle behind him.

His men made several passes among the deserters, cutting them down. He reigned in his horse to catch a breath. Fourteen riders remained.

The battle in front of the gates raged. The phalanx had pushed forward, using brute force to separate the Vulture lines. Members of the Traxx Guard used swords to slash and stab into their enemy. It was carnage.

"Far side. They're trying to flee on the far side!" one of his men yelled.

Garrett grunted in acknowledgement. "Far side. Go!"

His men gave a weak battle cry and they cantered the horses back across the line. They ran down a few retreating Vultures and continued circling to finish off the threat to their city.

The king's heart leapt for joy at the sight of the enemy, broken and dead upon the field. This day could have gone very differently. Normally, during the siege, the militia worked in shifts to cover both the day and night instead of everyone present for duty as they were this morning. Nicholas had massed the troops around the gates as a safeguard for when they were opened. If he hadn't led the force outside of the walls, foiling the Vulture surprise attack on the back gate....

Garrett sat back heavily in the saddle, his injuries protesting the movement. He ignored them as best as he could. All of the events of the past week led them to this moment. If Jade hadn't been kidnapped, they wouldn't have changed anything in their defensive routine. Tanya's subsequent escape and Nicholas' inability to get a search party beyond the walls... *Everything happened for a reason. Those things are no coincidence. What does that mean?*

He flicked Champion's reigns softly and the big horse started walking toward the gates. As they crossed the battlefield, the king pondered the implications that it had all been interwoven to culminate in this fight. Finally, he met Nicholas in front of the gates. "You've saved the city this day, Nicholas," he praised.

"*Aaah Uhh!*" the militiamen standing nearby shouted exuberantly.

Nicholas grasped Garrett's hand, saying, "If it hadn't been for your cavalry's bravery when they chose to charge out of the city with you, My Lord, the Vultures would have attacked in the dark before our troops were ready. We'd be stuck behind the walls trying to repel them instead of celebrating our victory on the fields surrounding the city."

"No, Captain. The infantry won the day!"

The men cheered his praise. "*Aaah Uhh! Aaah Uhh! Aaah Uhh!*"

Garrett stood in the stirrups and shouted, "You have won a great victory this day. Be proud! Because of your glory, the city of Homelake is saved from these animals!"

He waited until the cheering militia quieted down before continuing. "There is still much to do. We must tend to our wounded and hunt the remaining Vultures who escaped. We can't afford for any of them to live to spread their message of irrational hatred of our people. We must eradicate them from the earth!"

Champion stamped his hooves impatiently and the king turned him toward the city. "Nicholas, meet me at The Keep in two hours. I'm still going after my family."

*****

Scratch ran headlong through the underbrush, heedless of the clinging limbs and catch-a-fellow vines as he held his hand against the massive wound in his side. He'd taken a spear during the initial Traxx charge from the city and now he leaked like a pierced rain barrel.

The Vulture leader shrieked his frustration at the wilderness around him. It had been a perfect plan. They'd successfully built enough ladders and contraptions to breach the walls and maneuvered them into place in the night. They'd given them enough time to think it would be an extended siege. The Traxx should have been caught totally unawares, but they'd charged into his lines, disorienting his troops who'd been led to believe that they would be the attacker, not defending against a suicidal cavalry charge.

The ground rushed toward his face as he fell into the snow. He grunted in pain and grabbed a handful of slush to pack against the wound. The bitter cold shocked him awake and he surged to his feet. He had to get farther away from the city before he could attend to his injuries.

Nearby, the sound of men shouting startled him. *Are those my people or Traxx?* Soon, the voices became distinct and he knew it was the Traxx; they were hunting his people in the forest and slaughtering them like dogs.

"The blood trail, she heads this way," a rough, weather-hardened voice called. "Come on, boys!"

"Rolf, slow down. You don't get yourself separated from us."

Scratch twisted around at the sound of a breaking branch directly behind him. A bear appeared and he screamed in fear. The giant grinned at him and said, "Got you, I did. You left a trail wider than a demonbroc's ass."

None of his troops were around, they wouldn't know that he surrendered. "Mercy! Mercy, I beg you," Scratch pleaded. "I'm the leader of the Vultures. I deserve to be treated with respect and you need to treat my wounds."

The man stepped closer and kicked him in his injured side. Pain exploded across his body and he threw up as the edges of his vision went dark.

"Old Rolf don't need to do nothing for ya, savage," the bear whispered hoarsely. He pulled a wicked, hooked-end fisherman's dagger from his belt.

Scratch screamed more than he thought he would before he died.

SIXTEEN

Water. It's all she could think of. Drinking it, bathing in it, swimming in it. Instead, grime covered Tanya from head to toe. The fine, powdery dust of the desert floor infiltrated every crevasse and irritated her skin in a hundred places.

Three days ago, they'd passed the remains of a large city on the edge of the giant lake. The buildings seemed intact, without evidence of damage from the massive weaponry of old or from fire, but it was abandoned nonetheless. Tanya wondered how anyone had ever lived out here in these conditions.

They thought the lake that the Mistress had annotated on their map would provide much-needed relief from the dry, dusty climate, but the water had been contaminated, too salty to drink, so they'd been forced to look elsewhere. After a few hours of searching along the lakeshore, they found a small tributary where they were able to drink and to fill their canteens.

The horses were doing much worse than the travelers. Frederick's had stumbled badly a few hours ago, splitting one of its rear hooves. It wasn't bad enough that they had to abandon the animal, but they had shifted all of the saddlebags to it while Frederick rode double with Tanya—which only added to the heat, sweat and filth plaguing her.

She'd never been in the desert before, none of them had except for Darci, so they relied on her experience. Luckily, they were crossing in the beginning of winter, so the archer told them that the weather was the best they could have hoped for. They wouldn't have lasted more than a day in the summer heat with their limited water supply. However, in the dead of winter, the winds were dangerously cold and stirred up giant clouds of dust, which disoriented travelers. The spring was no better as the snows of the surrounding mountains melted and the rains came, creating massive flash floods of deadly mud.

Tanya pried her lips apart. Darci may have told them that early winter was the best time to cross, but she was still miserable. "Water," she croaked.

She felt Frederick shift behind her and then the plastic green canteen appeared beside her face. "Here," he replied as hoarsely as she had.

The princess fumbled with the cap, unscrewing the lid, careful to keep hold of it, lest it fall to the ground. She wasn't certain that she had the energy to retrieve it if it did. A tiny trickle of fluid tumbled out of the canteen when she tilted it up. "More?"

"Gone," he stated. Their attempts at conversation had long ceased. Opening their mouths seemed to further dehydrate them, so they spoke as sparingly as possible.

Tanya screwed the lid back on in frustration. They needed to find a source of fresh water. They wouldn't last much longer without it.

*****

Water! It's all she could think of. She drank it, bathed in it, and even swam across the little pond. She stood and ducked her face into the water, drinking deeply beside the horses. She didn't care that their slobber mingled with the life-giving fluid. Her friends back in Homelake would have been horrified to see her this way, soaking wet, drinking water like an animal. Quite unbecoming of a princess.

Tanya pulled her head out of the water and laughed. She hadn't known that something so simple as a little pool of water could make her so happy. She'd always taken it for granted that there'd be enough water. Never again.

"We're going to camp here for the night," Darci announced.

"But it's only mid-day," Frederick protested. "Every moment we delay means that Jade is with that monster longer."

"I understand your concerns," the archer replied. "But, we need to hydrate our bodies for the next leg of the trip across the Skull Lands." She paused, then hesitantly said, "And... Something has changed. I can feel it."

"What do you mean?" Tanya asked, splashing across the water as she made her way to the edge of the pool.

"I don't know yet. When you were drinking, I saw a new moon overhead and you tumbled into the pool... Only, you didn't splash in the water, you continued to fall, farther and farther away."

Frederick thrust his canteen at Darci. "Here. Drink some more water. You're delusional."

"No, that's not it. I— I have a secret that only the Mistress knows."

"What is it?" Brandt asked, edging closer.

Tanya watched emotions war across Darci's face as she struggled to decide whether she'd tell them her secret.

Finally, she relented. "I have visions sometimes. I see things that might happen."

"You're a *Seer*?" Tanya blurted out.

Darci looked at her, clearly annoyed. "No, I'm not a Seer, but I do have visions—rarely of anything nice, mostly of death."

"And you've had visions of death about our trip to find Jade?" the princess choked.

"Yes—and no." She sighed and then continued, "It's difficult to explain. Yes, I saw an ocean of blood long ago when the Mistress first told me that I would help the Traxx family, but that may be about the war, not about this journey. Besides the vision of you falling into the pool, I haven't seen anything specific regarding our quest at all; everything has come from the Seers."

Darci unbuckled the saddle from her horse and set it on the ground with a soft grunt. She began to rub her hands deeply into the muscles on the mare's hindquarters, working out the lactic acid, which could cause the beast to go lame if it built up over night. "Plus," she continued, "the things I see don't always come to pass. The future can be altered by our actions in the present."

Tanya accepted what the woman said at face value, she didn't know anything about visions. Instead, she tried to get the archer to expand on her statement from earlier. "So you said something's changed, but you don't know what that is. How do you find out?"

"Since my normal visions aren't clear enough to use as a guide, the Mistress gave me Calamus to aid in coaxing a vision when I felt like the time was right." Darci must have seen the confusion in everyone's eyes because she amended, "It's a drug that gets burned and I'm supposed to inhale the fumes."

"Like a pipe?" Brandt asked.

"Sort of," she nodded. "The Seers use a sealed room and burn it in a brazier, but I suppose smoking it would give the same effect."

Tanya was skeptical and she told the archer so. "I don't know. Smoking it from a pipe seems like you'd get a lot of it directly into your lungs. What if it's dangerous and you take in too much? There's got to be a reason the Seers burn it and not smoke the stuff."

Darci shrugged. "See any sealed rooms around here?"

"There are abandoned houses all over the place," Frederick said. "Why don't we use one of those?"

"Because I don't have much, only a handful of leaves. They burn twice what I've got per session and I expect that I'll need to use it again once we get closer."

She had a point. They were just past the midway point on the Seer's map, but there was no way of telling how accurate the distances between the Skull Lands and the forests were, or how big this desert was. They couldn't afford to go to the place annotated on the map if it was no longer a valid location.

"Okay, what do we do?"

Darci smirked. "We wouldn't be lucky enough that one of you has a pipe, would we?"

Tanya and Frederick shook their heads, but Brandt held up his hand meekly. "I've got a pipe in my saddlebag."

"Why do you have a pipe?" Tanya asked and threw her hand up to her mouth. "You said you quit."

"It helps me relax in the evenings. The siege has been stressful."

"You're smoking that shit while you're on watch, when we're sleeping out here, aren't you?" Frederick accused.

"Smoking what?" Darci asked.

"It's harmless," Brandt said. "There's a plant that grows all over the place called Cannabis. A lot of people in Homelake smoke it to calm their nerves."

"Yeah, but it dulls your senses," Frederick stated. "We've outlawed its use in the Guard. The militia uses it quite a bit, though."

"You told me you stopped," Tanya said.

"I *did*. Then the siege started and all those people died. I just needed some help getting to sleep at night. I'm sorry, Tanya."

She was furious at her cousin. He shouldn't need to take drugs to balance him out. "Get your pipe," she ordered. "Darci needs it so we can find out where Jade is."

He pushed himself up away from the pool and rifled through his saddlebag, digging deep, past all of the stuff he'd hidden the pipe under.

"Here you go," he said glumly, handing the hand-carved bone pipe to the archer.

The three of them busied themselves with filling their canteens and preparing the midday meal while Darci gathered her supplies. It wasn't much, but the little bit of privacy they offered her was likely needed. She spent several minutes removing various knives and weapons from her clothing and securing them tightly inside her saddlebags.

Tanya saw how uncomfortable it made the woman to talk about her visions and made her seem almost vulnerable. The fact that the archer had demons she hid from softened Tanya's heart toward her. Maybe she was such a hard-ass because of the things that she'd seen and the visions that plagued her. She decided that she should give the woman another shot at becoming more than just guide and protector to the princess. Maybe they could even become friends.

They ate their meal quickly and Darci spread the map out on the ground. She handed Tanya an old pencil. "Here, make any annotations on the map as I say them."

The princess accepted the tool solemnly, like she'd been given a delicate flower instead of a simple pencil.

Once Darci was ready, she handed a length of rope to Frederick. "I don't know how I'll react to the Calamus," she cautioned. "I've only been in the sanctum with the Seers when they performed the ceremony once…"

"Is everything alright, Darci?" Tanya asked as the archer trailed off.

"Hmm? Oh, yes. I just— I don't trust myself, so I need Frederick to bind my hands. Which means I'll need one of you to hold the pipe up to my lips."

"I'll do it," Brandt volunteered.

She looked at the younger Traxx with a smile. "I'm too old for you, junior."

"I— That's not…" he trailed off, an embarrassed flush spreading across his cheeks.

"Darci, what does this stuff do to you?" the princess questioned. "I couldn't help but see you put all of your weapons away so they'd be difficult to get to."

"It made me go nearly insane the only time I've inhaled it. I nearly killed a petitioner in the sanctum, which is why I stay outside when they go into the lodge. I don't want to take any chances, so that's why I secured my weapons and will have my hands tied behind my back."

"Good to know," Frederick muttered and cinched the ropes a little tighter. A momentary grimace of pain registered on the archer's face and then she nodded for Brandt to begin.

"I'll be here for you," Tanya assured her and sat directly in front of Darci so she could attempt to soothe her if she started to panic or become violent.

The Calamus smelled awful as Darci sucked on the end of the pipe. The smoke exhaled from her lungs seemed to hang low over the water like a fog and Tanya couldn't help but breathe it in as well, causing her to cough. She saw the archer's pupils begin to expand and reached across to rub her shoulders. *Sitting in that position must be hell on her joints*, she thought.

Darci shook her head violently and Brandt pulled the pipe away. She stared at him for a moment and then turned back to Tanya. "The game is afoot."

"What?" Tanya asked in confusion and looked to her Guard.

Frederick shook his head, mouthing the words, "*Be quiet.*"

"The Deceiver will travel to the pit before the Winter Solstice. The earth is sick and must— Your land is saved! A mighty victory— Death!

An ocean of blood. The Taker of Souls is not finished. His never-ending hunger demands more."

Darci kicked out. Tanya didn't expect any violence from her and took the boot to her face. She flew backward, gore pouring from her nose. She struggled to sit up, lightheaded.

Frederick and Brandt fought to restrain the archer. She screamed obscenities and said a few awful things about their mothers.

"What the hell is wrong with her?" Tanya asked, wiping away the blood oozing from her injured nose.

"Nothing!" Darci screeched and ceased fighting them. "This is the truth you asked for. The cleansing is almost complete. The Mother is ready to come back from the depths. The blood of billions has satisfied humanity's debts."

"Darci?" Tanya asked hesitantly. "Is that you or are you still under the vision?"

The archer sat back and relaxed, seemingly normal once more. "You must go to Washington before the new moon at Yule. There is a place known as Manastash Ridge where the Mother awaits. Your daughter will be there with another Traxx. Beware of treachery for the Deceiver always tries to come out on top."

"I don't—" Tanya stopped as Darci slumped sideways to the ground. She was unconscious. "What are we supposed to do now?"

"You heard her. We have to reach this Washington place in a few weeks," Frederick answered.

She held up the pencil. "I didn't get anything that she said. How do we know which way to go?"

"Uh, guys?" Brandt muttered.

"What?" Frederick asked.

"Look at the map."

Tanya shifted and did as he asked. Blood covered parts of the map from when the archer had kicked her, breaking her nose. "Yeah, it's ruined."

"No, Tanya. *Look* at it," Brandt insisted.

She wiped away more blood and snot from her upper lip and stared at the map. A glob of drying blood sat on the edge of the Skull Lands. A line of blood bisected their old destination and the pencil ran perpendicular to that, forming a giant "X" over the River Valley. Instead, a different line of bloody mucus stretched away from the midway point of the Skull Lands toward northwest and ended at another mass of blood. A small clod of black dirt had flown up during the struggle and rested next to the second mass.

"You don't think…"

"That's our map," Brandt asserted.

"You've got to be kidding me," Frederick muttered, staring over her shoulder.

"If you're wrong, we won't arrive at this place in time," Tanya warned her cousin.

Brandt shook his head. "I don't know how, but I know I'm not wrong. This is our map to the ridge she spoke of."

They didn't have any other options. The new path led them north of their original destination, but not by much. Darci had clearly stated that Jade wouldn't be at the River Valley that was marked on the map and that they needed to arrive at the ridge by the new moon. *Is this the right path?*

She glanced at the unconscious archer, wishing she were awake and could offer some advice. If she guessed wrong, it could be disastrous. Her head pounded from the lack of water and the importance of her decision.

"Lash Darci to her horse," Tanya ordered. "I can't believe I'm saying this… Let's follow the blood."

SEVENTEEN

The path looked the same as it had eight years ago when Garrett went to the Valley Lodge with Nicholas and Brandt. Back then, he'd wanted to know if he was the right choice for a long-term leader for the people of Homelake. That's when the Seers had told him that the Vultures would return and burn everything. Recent history would prove that they hadn't been wiped out like previously thought, and they'd certainly mastered the art of burning villages. *So, who will betray me?*

His small group crested the path and the valley spread out below him like he remembered. Little had changed. The last time he'd been here, the fall chill had already turned the grasses brown, this time a few inches of snow coated the valley floor. The old lodge sat in the middle, a thin trail of smoke coming from the central chimney.

"Looks just the same, doesn't it?" Nicholas said from behind him.

"Yeah." He paused and looked up at the chimney where the woman with the crossbow was likely watching them right now. "Let's go."

The party of five men walked down, following the depression in the snow that indicated the path. They were the first ones to walk this way since it had snowed, a good sign that they'd be the only ones at the lodge and would be able to see the Mistress right away. He stopped at the old metal pipe sticking conspicuously from the snow and waited for the guards to tell him it was alright to walk past that point.

It took a while for someone to speak to them, but finally, a male voice emerged from the pipe. *"You are under observation. Follow the path closely and do not stray into the snow."*

"A little different than last time," he muttered, leading the men down the path.

A familiar face met them at the fence that kept the lodge's livestock safe from the traps in the fields beyond. "Hello, King Traxx. I'm sorry, I don't remember your first name," the man said.

"It's fine. I can't remember yours either," he chuckled. "Garrett."

The guard snapped his fingers and pointed at him. "That's right. It's been a long time."

"That it has," Garrett replied.

"Garth," the man answered with a hand to his heart. "The Mistress has been expecting you."

"Good," the king smiled. "That means we'll be able to get on with our quest sooner than I'd expected."

The guard unlatched the gate and invited everyone inside before locking it securely behind them once more.

Garth talked as he led them toward the lodge. "Darci's been gone for about two or three weeks. I wasn't privy to her mission other than she was going to help you. I guess she didn't survive the battle?"

"I honestly have no idea what you're talking about," Traxx answered truthfully. Darci was the woman who'd been the head of security when he was here the last time.

"Hmm… She said she was going to help the Traxx family. Surely she would have gone to you."

"Until two days ago, Homelake was surrounded by an army of savages. If she tried to reach us a couple of weeks ago, then I'm afraid she didn't make it."

"Then that's a mighty loss to the Valley Lodge. I knew it was a fool's errand." Garth opened the door for them and bid his farewell to return to his post on the roof—Darci's old spot.

A young girl sat them in the lobby and went to fetch the Mistress. As Garrett looked around the room, he was hit with the feeling that it had all happened before. *What's the point of all this? I keep coming to these ladies for advice and nothing changes. Here I am with another request...*

"Garrett Traxx," a ruined voice called from the doorway where the girl had disappeared. "I foresaw your arrival, but I didn't know that you'd press on through the snowstorm."

He rose and kissed both of Diane's cheeks. "Mistress. You look as stunning as you did the last time I was here."

"And you still have a silk tongue, King of Homelake."

"For you, the compliments come easily."

She smiled and the scars on her exposed neck dimpled inwards. "I like you. There is too much estrogen in this household. We could use someone like you around here."

"Alas, I'm committed to my wife, Peyton."

"Pity," the Mistress mumbled, her eyes traveling down his body and back up. "Come, let us talk, Garrett. Bring your man—Nicholas, is that right?"

"Yes, ma'am," Nicholas replied, following behind the retreating pair obediently.

Instead of leading them to the sanctum as Garrett expected, she took them to a small office, set with two couches facing one another and a short table between them. The table was set with a steaming kettle in the center and three empty mugs beside a plate of warm bread.

Diane took the guesswork out of where they were to sit by moving around to the side with only one mug. "Please, sit," she said. "Coffee?"

"*Real* coffee?" Nicholas asked.

"Yes. It's over a hundred years old, but the people of the old world had ingenious ways of preserving their foodstuffs."

The girl reappeared and poured each of them a cup of coffee before disappearing again. Garrett took a sip. It was hot, but one of the most wonderful things he'd ever drank. In Homelake, they used different berries, roots and tree barks to make a version of coffee, but it was nothing like what the Seers served.

"I'm glad that the siege of your city has finally ended," the Mistress stated, breaking the silence. "You should visit me more often."

Garrett frowned. That damned lady was frustrating. She was beautiful and certainly as sexy as any woman he'd ever met. But, did she have to lay it on so thick? He knew her game from past interactions. She used her femininity to get what she wanted from men. What did he have to offer her?

"Thank you, Diane," he replied. "We lost a lot of our citizens to the Vultures, but it could have been a lot worse. If it hadn't been for your warning that they were coming, we'd have never prepared like we did. Homelake has an established military culture, all because of you."

She inclined her head slightly and her robe slipped open as she did, allowing the men a view of her ample cleavage. "I'm glad to help. Could you possibly repay the debt by sending a shipment of supplies to the Valley Lodge?"

There it is, he thought. "Of course, Mistress. Homelake wants to remain in the good graces of the Seers."

"You will always be in our good graces, Garrett Traxx," she laughed, causing the gold and silver bracelets she wore on both wrists to jingle. "But the services we provide keep us locked away in the mountains without the ability to produce our own food. So, we do ask for help from time to time."

Garrett nodded. "I understand." He took another sip of the wonderful coffee and then continued. "The reason I'm here is—"

"Jade Traxx."

"Ah, so you *do* know."

"Yes, I know of your granddaughter's kidnapping by the people from the River Valley."

"River Valley?" Nicholas asked in confusion. "Maybe you should start telling us what you know so we can go after the princess."

She glanced at the captain, her eyes blazing. "You forget your place, Nicholas. You are a guest in my home and in audience with me at my invitation. I don't *have* to tell you anything. I could send you on your way and ban you from the valley on penalty of death, forever."

Diane waited for him to respond. When he didn't, she smiled, saying, "There. It's always best when one remembers their station. People who live far to the west, beyond the mountains and deserts, abducted Jade."

"People?" Garrett asked. "Tanya saw him. She said he was more like a giant lizard than a man."

She leaned back and crossed one leg over the other, exposing even more skin. "They are people, make no mistake, but they've suffered terribly. Their injuries caused the mutations, which your daughter mistook as the features of an animal.

"I sent Darci to your daughter with horses and food. She will lead Tanya and the others to your granddaughter."

"Four people?" Nicholas scoffed. "I have a force of fifty men, all skilled in horsemanship, fieldcraft and combat, waiting in the village below. We can go after them and force these people to return Jade to us."

"Tanya Traxx is beyond your ability to assist, Nicholas. And yours, Garrett. You must trust in your family's ability to love unconditionally."

"What does that mean?" Garrett asked for clarity. It seemed like every time he spoke with this woman, he had more questions than answers. "The last time I was here, you told me that someone close to me would betray me. Now you want me to trust in my family's ability to love?"

"The future is always in flux, Garrett Traxx. Our actions can change what happens, for good or bad. The travelers have moved beyond my abilities to see them," she continued. "Something has happened. A force much more powerful than me has intervened. I know that Darci leads them westward still, but their destination has changed..." she trailed off and then said. "I don't know where she's going."

"Then we'll go west, to their original destination," Garrett decided. "We'll go to the river valley that you spoke of and find out where they went."

"Good idea, My Lord," Nicholas agreed.

"No. If you travel into the desert, Homelake will lose its king—immediately."

"I can't leave my daughter alone out there."

Diane uncrossed her legs and leaned across the table, grabbing his hand. "Garrett, your daughter isn't alone. She has the greatest archer alive today with her and the swordsman, her lover. They will meet an even greater warrior and the... the Mother."

"Who's the mother?"

"I don't know. That's just the word comes to mind when I have visions of her. She reminds me of my mother, caring, fair and just, but don't get on her bad side."

"Even with all of those people to help her, I need to go to her."

"You *need* to return to your city, Traxx. Your people need you. The Vultures may all be dead, but the wounds they inflicted are still hurting your people. They need you to help heal those wounds."

"But my family..."

"Is in the most capable hands that I know. Darci will do everything in her considerable power to ensure the safety of your family."

"Will it be enough?" Garrett asked.

"That is beyond my knowledge," she replied. "Like I said, the quest has moved beyond us. My visions for the Traxx family have told me that you're needed back in Homelake, not searching the entire west for your granddaughter."

"But, Mistress, I—"

She released his hand and placed a finger against his lips. A look of sadness passed over her face, marring her beauty for a moment. "Shhh, Traxx king. Enjoy your coffee and flirt with me some more. It might be the last time you're able to do so."

What the hell does she mean by that? he wondered.

*****

The trip to The Devil's Hole was uneventful compared to the events leading up to the journey. Freya was still uncertain just what had happened the night Grobahn tried to convince them to leave the Dominion over a month ago. The last thing she remembered, they were arguing with the priest about why it had to be such a sudden departure, and then she blacked out.

When she awoke the next morning, Varan told her that she'd put her foot down about leaving and decided on the Winter Solstice as the day to begin the healing. The high priest was pissed. Since that night, he'd taken his anger out on anyone who came within five feet of him. Her minor irritations with the man's personality became full-blown dislike, bordering on hatred by the time they left the Dominion last week.

Why did he need to be such an ass? Freya wondered for the thousandth time as she stared at Grobahn's back. She and Varan—even Brahm at one point—had discussed the possibility of leaving Grobahn behind and traveling to the Hole on their own. She knew instinctively that she didn't need him for any type of ceremony or communication with Gaia.

Unfortunately, even if they could have found additional maps, he had their only working compass. They were stuck with him.

Of the original thirteen that Grobahn suggested, he'd recanted, saying that they only needed five, which represented the four seasons and the sun, which they were trying to welcome at the rebirth. That meant Freya, Varan and Jade, plus Grobahn and Thistle. Brahm stayed behind to watch over the Coven in the Dominion.

"I need a quick break," Varan confessed beside her.

The high priest turned and asked, "Again? What do all of those muscles do for you if you can't even walk a few miles?"

"You try pushing this thing for the hundred or so miles that we've gone in five days," Varan spat, gesturing to the wheelchair that Jade rode in. The little girl walked when she could, but twenty-plus miles a day was simply too much for her, so they'd used what they had on hand in the Dominion.

"We just took a break two hours ago," the priest seethed. "We've still got five or six miles to go until we reach The Devil's Hole and only a few hours to get there."

"I've pushed this chair across fields and woodlands, carried it across rivers…" the warrior trailed off, likely sick of arguing with the man. "I'm tired, Grobahn. I just need a rest for a few minutes."

The priest wheeled on Freya, causing Varan to step in between them rapidly. "Oh, call off your dog, *Freya*. I'm not going to hurt you."

"Freya? What happed to calling her Mother?" Varan asked.

"Yes, of course. I'm sorry, Mother," he replied. Freya felt the sarcasm dripping from his words. "Forgive me. I spoke in the heat of the moment. Surely you don't agree with another stop?"

"We've all got to make it to the Hole by Yule, not just a few of us. Jade's put forth a valiant effort, but the walking has torn up her feet. If we push her much faster, she'll be lame when we reach our destination."

"It won't—" Grobahn stopped and turned away.

"What was that?" Freya asked.

"Oh, nothing. I'm just frustrated, *Mother*." He stalked off and sat heavily in the dirt beside the road they currently followed. The priest pulled out the compass and turned toward where Freya assumed Gaia waited for them, positioning himself on his knees to pray while Thistle, their only other companion, stalked into the grass to relieve himself.

"What's up with him?" Varan asked.

"Someone jammed a stick up his ass and left it there," Freya replied. "Oh! Sorry, Jade. I didn't mean to say that."

"It's okay," she said. "I don't like him either."

Varan laughed at the girl's comment. "I *knew* you were related to me, little one!"

He pulled a canteen from the small pack attached to the back of the wheelchair and took a swig. "Want some?" the warrior asked, holding it out to Freya.

She accepted with a smile, taking two swallows before passing it back. He gave the half-empty canteen a shake and frowned. "I hope we find a stream soon," Varan muttered as he put it away.

The land they traveled through wasn't completely arid, but it was dry and left her throat parched, even after she'd taken a drink. Grobahn assured her that they were headed in the right direction, but what if they got there and ran out of water? *What would the self-assured high priest do then? What would any of them do?*

"Alright, you've had your rest," Grobahn's nasally voice interrupted her thoughts. "It's time to go. The Mother awaits."

Freya looked over to where Varan stared after the retreating priest. "Hey, you okay?"

"Yeah," he replied. "I just think he's acting strange. And, what happened to you being the Mother?"

"Guess I was a good enough stand in for a while, but nothing compares to the real thing."

"Heh," he chuckled. "Yeah, I guess you're right."

Varan pushed himself to his feet with a grunt and began pushing Jade's chair down the road. Freya waited as the others slowly passed her by and watched as they went around a curve in the road.

Then she was alone. It was the first time she'd been by herself, without another living soul within sight since she'd came to the Dominion. She spun in a circle on the old road, her arms held out wide, relishing the silence for a moment before hurrying after everyone else.

*****

"We're almost there."

"How do you know?" Tanya asked.

"I saw this ridgeline in my vision," Darci replied. "We follow it until we find the Mother."

"And Jade."

"And your daughter," Darci amended.

They'd traveled for weeks, pressing hard to make it to the ridge before the Winter Solstice. Except for the breakneck pace that they drove the horses to, it had been rather uneventful after the pool where Darci's vision changed their course.

Who the "Deceiver" and "Mother" were remained a mystery, while the Taker of Souls seemed straightforward. Repeated attempts at inducing another vision with the Calamus had failed. Tanya thought that maybe Darci's vision meant that she was the mother since they *were* going after

Jade, but she couldn't even begin to guess whom the first person was supposed to represent.

"I—" Darci started to say something and then stopped.

"What is it?" she asked.

The archer shook her head. "I don't know. I just got the feeling that we need to dismount the horses and tie them up. We need to walk from here."

Frederick glanced over his shoulder at the two women riding side-by-side. His horse's hoof had healed enough to allow him to ride her, which meant they'd been able to go faster than they had through the desert. "What was that?" he asked.

"We need to halt," Darci answered, pulling on the reins of her horse to stop.

"Why's that?" Frederick inquired as his mare stopped suddenly, threatening to throw him. "Geez!"

"I don't know," the older woman replied. "I've never mistrusted my feelings before and that's served me well over the years." She smirked, adding, "Besides, it looks like your horse doesn't want to go any further."

He looked to Tanya for guidance. The Seers had sent Darci to them because they trusted her instincts, and she was obviously in tune with *something* that the princess and the others couldn't feel. "Okay," she replied. "Let's find a place to stash the horses and continue on foot."

Frederick searched ahead for a few minutes and returned, saying he'd found a place to tie the horses, and grasped the reins to lead the mare to where he'd indicated. The horse dug her front hooves into the dirt, throwing her head backward in an effort to pull the reins from his hand.

"Hey," he hissed. "What the hell's wrong with you?"

"I *told* you she doesn't want to go any farther," Darci reiterated.

Tanya tried to walk her horse forward as well, getting a few feet farther than Frederick before her mount refused to cooperate. "Alright, let's find somewhere to tie them up back that way," she said, waving toward the way they'd come from.

It didn't take long to find a small stand of stunted trees where they could tie the horses up without fear of them getting their leads tangled or strangling themselves on something.

They took the saddles off and hid them in the bushes a few yards from the horses before performing a quick rubdown. It was unlikely that anyone was out here, but there was no point in taking the risk of someone stealing their food stores.

Tanya verified that the animals each drank some water from a canteen before she left them under the trees to join the others. They turned back along their original route and began walking. They still didn't have a definitive description of where they were going, but Darci was sure that they'd know it when they got there.

Behind them, the horses neighed forlornly. They didn't like the prospect of being left out in the cold, dry plain any more than Tanya did.

EIGHTEEN

"Hurry! It's almost midnight," Grobahn called to the others excitedly. The priest practically danced with anticipation of the end of their journey. *The Mother will take their souls and I'll be the one who helps to return Her to the earth!* "Come on, we need to get there before the Solstice."

Behind him, he heard that idiot, Freya, mutter, "Why is he in such a hurry? The Solstice didn't hold any significance to him until I said something about it."

Because the sooner I can be rid of you, the better, he thought. He hated the woman and her dog, Varan. How he'd ever let Brahm convince him that the woman should be called the Mother was beyond him. He hadn't specifically agreed to it, but he'd stood by and let the other priests call her that, and then the People learned of it and they adored her. Now the bitch actually thought she was important.

Oh, but she is! The Mother demands their souls. He fingered the athamé under his robe. He'd use the ceremonial blade on the warrior first and then the woman. The child would be last. He'd have to work quickly, but with the Mother's help, he knew it was possible. The key was to dispatch Varan without the others seeing, then he'd slice open Freya's throat, spilling her life force onto the deity waiting below.

His vision had shown him the layout of The Devil's Hole; those other fools who called themselves priests didn't know anything besides the name of the place, which was the piece that he'd been waiting for. As long as they stayed out of his way and let him do the Mother's work, he would tolerate them.

The more he thought about Freya's proclamation to arrive at the Hole during Yule, the better he liked the idea. First, because the Winter Solstice was significant to the Coven and signaled the promise of rebirth from the winter, even though the worst of the weather was yet to come. The primary reason he liked the idea was the darkness that midnight would provide. The Solstice fell on the night of a new moon this year. It would disguise his actions well as he slid their lifeless bodies into the Hole.

"Come, come!" Grobahn tried unsuccessfully to hide the sinister tone in his voice as he continued with a grin, "Our destination is just over this rise."

*****

"Come on, we're almost there," Darci said, forcing the words between ragged gasps for air. They'd sprinted the last mile, uphill, leaving the heavier men behind, breathless.

Tanya felt the urgency hanging in the air, as if it were a dense fog. She'd never felt the need to arrive at a location as keenly as she did now with the moments ticking away toward midnight. *Why is it so important to reach this place—wherever it is—exactly at the Winter Solstice?*

They finally topped the rise they'd climbed. Shadows filled the valley before them and Tanya couldn't see anything. "I— I think I'm going to pass out," she confessed.

"Breathe— deep. In your nose— out your mouth," Darci answered haltingly as she struggled to catch her breath. The older woman sat down, tucking one leg in and bent the other so her knee was at chest height. She rested her elbow on that knee and peered through the scope on her crossbow at the darkness below.

Tanya focused on breathing. She couldn't be certain if the black circles around the edges of her vision was the night or from the lack of oxygen during their run. *What is she looking for?* the princess wondered. *Does she think there's a threat in the valley?*

Finally, her breath stopped coming in ragged gasps, enough that she could ask, "What are you looking for?"

"There's something about the vision that's bothering me," Darci replied. "Why did we both feel that it was so important for us to reach this place before *somebody* else?"

Tanya waited a moment. When it became evident that the archer wasn't going to elaborate without prompting, she asked, "So, what's bothering you?"

Darci didn't speak for a moment. When she did, she went over what they'd already discussed, many miles ago. "You said I mentioned the Deceiver and the Taker of Souls."

"Yeah…"

"I think it may be both figurative and literal."

Tanya shook her head. "I'm sorry, I just don't understand."

"I think somebody down there is a murderer."

*****

Freya surveyed the depression they'd entered. A ridgeline ran across her sight to the front, while a few stunted trees dotted the landscape behind. Rusted metal poles marked the perimeter of The Devil's Hole, a nine-foot wide circular pit that ran deep into the ground. A narrow circle of sand-colored brick ran around the ledge and disappeared into the Hole.

She wondered what it had been used for in the past. It looked manmade. Had humans found the pit and placed the bricks around the sides, making it perfectly circular or had they possessed some type of machine that could bore straight down into the earth and designed the Hole for some other purpose? She'd never know, obviously, but she wanted to see the place in the daylight so she could get a better understanding of what had gone on here in the old days.

While the Hole looked manmade, it *felt* like something entirely different. Freya couldn't think of a proper way to describe her feelings about the gaping black pit. She should have been afraid, or at least slightly nervous, about what possibly lived in the darkness below. Bats, demonbrocs, mountain lions, all kinds of animals could have taken up residence there. But, it wasn't like that. When she gazed down into the inky blackness, she felt warm inside and her heart fluttered slightly in her chest.

"Scary place, huh?" Varan said, startling her.

"Hmm. That's not how it makes me feel. I feel like I've been searching for this place my whole life. Like everything that I've ever done and all that I've endured were to bring me to this moment." Freya paused and glanced at Varan's silhouette. She grasped his hand in hers, searching for a way to describe her feelings. "I feel like I'm... *home*."

He laughed and squeezed her hand. "Well, the priests say that you're Gaia incarnate and this is where the spirit of Gaia is supposed to reside, so maybe you are home in a way."

Is that it? she wondered. Did she feel so comfortable in this barren place because of her connection with Gaia? *Does that mean... Does that mean that I really am Gaia?* It was a heavy thought, one that she'd dismissed before as religious superstition.

"Varan, I don't know. It feels blasphemous to say that I'm a goddess."

He smiled. "I'm the biggest skeptic that there is, but maybe there's something to this. There seems to have been a lot of— *Ungh!*"

The warrior started to fall forward, his dead weight threatening to drag Freya into the depths. She reacted, pulling against him and fell onto her back. His body flopped limply on top of her.

"What? Varan! Help!" she cried, trying to push herself out from underneath him. As she did so, she found herself staring at the handle of a knife jutting from Varan's back.

"Well, hello there, *Mother*," Grobahn spat as he stood above her.

She shook her head side-to-side in disbelief. "What have you done?" she screamed.

"Gaia—the real Mother—demands blood as a sacrifice... Your blood."

Freya pushed ineffectively against the dead weight of Varan's body. It was no use; he was too heavy for her. She craned her neck to see what had become of Jade. Thistle stood behind her wheelchair, both hands pressed down on her shoulders. She wasn't going anywhere with him there.

She flicked her eyes back to the high priest. "Is this why you insisted that only Thistle come along?"

"Of course, you idiot. The Watcher of the Coven obeys my bidding. He wouldn't dare question me like the others do. They've been questioning me for years, but now I have the truth and the Mother speaks to me!"

She pushed against the body, gaining a few inches of freedom. "Brahm said that we'd discover what we needed to do once we got here. He didn't say anything about Gaia's requirement for blood."

"The Summoner only received part of the vision. Gaia graced me with the entire thing." His eyes sparkled strangely in the sliver of light coming from the new moon. "Once your blood is mingled with her spirit below, the earth will be healed!"

The priest bent over and pulled the knife from Varan's back. Blood splattered across Freya's face as the curved dagger came free. "Ugh... Grobahn stop! You don't have to do this."

"Oh, but I do. The Mother has been training me for this moment for years, hardening my heart by not speaking to me until recently. Those years of solitude prepared me for this moment. She has made it so I'm no longer afraid to do what must be done."

He looked up at Thistle. "Bring me the girl."

Grobahn sneered at Freya. "I want you to watch me cut her to ribbons. The Mother demands suffering." Jade screamed as the hulking Watcher picked her up.

"No!" a woman's voice carried on the wind as Thistle stumbled, an arrow sprouting from his scapula.

"What? What's—" Another arrow appeared in Grobahn's leg, causing him to fall. From her vantage point, she could see the priest press up close against Varan's body, using him as a shield.

The shadows came alive around Freya. Two men materialized from the darkness, swords held across their bodies in a guard as they advanced toward Thistle. A thin, dark-haired woman dashed into her line of sight, scooping up Jade in one motion and continuing back into the night.

The men began to fight with Thistle. He used the thick scales on his arms to absorb and deflect their sword thrusts, backing dangerously near the edge of the pit until a large dagger appeared in his hand. He pressed forward, attacking the two swordsmen.

The battle raged backward and forward for what seemed like minutes, then the Watcher's knife slipped past the parrying thrust of one of the men, sliding down the length of the sword until it plunged hilt-deep into his chest. He collapsed instantly, freeing the blade.

Thistle stepped back to reposition his feet and another arrow embedded into his neck. It severed his windpipe, impeding his breathing, but missing his jugular. His breath came out in wet gasps through the hole. The dagger wavered in his grasp momentarily and then tumbled to the ground.

The remaining swordsman used the damage to press the advantage. He ducked inside the Watcher's upraised arm and jammed the tip of his sword through the underside of Thistle's jaw. The blade slid home, emerging from the top of the bigger man's head.

Thistle fell to his knees, the lifeless body held up by the blade in the swordsman's hands. The newcomer placed his foot on Thistle's chest and pushed. His body toppled over the edge of the Hole, lost forever.

"Help!" Freya shouted.

The swordsman spun, dropping into a crouch as he turned. His expression was one of determination, not of anger like she'd have thought it would be. He looked much younger than she'd expected.

"Where's the other one?" he asked.

"He got shot," she replied. "He was here, but I don't know where he went. I can't get out, can you help?"

"Of course. Let me *help* you."

She didn't expect Grobahn to answer her. He jerked her roughly from underneath Varan and wrapped an arm around her waist. The tip of his knife jabbed into her neck as he backed toward the pit.

"You've ruined everything," he spat at the swordsman, shifting Freya slightly with each step. *He knows the archer is still out there, but he doesn't know where.*

"Let her go," the man who'd killed Thistle growled. "You kill her and you're dead the second she falls."

"If I am to be sacrificed for the greater good, then so be it. I just need to—"

THUD.

"Ungh…"

The fletching of another arrow appeared over her shoulder. *The archer!*

"You're going to ruin everything!" Grobahn shouted, the hatred in his voice evident. "Gaia demands this woman's blood."

Grobahn's body jerked awkwardly and the knife fell away from her neck, clattering to the brick below his feet. His hand clutched her stomach and then dropped.

"That's for taking my daughter," a girl said behind her. Grobahn shuddered once more as he was stabbed again. "And that's for Brandt."

Freya pushed away from Grobahn and he fell to the edge of The Devil's Hole. The dark stain of his blood spread slowly across the brick, flowing down the grooves and running over the edge. The woman who'd grabbed Jade earlier stood nearby, holding a dagger covered in the priest's gore.

She stared defiantly at Freya. The former slave held up her hands to show that she was unarmed. "Where's Jade?"

"She's safe."

"Did you say she was your *daughter?*"

"Yes, she is."

"Then you must be the princess, Tanya," Freya stated.

The woman's posture relaxed slightly. "Yes. How do you know?"

"Jade told us about you. We've spent a lot of time together."

"Who are you?"

"My name is Freya and…" she trailed off. What did Grobahn's treachery mean? Was this past year just a lie? "And, up until a few minutes ago, I thought I was someone important. Now I realize that I'm just a slave who escaped a brutal master."

"Tanya! I'm so sorry," the swordsman said from behind her.

The princess looked beyond Freya to where the fight with Thistle had occurred. "Brandt's gone, isn't he?"

"I'm sorry," the swordsman reiterated.

Tanya refocused on Freya. "Are you in league with this monster? We've traveled thousands of miles to find my child. Now that I have her, I'm not going to let anything get between us again."

Freya shook her head vehemently. "No. I'm not with him. He… He lied to us; said that if we came here with him, the earth would be healed."

"The Deceiver," Tanya muttered.

To emphasize her point that she wasn't with Grobahn, Freya kicked the priest's foot. It was enough force to send him sliding over the edge of the pit to the waiting darkness.

"*Ungh...*"

"Varan?" Freya cried in shock. She ran to her lover's side and knelt beside him, she'd thought he was dead.

"Varan?" the princess and swordsman both repeated at the same time.

Freya felt along his neck until her fingers found the groove between his muscle and Adam's apple. A weak, intermittent pulse met her touch. "Still alive," he muttered with a lopsided grin.

The others walked up behind her and she asked, "Are either of you healers? Grobahn stabbed him in the back. He's going to die."

Tanya whistled with two fingers in her mouth, waving her arm above her head. "Darci is trained in the ways of healing battlefield wounds," she said. "If there's anything that can be done for him, then she'll do it."

"Thank you." She leaned down to whisper into the warrior's ear. "Don't you die on me, Varan. We have so much to live for. I'm... I'm pregnant, Varan."

His head lolled toward her. "Pregnant?" he asked feebly. "I've been hurt worse in the Contest."

Another woman jogged up to the group, Jade close behind her. "Uncle Varan!" the little girl called out as her mother tried to corral her into her arms.

"Don't look, honey," the princess said.

Freya stepped away as the woman crouched down to examine Varan. She set aside a giant crossbow to probe the wound and the area around it, pressing down with her fingers on both sides of the injury. Dark, maroon blood oozed out. "Not arterial," she mumbled and reached into a pouch on her belt.

A hand fell on Freya's shoulder, exerting enough pressure to spin her around to face the swordsman. Tanya stood beside him with her hands crossed over her chest. "Who *are* you?" the princess demanded.

"I'm Freya. I was a slave girl when I was given to Varan Traxx, Primus of the Contest."

"My cousin Varan is alive?" Tanya cried, falling to her knees before crawling over to the warrior's prone body.

*****

Far from the family reunion, miles below the surface of the earth, Grobahn's body splattered against the rock, feeding seeds that had remained long dormant in the darkness among the remains of humanity. They sprouted forth vines, growing rapidly to cover the floor of the entry to the Mother's realm.

The Taker of Souls emerged from between the growing vegetation. He inclined his head in respect to the Mother before claiming both Grobahn and Thistle's bodies for his own. He slid backward into the vines, disappearing once more. She knew that he required one more soul for the fulfillment of their pact.

Gaia stood from the throne where she'd been confined for so long, renewed by the energy of growth and hopeful for the new world that would spring forth. She decided that it was time for her to walk along the surface of her world once again. She'd been much too lenient with previous generations of humanity and they'd almost eradicated themselves and all of her other creations. She had to ensure that they didn't make the same mistakes.

The vines crawled toward the image of the New Moon, directly overhead. It was now the season of rebirth and the Mother allowed the expanding vegetation to carry her from the darkness into the light.

EPILOGUE

"The princess! The princess has returned!"

The words echoed across the border city of Homelake, mingling with alarm bells from the watchtowers. The city came alive, needing the boost to their morale like never before.

"Your Eye-ness," a member of the Traxx Guard greeted her at the gate.

"Rolf!" Frederick shouted in surprise, practically falling off his mare to give the fisherman a hug. "Wait. What are you doing in the uniform of the Guard? And a sergeant to boot!"

"Lot's changed since ya left, Frederick. We had ta militarize the entire city, that ain't somethin' ya come back from easily."

"But the Vultures are gone, right?"

"Aye, boy. Killed their leader myself, I did." He placed an arm around Frederick's neck and the two of them turned away from Tanya and her companions.

She couldn't hear what they whispered, but Frederick looked over to her several times with a pained expression. He separated from Rolf and thanked him before stepping up into the saddle once more.

"What was that about?" Tanya asked.

Frederick shook his head. "We must return to The Keep as soon as possible."

They rode through the gate and it clanked together behind them. She turned to watch the Guard secure the iron with locks. *The gates were always open before the Vultures came, but if we beat them, why are they locked once again?*

The clattering of hooves announced an escort, hastily dispatched to be their honor guard. The riders were more heavily armored than a simple ceremonial escort. \

"What has happened?" Tanya asked Frederick, pulling on the reins.

"Princess?" a familiar voice called from the behind the honor guard.

The soldiers' horses parted and Nicholas, Captain of the Traxx Guard, rode through the press of bodies. His eyes swept across Tanya's ragtag group. Freya and Varan rode double on Brandt's horse, while Jade sat in front of her and Frederick rode alone. Darci had returned to the service of the Seers after a tearful goodbye in the town of Creede.

"Hello, Nicholas," Tanya replied. "What's the meaning of this?"

His eyes dropped and then he looked back up. "Where is Brandt?" the captain asked.

"He didn't survive our journey."

"I'm sorry to hear that. Blake will be overcome with grief. He was a special young man, destined for greatness. So many lives cut short." Nicholas took a deep breath and let it out slowly. "Tanya, there's no easy way to say this… Your father is dead. He was killed a week ago by a broc when he was on one of those trading missions of his. Your uncle has been acting as the regent until your return."

The world seemed to fall away from Tanya and she became lightheaded. It certainly wouldn't do for her to pass out on her horse. "I must sit for a moment," she stated and slid awkwardly to the ground.

The princess stepped a few feet away from the street and sat in the vibrant grasses of the city. It seemed like spring had made a comeback everywhere they went. The grass made a soft cushion under her and she dropped her head between her knees.

"What of my mother?" she asked.

"Suicide," Nicholas replied, thin-lipped. "She jumped from the battlements two nights ago."

They'd been through so much. This wasn't the reception that Tanya had anticipated upon her return. She'd expected to return to an exuberant party in celebration of Jade's rescue and the return of Varan from the dead. Instead, it was more of the same: Death and sorrow.

Is pain all that life has to offer to humanity?

A thick shadow appeared over her and she looked up into the face of her red haired companion, whose stomach had extended now that she was in the sixth month of her pregnancy. "Do not be sad for your father, child," Freya said hollowly. "The Taker required a few more for our bargain to be complete. The deal was struck long ago and the Traxx family has paid my debt. For that, I am eternally grateful."

"Freya, what do you mean?"

In her periphery vision, she saw Frederick motioning to keep the Guard at bay. "As repayment for the burdens I placed on your family for the last century, your children and grandchildren are now immune from all the illnesses and harm of this world. They will each live to a ripe, old age, dying on the last day of their ninety-ninth year. The Traxx will rule the entire region through diplomacy and bring peace to all of your partners."

"I'm not sure what you're talking about, Freya. You're not making any sense."

"Freya is connected to me in an unexplainable way; she is the vessel who delivers my message in a fashion that everyone can understand," the redhead detailed. "I am Gaia; and I have returned to this world, *Queen* Tanya.

"The old world was purged by fire," Gaia continued. "The coals have darkened; the embers are extinguished. In their place, the world will be made new again and the Traxx will carry my message of love as far as the oceans. Your family will be my voice for generations to come and my generosity will flow through you to all the people of Homelake."

She stared at her new friend. The things she said were crazy—and yet, they felt *right*.

Tanya was now the head of the Traxx family. Mother Gaia guaranteed them safety and prosperity, but it was up to her to ensure that her family wasn't corrupted by that power. Humanity couldn't afford to slip into the chaos of the old world ever again.

"I will make you proud of your creation once again… Mother."

"I know you will. I will always be watching."

The End
this concludes *The Path of Ashes* series

If you enjoyed this book, please leave a review online.

For additional books by Brian Parker, type the following link into your web browser. This will direct you to his author page on Amazon where all of his titles are listed

www.amazon.com/author/BrianParker

ABOUT THE AUTHOR

A veteran of the wars in Iraq and Afghanistan, Brian Parker was born and raised as an Army brat. He's currently an Active Duty Army soldier who enjoys spending time with his family in Texas, hiking, obstacle course racing, writing and Texas Longhorns football. He's an unashamed Star Wars fan, but prefers to disregard the entire Episode I and II debacle.

Brian is both a traditionally- and self-published author with an ever-growing collection of works across multiple genres, including sci-fi, post-apocalyptic, horror, paranormal thriller, military fiction, self-publishing how-to and even a children's picture book, Zombie in the Basement, which he wrote to help children overcome the perceived stigma of being different from others.

He is also the founder of Muddy Boots Press, an independent publishing company that focuses on quality genre fiction over mass-produced books.

FOLLOW BRIAN ON SOCIAL MEDIA!

Facebook: www.facebook.com/BrianParkerAuthor

Twitter: www.twitter.com/BParker_Author